MARTIANS ABROAD

MARTIANS ABROAD

CARRIE VAUGHN

TOR

A TOM DOHERTY ASSOCIATES BOOK
NEW YORK

MARTIANS ABROAD

Copyright © 2016 by Carrie Vaughn, LLC

A Tor Book
Published by Tom Doherty Associates
175 Fifth Avenue
New York, NY 10010

www.tor-forge.com

Tor® is a registered trademark of Macmillan Publishing Group, LLC.

The Library of Congress Cataloging-in-Publication Data is available upon request.

ISBN 978-0-7653-8220-7 (hardcover)
ISBN 978-1-4668-8647-6 (e-book)

Our books may be purchased in bulk for promotional, educational, or business use.
Please contact your local bookseller or the Macmillan Corporate and Premium Sales
Department at 1-800-221-7945, extension 5442, or by e-mail at Macmillan
SpecialMarkets@macmillan.com.

First Edition: January 2017

Printed in the United States of America

0 9 8 7 6 5 4 3 2 1

For my brother, Rob

MARTIANS ABROAD

1

There are a thousand shades of brown.

My scooter skimmed above the surface so fast the ground blurred, kicking up a wake of dust that hazed from the color of dried blood to beige, depending on the angle of light. Ahead, rust-colored hills made chocolate-colored shadows. The plains before the hills were tan, but in a few hours they'd be vivid, blush-colored, beautiful. Right now, the sun was low, a spike of light rising from the rocky horizon in the early morning. The sky above was pale cinnamon.

I had nothing to do today. Classes were over, I hadn't started my internship at the astrodrome yet. So I went riding, just out, as far and as fast as I could. A track ran around the perimeter of the colony—a service road, really, but no official vehicles went out at this hour, so I had it to myself. Made one circuit, then headed to the open plain, avoiding weather stations, mining units, and other obstacles. I revved the engine, the battery did its job, and the lifts popped me half a meter into the air. Dust flew behind me, and I crouched over the handlebars, sucking air through my mask, blinking behind my goggles. The wind beating against me would be cold, but I was warm and safe inside my environment suit. I could ride around the whole planet like this.

"Polly? Are you there?" The voice of Charles, my twin brother, burst over the comm in my helmet. Of course it was Charles. Who else would want to ruin my perfect morning?

"What?" I grumbled. If I could turn off the helmet radio I would, but the safety default meant it stayed on.

"Mom wants to see us."

"Now?"

"Would I have bothered calling you otherwise? Of course now. Get back here."

"Why couldn't she call me herself?"

"She's a busy woman, Polly. Stop arguing."

Charles and I were only nominally twins, in that we were un-corked at the same time and grew up together. But I'm really older because my embryo was frozen first. My unique collection of DNA has been in existence in the universe longer than his. Never mind that Mom decided later that she wanted a girl *and* a boy rather than just a girl, and that she then decided that it would be fun to have them together instead of one after the other. Or maybe she thought she'd save time that way, raising two babies at once. At any rate, I was frozen first, then Charles was. I'm older.

But as Charles always pointed out, we've been viable human beings for exactly the same amount of time. The seals on our placental canisters were popped at exactly the same moment, and we took our first breaths within seconds of each other. We watched the video twenty times to be sure. I didn't even have the benefit of being five minutes older like a natural-born twin would. We were twins, exactly the same age. Charles was right. He was *always* right.

I would never admit that out loud.

"Okay. Fine." I slowed the scooter, turning in a wide arc and heading for home. I'd gone farther than I'd thought. I couldn't see the bunkers over the garages, air locks, and elevators leading down to the colony, but I knew which way to go and how to get there, and if I got off track, the homing beacon on the scooter would point the way. But I didn't get lost.

I took my time cleaning up and putting things away, waiting in the air lock while vacuums sucked away every last speck of Martian dust from my suit, putting the scooter through the scrubber so not a particle of grit would get into the colony air system. Once everything was clean, I checked the scooter back into its bay and folded my suit and breather into my locker. I put the air tank in with a rack of empties for a technician to refill. I carefully double-checked everything, because you always double-checked everything when things like clean air and functional environment suits were involved, but no matter how long I took with the chores, it wouldn't be long enough. I couldn't put off talking to Mom forever. So I brushed the creases out of my jumpsuit and pulled my brown hair into a tail to try to make it look decent. Not that it helped.

The office of Supervisor Martha Newton, director of Colony One operations, was the brain of the entire settlement, oversee-ing the engineering and environmental workstations, computer banks, monitors, controls, and surveillance that kept everything running. The place bustled, various department heads and their people, all in Mars-brown uniforms, passing along the corridor, ducking into rooms, studying handheld terminals, speaking urgently. It was all critical and productive, which was exactly how Mom liked it. Supervisor Newton herself had a private room in the back of operations. Her office as well as her house, practically—she kept a fold-away cot there, and a stack of self-heating meal packets in one of the cupboards for when she worked late. Some days she didn't come home. Usually, when she wasn't sleeping or fixing casseroles, she kept the place clean, spotless, like a laboratory. Nothing cluttered her gray alloy desk except the computer screen tilted toward the chair. Two more chairs sat on the other side of the desk. The cot, her jacket, and emergency breather were tucked in a closet with a seamless door; her handheld and other office detritus remained hidden in a drawer. A window in back looked over the central atrium gardens. Anyone entering, seeing her sitting there, expression serene, would think she ran all of Colony One by telepathy. I wouldn't put it past her.

When I finally arrived, sliding open the door, she was sitting just like that, back straight, her brown hair perfectly arranged in a bob, wearing neither a frown nor a smile. Her beige-and-brown uniform was clean, neatly pressed, buttoned at the collar—perfect.

Charles was already here, slouching in one of the extra chairs. My brother had grown ten centimeters in the last year, and his legs stuck out like he didn't know what to do with them. I'd been taller than him before last year. Now he stared down at me and made jokes about my scalp.

They both looked at me, and I felt suddenly self-conscious. My jumpsuit was wrinkled, my hair was already coming loose, and I could feel the chill morning air still burning on my cheeks. I couldn't pretend I hadn't been out racing on the scooter for no reason at all. Maybe she wouldn't ask.

"Polly, thank you for coming," Mom said. As if I'd had a choice. As if I could find a place on the whole planet where she couldn't find me. "Have a seat."

I pulled up the other chair and sat; the three of us were at the points of an equilateral triangle. I wondered what Charles and I had done to get in trouble. This wasn't about taking the scooter out, was it? I couldn't think of anything else I'd done that she didn't already know about. Charles was usually too smart to get caught when he did things like hack a mining rover or borrow gene-splicing lab equipment to engineer blue strawberries just to see if he could. I glanced at him, trying to get a hint, but he wouldn't look at me.

We waited, expectant. Mom seemed to be studying us. The corners of her lips turned up, just a bit, which confused me.

"What's wrong?" I asked.

"Nothing at all," she said. "Just the opposite, in fact. I'm sorry— I was just thinking about how quickly time passes. It seems like yesterday you were both still learning how to walk."

This was starting to get weird. She usually talked about how much better she liked us once we started walking and talking and acting like actual people instead of needy babies. Mom wasn't a fan of neediness.

She rearranged her hands, leaned forward, and even seemed excited. Happy, almost. "I've got some really good news. I've secured a wonderful opportunity for the both of you. You're going to the Galileo Academy."

Frowning, Charles straightened. I blinked at him, wondering what he knew that I didn't. I said, "What's that?" The way she said it made me think I should have heard of it.

"It's on Earth," Charles said flatly.

"You're sending us to Earth?" I said, horrified.

Earth was old, grubby, crowded, archaic, backward, stifling—the whole point of being on Mars, at Colony One, was to get away from Earth. Why would she send us back there?

"This is a wonderful school, the best there is. Kids from all over the system go there, and you'll get to learn and do so many things you'd never have a chance to if you stayed here." She was eager, trying to sell us on the idea. Trying hard to make it sound like the best thing ever and not the disaster it was. This was clearly for her, not us. This was going to be good for *her*.

I wanted to get up and throw the chair into a wall, just to make noise. I wanted to either scream or cry—both options seemed reasonable.

But I only declared, "No. I don't want to go."

"It's already settled," Mom said. "You're going."

"But what about my internship? I'm supposed to start at the astrodrome next week. I'm supposed to start flying, really flying—" No more skimmers and scooters and suborbital shuttles, I was going to bust out of the atmosphere, get into pilot training and starships. I didn't want to do anything else, much less go to school on Earth.

"The astrodrome will still be there when you're finished," she said.

"Finished when? How long is this going to take?"

"The program is three years."

I had to do math in my head. "Their years or ours? How long is it really?"

"Polly, I thought you'd be excited about this," she said, like it was my fault my life was falling apart before my eyes. "It'll be your first interplanetary trip—you're always talking about how you want to get into space—"

"As a *pilot*, not as baggage, just to end up dirtside on Earth. And you didn't even ask! Why didn't you ask if I wanted to go?"

Her frown hardened. The supervisor expression—she was right, everyone else was wrong. "Because I'm your mother, and I know what's best."

How was I supposed to argue with that?

I crossed my arms and glared. "I don't want to go. You can't make me."

"I've already let the supervisors at your internships know that you won't be participating. The next Earthbound passenger ship leaves in two weeks—you're allowed five kilos of personal cargo. Most of your supplies, uniforms and the like, will be provided by the school, so you shouldn't need to take much with you."

"Five kilos on Mars or Earth?" Charles asked. He'd been scheduled to start an internship in colony operations. He'd run the planet within a decade. We both had *plans*.

"Mom, I'm not going," I said.

"Yes, Polly, you are."

Charles hadn't moved, and he still wouldn't look at me. Why wasn't he saying anything? Why wasn't he arguing with her? He didn't actually want to go, did he?

If he wasn't going to help, I'd have to do this myself, then. "I'll submit a petition to the council. I'm old enough to declare emancipation, I can still get that internship—"

"Not without my approval—"

"If I declare emancipation I won't need your approval!"

"—without my approval as director of operations," she said.

That was a really dirty trick. That was pulling rank. And it wasn't fair. Charles raised a brow, as if this had suddenly gotten interesting.

Mom took a breath, indicating that I'd riled her, which was a small comfort. "Polly, you need to plan long term here. If you finish at Galileo Academy, you'll be able to pick your piloting program. You'll qualify for a program on Earth. You'll be captaining starships in half the time you would be if you went through the astrodrome program here."

Right now my plan was interning at the astrodrome between semesters learning maintenance, traffic control, and support positions like navigation and communication. I'd have to finish school, then try for an apprenticeship while I applied for piloting-certification programs—and no one ever got into a program on the first try, the process was so competitive. I'd have to keep working, adding to my résumé until I finally made it, and then add on a couple of years for the program itself.

If what she said was true, this Galileo Academy was impressive enough that I could get into a piloting program on my first try. Which sounded too good to be true. She held this out as the shiniest lure she could find, and I was furious that I was ready to buy in to the scheme.

I'd had a plan. She could have at least warned me that she was plotting behind my back.

"But why does it have to be Earth?" My voice had gotten smaller, like now that the shouting was done I was going to have to start crying. I clamped down on the impulse.

"Because everything goes back to Earth eventually." She looked at my brother. "Charles? Do you have anything you want to say?"

"No," he said. "You're right, it sounds like a wonderful opportunity." I couldn't tell if he was mocking her or not. He might have been serious and mocking at the same time.

Her smile was thin. "I'll be home for supper tonight. We'll talk more about it then."

Dismissed, like a couple of her underlings. I stormed out of the office, Charles following more calmly, and the door slid closed behind us. We walked home. A straight corridor led to a another corridor, long and curving, that circled the entire colony. Plenty of time for stomping before we got to the residential section and our quarters. Not that Charles stomped. He seemed oddly calm.

"Why?" I asked him. "Why is she doing this to us?"

"You should look at it as an opportunity, not a prison sentence."

"That doesn't answer my question."

"My guess? She wants us to know what Earth is like. For real, not just in the propaganda."

That actually made sense. "Okay. But why?"

He looked at me down his nose. The don't-you-ever-think? look. "It's where we're from."

"We're from Mars," I said.

" 'We' as in humanity are from Earth. The dominant political, social, and economic structures that define us are still dependent on Earth."

"So we're just supposed to automatically think Earth is great."

"It might not be so bad. It might even be interesting."

"There's got to be a way we can get out of it."

We walked a few steps, and I thought he was thinking, coming up with a plan to get out of it. I was depending on him coming up with a plan.

"I don't think I want to get out of it," he said, and my heart sank.

"Charles—"

"It's only a few years. And you'll get into a piloting program afterward. Why are you arguing?"

I was arguing because my world had been turned upside down and shaken in a way it never had before, and I didn't much like it.

Two weeks at home before I had to leave for years. *Years.* Nobody left Mars. People came *to* Mars, because it was better, for the jobs and the wide-open spaces and the chance to be part of something new and great like the colonies. That was why our grandparents had come here. Mom was one of the first of the new generation born on Mars, and Charles and I were the second. Mars wasn't a frontier anymore, it was *home.* People came here with the expectation that they would never leave. And why would they? Going back and forth was hard enough—expensive enough—that you couldn't just pop in for a visit. If you came, if you left, it was for years, and that was that.

But people did leave, because a ship departed for Earth every two months. Mom must have known about this for a while to book me and Charles far enough in advance. She didn't tell us about it because she knew we'd try to dodge. Or, I would try to dodge. She didn't want to spend months arguing with me.

I lay on the grassy lawn in the middle of the colony's main atrium. Partially sunk underground, a lensed dome let in and amplified the sun, feeding the lush plants, trees, flowers, and shrubs. The light above me was a filtered, golden glow, and beyond it lay pink sky. I wanted to memorize the scene.

My best friend, Beau, lay beside me. We held hands. I didn't want to ever let go. I'd told him the news, and he'd taken it like Charles had—matter-of-fact, maybe even curious. "You'll get to see the ship. Aren't you even excited about that?" I was, but after all the carrying on I'd done, I wouldn't admit that. The ship would be carrying me away from home, which put a damper on the whole experience.

"What if I pretended to be sick? If they think I have a cold or the flu or something they won't let me on the ship."

"They'll test to see what you have and find out you don't have anything."

"I could catch something for real. There's got to be some virus culture in the med lab."

He glanced at me. "You try that, you'll catch something worse than a cold."

He was right. The lab mostly had cultures of bacteria collected from under the polar ice caps—Martian microfauna. It probably wouldn't do anything to me. Or it'd kill me outright.

I sighed. "I'm supposed to want to go. Mom keeps telling me what a great opportunity this is. I think she's just trying to get rid of me."

"Then maybe you should look at it that way—you won't have your mother looking over your shoulder every minute of the day anymore."

I had to smile at that. Communications between Earth and Mars had a ten- to twenty-minute time lag. She'd never be able to interrogate me like she did here. She'd still keep an eye on me, sure, but the news she got would always be at least ten minutes old. That was something.

"Yeah, but she'll just make Charles keep an eye on me."

Beau reflexively looked around, an instinctive check to see if Charles was eavesdropping. I couldn't have said whether my brother was or wasn't. I couldn't do anything about it one way or another—if I caught him at one trick, he'd find another—so I let it go. But Beau hadn't grown up with him, so he wasn't used to it. After a moment, he settled back down.

"Your brother's kind of weird."

"He's just Charles," I said.

We stayed silent for a long moment. A vent came on, and the leaves on the tallest tree fluttered. I listened to Beau breathe, soft and steady.

"I'm going to miss you," he said.

I looked at him, tears stinging my eyes. I didn't know what to say or do, so I rolled over, put my arm around him, and rested my head on his chest. He put his arms around me, and we stayed like that until we had to go home for supper.

2

My bunk on the *Lilia Litviak*, about half a meter wide and two meters long, wasn't too small for sleeping, but it was too small for just about anything else—like lying back to stare at the ceiling and feel sorry for myself. There was another bunk just like it underneath, which belonged to Charles. They folded up during the day when we were moving around the cabin. Mine was supposed to be folded up now, in fact, but I was lying here instead.

Filtered recycled air ought to smell the same no matter what, but the ship smelled different from the colony. It must have been the gardens—the colony could pull fresh oxygen from the gardens, using natural filtration. Here, all I could smell was the ship, steel and rubber and a tinge of sweat that never went away. I breathed slowly, getting used to it, thinking, *This is what space smells like.*

I had to figure out a way to sneak onto the bridge. Just to watch. Beau was right, I was finally on an interplanetary ship, I ought to be enjoying it. But between the passenger quarters and the bridge lay the galley, cafeteria, gym, infirmary, and crew quarters. How was I supposed to sneak through all that? So I had to figure out a plausible way to ask if I could go watch. I had to meet the captain and endear myself to him. The required safety video introduced him as Captain Arlan McCaven, a dashing name to go with a dashing figure, everything a captain ought to be—he was in his forties, perfectly keen in his pressed blue uniform, looking off into an unseen distance with sparkling gray eyes. Everybody on the ship was smitten with him. He wouldn't even notice me. I had to think of something clever to say, I had to tell him everything I knew about the *Lilia Litviak*, the thrust capabilities of the Mand-propulsion engine that powered the ship, or the trajectory that was the most efficient route to Earth. Surely that would impress him.

No it wouldn't.

The bell rang for dinner in the mess hall. Feeling like my limbs were too heavy, I rolled out of the bunk and dropped to the floor. The ship's acceleration was meant to simulate half-Earth gravity; I shouldn't have felt too much difference from the Martian gravity I was used to, which was one-third of Earth's. But I did. I felt like I was wearing weights on my limbs. If I was having trouble now, what was Earth going to be like?

When I folded and secured the bunk against the wall, I found a note on the underside of it, stuck in one of the seams.

Polly's eyes only.

Like who else was going to find it?

Anyone else would send e-mail, but Charles had to scrounge up a piece of actual vegetable-matter-based paper and a graphite stylus that would write on it. Nobody used paper but artists and scientists. I asked him about it once, and he said that the trouble with e-mail was that people could ignore it, delete it, file it, and you, the sender, were at their mercy. But you stuck an old-fashioned paper note in front of somebody's nose, and it was important. They couldn't possibly ignore it. It was intrusive. Just like Charles.

I unfolded the note and read. *"This place has the most* interesting *people. Get off your ass and come talk."*

I had only two goals for the trip: to see the bridge, and to get through it without letting anyone bother me. The less I talked to people, the more likely that would happen. Charles was the amateur sociologist, not me. But a person had to eat, and food was available in the ship's galley only during mealtimes, so I went.

The galley was plain, with beige padding on the walls, floor, and ceiling, all to prevent injury when the ship was in zero g. No one was supposed to be walking around when the ship was in orbit and near weightless, but the precautions were everywhere. My attitude was you ought to know better and not depend on padded walls to save you when you went spinning uncontrollably across corridors. The ladders and handholds scattered everywhere were for *holding on.*

The chairs and tables were bolted to the floor, and the buffet-style galley opened out of one wall to serve freeze-dried delicacies like protein casserole and mixed vegetables. The line of passengers had mostly filed through already. I was late. I also couldn't see Charles anywhere. I thought surely he'd be here, waiting to pick on me.

The ship carried a greater variety of passengers than I had been expecting. Earth officials returning from visits to Mars were noticeable in their complicated close-fitting suits with colored sashes, scarves, and ties. Outer-colony folk—miners, pilots, surveyors—often stopped at Mars on their way to the inner system, and they tended to wear blue or black jumpsuits, plain and practical, with lots of pockets, handhelds strapped to belts, and ship or station patches sewn on the sleeves—a throwback to the really old days when each mission into space was important enough to have its own patch. They also tended to be taller and bonier, with ropy muscles attached to thin limbs—the build of people who lived their lives in low gravity. Those of us from Mars fell somewhere in between the outer-colony folk and the stouter, fleshier people from Earth. My own clothes also fell somewhere in the middle—a white T-shirt, brown jacket, tough trousers, and thick boots. No one would think I came from Earth.

I went through the line, put food on my tray, found a table off by myself, and there was Charles, sitting across from me, like he'd been hiding around a doorway waiting for me.

I glared at him. "You don't have to sneak up on me."

"See that guy? In the jumpsuit, real tall, dark skin, and curly hair—don't stare at him." Charles pointed over his shoulder, getting me to look, then chastised me when I craned my head around. So I ducked my gaze and tried to find him out of the corner of my eye.

He was young, an outer-colony guy, smooth skinned, nice smile, wearing a blue jumpsuit with the patch of a mining company logo on it. He was sitting with a handful of other outer-colony men and women—they stuck together.

"That's Ethan Achebe, part of the Zeusian Mining Enterprise Achebes, and he's also headed for Galileo Academy."

"How do you know all this?"

"I got a copy of the passenger manifest—"

"That shouldn't be public—"

"—and I've already met him. He's real nice. You should talk to him. Get to know him. Maybe find out why he's going to Earth for school."

"Why would I do any of that?"

"Because I told him you have a crush on him."

"Charles!"

The guy, Ethan, glanced over and offered a bright, cheerful smile. I looked hard at Charles, leaning on my hand to hide my face.

"I hate you."

Charles smiled, but the expression was sinister. "No you don't."

I stayed hunched over my dinner and didn't have to say much of anything else while Charles schemed. I wasn't interested in him, in Ethan Achebe of the Zeusian Mining Enterprise Achebes, or any of his other projects. All I had to do was figure out how to get a glimpse of the bridge before the trip ended.

Past the galley was a gym, a boxy room filled with equipment that looked like it might be fun to play with, or torture devices, depending. Lots of machines for weight, resistance, and cardio training, so people like us from the colonies could build up muscles and stamina for dealing with Earth's high gravity. I had a whole schedule of exercises I was supposed to be doing, along with the nutritional supplements and muscle and bone enhancers I was taking.

Beyond the gym was the observation deck, which was really just a pair of spongy foam benches and two small round view ports for nominal observers to look out. Halfway between Earth and Mars there was exactly nothing to see. Both planets were pinhead-size disks, one red, one blue-white. Monitors on the wall let you access external telescopes and cameras on the ship's sensor array—magnify the images, zoom in on features, take pretty pictures to send back home. But I could do all that on the monitor back in the cabin.

Next to the door on the far side of the observation lounge was a sign reading NO ADMITTANCE: CREW ONLY BEYOND THIS POINT. *That* was why I spent time here. Because on the other side of that door were crew quarters, and beyond *that* was the bridge. The bridge, where everything interesting happened, the only spot on the ship worth paying attention to.

The crew—that included the bridge crew, pilot, navigator, captain, everyone—ate in the same galley as the passengers, on alternating shifts. If I waited here long enough, they'd all pass by eventually. I'd see Captain McCaven, maybe even talk to him. And if I could just talk to him, get on his good side, then maybe, just maybe, I could ask him for a look at the bridge. Just a quick look. All I had to do was ask. How hard could it be?

At the right time I sat on the sofa and waited. Shifts would be changing soon. He'd have to come this way eventually. He had to eat sometime, didn't he?

I heard the voices first—two men in conversation, low and businesslike. This was it, the captain, had to be. I stood but stopped myself from running into the restricted corridor. I'd just get thrown out, get a black mark on whatever kind of records they kept, and I'd never get on the bridge. Stay calm.

Then they were there, at the doorway. He was tall, very tall. He actually had to duck to enter the observation lounge. His hair was mussed, his face set in concentration, so much more serious than in the official photo. The other man was shorter, sandy haired, with a trimmed beard—Lieutenant Yeltsin Clancy, second in command according to the ship's publicity. The two of them had their heads together, over a handheld.

They marched through the observation lounge without a sideways glance.

I opened my mouth, didn't say a word. Started to take a step forward and held back. Didn't know why. I could have said, "Hi," or "Hey, I'd like to be a pilot someday!" or "Gosh, I'm a fan." I could have waved, just a friendly hello to get their attention. But no. Not a word, and they were across the room and through the next doorway in moments.

I slouched back on the sofa. Real brave there, Polly.

I was still sitting, half fuming, half planning my next attack on the problem, when a gentle voice said, "Hey, mind if I come in?"

The voice was Ethan Achebe's—the outer-system guy Charles was so keen on. Also tall enough that he had to slouch to get through the doorway.

"It's a public lounge," I said. "Why ask me?"

He shrugged, moving into the ambient lighting. "You look a little pissed off, like you want to be alone. If you'd rather I go, I'll go." He spoke with an accent—the vowels round, the consonants clipped. Unfamiliar, kind of intriguing.

"It's okay," I said. "I'm not pissed off, I'm just . . ." I sighed, because I didn't know what I was, and I didn't want to tell him that I couldn't work up the nerve to talk to the captain. Or that

I was trying to talk to the captain, or why. He wouldn't understand. Or he'd laugh. I didn't know why I cared.

He sat on the other end of the sofa. Not next to me. I might have left if he had.

"You want to talk about it?"

"No," I said.

We stayed so quiet after that I could hear the ship's vent system hissing. I didn't know what to say. And why should I be the one to say something? I was here first. I figured if I sat long enough, staring at the glare and shadows outside the view port, he'd get bored and leave. It would be a contest to see who could stand the awkwardness longer.

"So," he said finally. "You're from Mars?"

Frowning, I looked at him. "And you're from . . ."

He leapt to the invitation, eyes wide, leaning in as he spoke. "I've spent most of my life on Zeus Four—that's the big station in orbit around Jupiter. It's huge, you'd need all day to walk around it, but it mostly looks just like this, you know?" He gestured to the hull around us. "All steel corridors and spun-up gravity. I landed on Europa once, at a research station, but the surface is so inhospitable we had to stay in the lander and couldn't do anything but look out the windows. We got to steer the rovers a bit, but it's not like really being there. But you . . . you've been on an actual planet. Grew up on one, even, with sky and ground and everything. So Earth won't seem all that strange to you, will it?"

He seemed to expect me to respond to all that. Maybe I should have told him I wanted to be left alone after all. "I didn't think much about Earth at all until a couple weeks ago. I have no idea what it's like."

"But aren't you excited?"

Was everyone at Galileo Academy going to be like this? "Going to Earth wasn't my idea."

He blinked. "Oh. No wonder you're angry."

"I'm surprised Charles didn't tell you the whole sad story."

"Charles—your brother, right?"

"Nominally—genetic material is about all we have in common."

"Have to admit he's a bit spooky. The way he looks at you like he's peeling back your skin."

"Don't ever let him hear you say that," I said. "He'll think he's won."

"Won what?"

"That's just it—we'll never know until it's too late." I pushed against the sofa back, sighing again as I stared at featureless space outside the window. Like it was my life stretching before me, a big blank nothing. "I don't think anything about Mars is like Earth. Sure, it's a planet, but no breathable atmosphere. It makes a difference."

"And gravity?"

"Earth has three times the gravity. I'm not even going to be able to walk right."

"Yeah, tell me about it. I got all these exercises I'm meant to be doing."

"Yeah, me, too. It's ratty." My frown felt even more surly at the thought.

He nodded back to the gym. "Jogging's more fun if you have someone to do it with. You game? Next day shift we can start."

"I don't know—"

"Come on. We're both more likely to get it done if we push each other to it."

Charles would have tried to blackmail me into doing something I didn't want. Ethan just looked at me with his big brown eyes beaming with enthusiasm bright as hand torches.

Voices traveled past us, tickling my attention, and I looked up in time to see the captain and his lieutenant exiting the observation lounge and heading back into the restricted corridor. I missed my chance *again*.

3

Hey Beau. I've only been gone a couple of weeks but it seems like months. There isn't a whole lot to do on the ship. I've been trying to figure out a way to get on the bridge, to at least get a look at the bridge, but it's pretty well separated from the rest of the ship, and the crew isn't around much. Still working on it.

Send back as soon as you can. I know you can't send messages all the time, but every little bit will help.

Miss you.

Polly

The ship was accelerated to half-Earth gravity, which was apparently seen as a good compromise among Earth gravity, Mars gravity, and gravity on the outer stations, which varied anywhere from near-Earth to zero g. I didn't notice the difference until I moved. Walking wasn't too bad if I took it slow. Jogging sucked. I felt like someone had slung weights over my shoulders, and my heart pounded hard as soon as I started. I leaned on the treadmill's arms, huffing with every step. I had only another two weeks to get into some kind of shape.

Earth gravity was going to hurt.

Ethan didn't complain. He stood tall and his steps pounded in an easy jog. He was smiling like this was easy, but sweat covered his dark skin and he huffed just as hard as I did.

"What's . . . what's Zeus Four . . . spun up to?" I panted at him.

"One . . . one-third . . . same as . . . as Mars."

So we were in exactly the same fix. At least I wouldn't suffer alone.

That morning, waking up in our cabin, I'd asked Charles if he was keeping up with the exercise routine and nutritional supplements we'd been assigned.

"Of course I am," he'd said.

"But I never see you in the gym."

"I go during the night shift," he said, in a tone that suggested it should be obvious. "I don't have to let everyone see me sweating buckets. What do you think I've been doing every night when I get back here an hour after lights-out?"

I shrugged, defensive. "How am I supposed to know? Rifling through everyone's cupboards?"

"Amateurish," he said, shaking his head.

The one thing I couldn't let happen was to step off the shuttle on Earth and collapse into a puddle of unconditioned muscles while Charles walked off like the king of the world. So I jogged. Ethan made it easier.

"What . . . are you most . . . looking forward to? On Earth?" he asked, glancing sideways to my treadmill.

"I . . . told you," I answered. "I'm *not*."

"I want to see . . . forests," he said. "I've . . . seen pictures. Millions of trees . . . they go on for . . . kilometers."

"We have . . . trees . . . on Mars," I said. "In the atrium domes."

"But millions of them?" he said.

"What's the difference?"

"That's just it," he said, laughing. And how could he laugh without any air in his lungs? "It's got to be different. I want to see it."

"Overrated," I muttered.

"There's got to be something you want to see," he said.

Nothing on Earth could possibly be worth this. "Less . . . less talking . . . please," I gasped.

I wrote a careful message to Captain McCaven, asking for a chance to see the bridge. I tried to sound intelligent and professional, eager but not too eager. I didn't have a number or address to send it directly to him, so I sent it to the ship's passenger-liaison office. I could sort of understand why they didn't publicize the captain's personal address. But it wasn't like I was going to be rude and send him a million messages.

All I got was an automatic response: "Thank you for your interest. We appreciate comments from our passengers." Whatever. I couldn't be sure anyone had even read my request. So I sent it again. And got the same automated response.

Maybe Charles was right about e-messages. So I tried a different strategy.

I tried to get into Charles's storage bin in our cabin, but he'd locked it with a thumbprint code. I briefly thought about waiting until he was asleep and trying to ease his hand over to activate the lock. But if I did that, he'd most likely wake up, and I'd have to explain. No way was I getting in there.

I found the note he'd written to me and tore a blank strip off the bottom of it. It didn't give me a lot of room, and the edges were rough and torn, unlike the nice clean square the page had started out as. For a pencil I had to use a stylus for a handheld terminal, dipping it in a brown sauce from the galley to use as ink. The result was rather horrible and would pretty much rot away in a couple of days. But it didn't have to look *pretty*, it just had to get noticed. This would get noticed.

> *Dear Captain McCaven:*
> *My name is Polly Newton, and I'm traveling from Mars with my brother Charles in cabin C32. I hope someday to be a ship pilot. I got top grades in astronautics in school. I would very much like to see the bridge of the Lilia Litviak during the trip to Earth, and I promise to be quiet and respectful and not get in the way. If such a thing can be managed, I would be very grateful.*
>
> > *Sincerely,*
> > *Polly Newton*

My writing was very tiny. He probably wouldn't even be able to read it. As long as he made out "Polly Newton," which I was sure to make legible, I ought to at least get attention from it. Maybe the kind of attention that would get me confined to quarters, but still.

Back in the observation lounge, I shoved a corner of the note into the NO ADMITTANCE sign that was bolted to the wall. The captain couldn't possibly miss it.

I was late to dinner and ended up sitting by myself in the corner. Until Charles brought his tray over and sat across from me. I'd have preferred sitting alone.

"What have you found out about Achebe?" he asked. Before hello, even.

"Who?" I said.

"Ethan Achebe, the Zeus Mining heir."

"I don't know. What am I supposed to be finding out about him?"

"Why's he going to Earth—and to Galileo? Is anyone traveling with him? Is anyone else in his family already there? Does he have a job with the company?"

"I thought you said you hacked into the passenger files. I'd have thought you'd have found out all this stuff already."

"The files don't say how he feels about any of it. So, how does he feel about going to Earth?"

"I'm not going to be your spy, Charles. Ask him yourself."

"He's more likely to talk to you."

I put down the fork and glared. "All right. What if I did ask him? What makes you think I'd tell you what he said?"

"You're being difficult to spite me."

"Yes, I am! Can you blame me?"

"Just remember, we're in this together."

I didn't even know what that meant. I scraped up the last of my protein and gravy and stomped off to put my tray in the chute.

Charles had some kind of plan going on. Clearly he did. Even if I could read his mind I probably wouldn't be able to figure out what it was. Jogging while angry actually felt good. I even did twenty minutes without Ethan.

So after jogging, I read about Galileo Academy and tried to figure out why Mom wanted us to go there.

Galileo Academy had been founded some thirty years ago by some of Earth's elite families. The stated goal was to create a "revolutionary new academic environment" in which the next generation of leaders "could be trained to confront and conquer the unique challenges of pan-solar system human expansion." Like it was building some kind of rampaging army. The rhetoric sounded like a sales brochure. Sales brochures were most of what I could find in my research. The school quickly established a reputation as cutting-edge, and its graduates had founded and run important companies, sponsored solar system–wide expansion projects, and held all kinds of political offices. A lot of very wealthy, very prominent families happily sent their kids to school there. The place was a status symbol, a way for rich and powerful families of Earth and beyond to keep showing off how rich and powerful they were, which didn't seem entirely fair to me. How was anyone else supposed to break in to that world? Maybe that was the point.

No Martian students had ever been enrolled at Galileo Academy, because Mars didn't really have rich and powerful families. Just a few thousand people trying to make sure the planet didn't kill them while developing hydroponics and mining industries. Charles and I would be the first.

That clinched it. This wasn't about what was best for me and Charles. This was about making my mother look good. She wanted *her* children to be the first Martians to attend Galileo. She would have been able to use her influence as Colony One's director of operations to make it happen. And now she'd get to brag about it. I wondered how she'd managed it. Mars was independent, with its own government and sovereignty exactly because its founders wanted to cut themselves off from Earth's established systems. We didn't even use money, exactly—not that we had all that much to buy. You earned credits by working and traded them for what you needed from colony stores. Nobody starved. Everyone had a place to live—because where else would they go? I wondered what kind of strings Mom had pulled, and how many favors she'd called in, to get us into Galileo.

I was suddenly glad Charles was here, so at least I didn't have to go through all this by myself. The assurance that I probably would have an easier time getting into a good piloting program—assuming I graduated with good enough scores—didn't make me feel all that better. Even that part of it was as much for Mom's benefit as it was for ours.

I started working out a plan where I could ditch at the transfer station in orbit around Earth and stow away on the next ship heading back to Mars. Or maybe earn my way on to a crew like some old-time Earth sailor.

A new message pinged on my handheld account: "Passenger Newton, please report to observation lounge at 2100 ship time."

An hour from now. I *raced.* I wasn't going to miss this chance. The note had worked. I was right. Captain McCaven couldn't ignore me.

The person who came through the corridor wasn't Captain McCaven but his bearded companion from the other day. His second in command.

"You must be Polly Newton," he said. "I'm Lieutenant Clancy."

"Hi, yes, I know, I read everything on the public manifest," I blurted, staring. "Did the captain—"

He shook his head. "The captain wouldn't approve of this. He's off duty right now, so we can sneak in for just a minute, as long as you're quiet about it."

I nodded quickly. "Absolutely. Dead quiet."

He led me through that authorized personnel only door into restricted territory.

Crew country, they called it, the opposite of passenger country, and I could tell the difference right away. The corridor was just as padded and marked with safety warnings as the rest of the ship, which surprised me. But the corridor and doors had lots of other markings, utilitarian rather than friendly. Not at all dressed up. We passed a couple of people who wore uniforms, and all the doors had serious labels, like ENGINEERING and QUARTER-MASTER. It was *beautiful.* At last, we reached a wide gray door at the end of the corridor, and Clancy pressed a button on a keypad. The door opened, and I was on the bridge. I'd made it.

He pointed to the bulkhead right next to the door. "Stay here. Don't move."

I'd have stopped breathing if I could.

The place looked like any engineering workstation on Mars, consoles with screens set into them, slim chairs bolted to the deck, panel after panel of indicator lights, toggle switches, fingertip-size buttons. There were speakers and vents, cabinets painted red and marked with emergency symbols, numbers scrolling on a monitor, thick binder notebooks stuffed full of pages hooked to a shelf with plastic cords. All of it was dimly lit with inset lighting to reduce glare. I'd seen lots of pictures of all kinds of ship bridges, from tiny shuttle cabins to the big cargo cruisers. This was my first time seeing one in person. The big difference between this and a planet-side workstation: the chairs moved. They were set into rockers so they could change orientation when the ship changed heading. This whole thing *moved*.

The bridge had chairs for six crew members. On the off shift, only one person was here working, probably one of the junior crew set to monitoring the systems. Once the rockets had been fired, taking the ship out of Mars orbit, momentum would carry it straight to Earth. There wouldn't be much piloting or navigating to do until we approached Earth orbit. I'd love to see that, all six chairs filled, the whole bridge busy. But this was better than nothing. I wasn't going to complain.

Lieutenant Clancy said, "That's the command station, where Captain McCaven sits when he's on duty—"

"It has data feeds from all the other positions on the bridge, and also engineering, communications, and the sensor feeds. The pilot sits there, and those are the thruster controls, right? For coupling with station-docking systems. The navigator sits there, that monitor displays the charts. That's the radio for short-range communications. That panel monitors M-drive activity, I think."

Clancy stared at me. "You really *are* into this."

"I told you, I'm going to be a pilot someday."

"Well. Good for you, kid."

The junior crew member might have chuckled.

I didn't know how long he'd let me stay here, so I tried to take it all in, to memorize every piece of it. There must have been a million buttons, and I wanted to know what every single one of them did. I took a deep breath. The place had a close, comfortable atmosphere, smelling of work and buzzing with the low hum of cooling fans. It *felt* like a place where amazing things happened. I was itching to sit in one of those seats . . . the captain's seat. That would get me booted out for sure, so I stayed where I was.

I almost wished that something exciting would happen while I watched. Not *too* exciting, of course, nothing like a hull breach or radiation-shield failure. Maybe a micrometeoroid hit that would set off an alarm and require some kind of damage report. But nothing happened. All the lights that were supposed to glow quietly to themselves kept glowing, and no alarms sounded. The crew member seemed to be reading a book on her handheld.

Finally, Clancy glanced at the panel on the captain's consol and clicked his tongue. "All right, I think that's enough. Time to go, Ms. Newton."

It had only been a couple of minutes. Wasn't nearly long enough. I thought about arguing—just a few more minutes, I wasn't hurting anything—then thought better of it. Best be polite. Maybe they'd let me on again before the end of the trip. Maybe they'd let me sit at one of the stations—

I thanked Lieutenant Clancy and let him escort me back to the observation lounge. The room seemed so . . . ordinary.

"Good luck to you, kid," he said. "I hope you make it."

"Thanks, I appreciate it. But, I mean—why wouldn't I?"

"Oh, you know. You're headed for Earth, and you're . . . Never mind. You'll do fine."

He turned back around for the bridge before I could ask what he meant.

I lay back on one of the sofas in the lounge, my eyes closed, and ingrained every detail of the *Lilia Litviak*'s bridge on my memory, every light and panel and switch, every readout and what it meant. I could have piloted the ship myself if I had to. Well, I couldn't really, I knew that. But I knew enough to qualify for pilot training. No way anyone could keep me from it. Clancy didn't need to sound so skeptical.

I cornered Charles at supper. "What's Earth like, really?"

He glared. "You've seen the same brochures I have."

He'd laugh if I told him about begging to get a look at the bridge, so I didn't tell him what Clancy said. "Are we going to have trouble there?"

"Oh, probably. We're from the hinterlands, why shouldn't they give us trouble?"

"Then why would Mom send us there? Besides to make her look good."

"Maybe so we'll get used to it."

"But if we were never going to leave Mars anyway—"

"It's a bigger universe than that, Polly."

I was crazy thinking he'd give me a straight answer.

4

We entered Earth orbit three days later. I entertained fantasies of getting to sit on the bridge to watch the maneuvering sequence that would use Earth's gravity to help slow the ship and nudge it into orbit around the planet. It was one of those common procedures I'd spent my whole life reading about, seen in countless videos—the kind of thing I'd be doing someday—but I'd never experienced it myself. How amazing, to watch it from the bridge. But all passengers were restricted to their cabins and required to strap into their bunks to brace for the banging and bouncing that happened when a ship changed acceleration and direction.

Even lying flat and belted in, the orbital maneuvering was *cool*. I turned on the commentary on my bunk-side monitor and got a rundown on the whole process, from the approach, to the calculations that determined the exact angle of approach that would result in an orbit and not skidding off into another trajectory, to the turn of the engines to face the opposite direction to decelerate . . . Simulated gravity shifted and faded, and my stomach flopped over. My bunk shook and my teeth rattled. When I laughed, my voice vibrated.

"Will you shut up?" Charles moaned from the bunk under mine.

I wiggled to the edge of the bunk so I could look down at Charles. His eyes were clamped shut and he was gripping the strap across his chest so hard I thought his knuckles were going to pop. Was he actually getting motion sickness?

"You going to be okay?" I called down. "Want me to get you a barf bag or something?"

"Shut. Up." I could barely hear him around his rigid jaw.

It really would suck if he got sick. I'd still mock him for it until the end of our days.

The topsy-turvy bouncing lasted ten minutes or so, until the *Lilia Litviak* settled into orbit. We'd arrived. It took another day to match orbit and spin with Ride Station, where we'd be meeting the shuttle that would take us to Earth. Once again, I had to follow along with the tourist commentary on the monitor in the cabin. They wouldn't even let us watch from the observation lounge. They didn't want untrained passengers bouncing around the corridors for some reason.

Before the maneuvering started, I complained about it to Charles, who suggested, "It's because if something goes horribly wrong they don't want us to see it coming." He was probably right.

Ride Station was a kind of giant cylinder made of connected corridors, rings, pods, and docking sections held together by a steel framework. The whole thing spun to create simulated gravity in the outer levels. It was mainly a transfer station—ships coming in from Mars and the outer system could dock here; short-range shuttles from Earth delivered supplies and passengers. The place was busy, ships coming and going, passengers arriving and leaving. The space around it was filled with blinking lights and silver hulls reflecting sunlight and then falling into shadow. The closer we got, the more the hull and framework of the station filled the monitors until I couldn't see anything else.

Then we docked. I expected to feel something, a big clanging ringing through the hull, a hum as the ship powered down, a vibration as thrusting engines guided us to the docking ring. But I didn't feeling anything—until the ship's gravity was taken up by the station's spin, and then what I felt was *tired*. Heavy. My steps moved slowly, and my breath dragged out of my lungs. The gravity was spun up higher here. Two-thirds of Earth gravity, double what it was on Mars. I was going to feel this heavy for the foreseeable future. No, I was going to feel *worse*—this wasn't even full Earth gravity. How did people on Earth live like this?

We got ready to leave the ship. My bag felt massive, and I hadn't even packed much. But that five kilos on Mars would be fifteen kilos on Earth. I wanted to go home. I never thought I would miss the ship, its cramped quarters, its mind-numbing routine. But at least I could breathe there. Bags over our shoulders, Ethan, Charles, and I gathered at the mouth of the boarding tube, the passageway that linked the ship to the station. Charles didn't look like he was having too much trouble, but he was probably just hiding it really well—don't show weakness, after all. Ethan walked with his shoulders slumped and didn't seem to be doing any better than I was.

I didn't bother hiding anything. I huffed my way through the tube and dropped my bag as soon as we reached the docking bay on the station.

"That bad?" Ethan said. He was smiling, gazing around with his eyes lit up.

"You're just going to have to pick it back up," Charles observed, and I sneered at him.

The ship had docked on the station's outer hull. Inside, a broad corridor curved in both directions. At the next docking bay, fifty meters along, crates were being loaded on a ship, some kind of cargo from Earth bound for the outer system. Pipes and cables made up the ceiling, and across from us a door led to a passageway and the station's inner corridors. It was all painted a pale, inoffensive beige, same as the ship, same as half the rooms at Colony One. The least aggravating color imaginable, which made it weirdly maddening.

This could have been the garage by the air lock back home—most wide metal rooms looked the same at some level. But this one was crowded, busy, worn. The rubber matting on the floor had a scuffed trail where hundreds of footsteps had passed. Noise echoed, and a regular current of people passed along the corridor in front of us, some of them carrying satchels, pushing carts, wearing hard hats, or talking with companions. I'd seen this many people on Mars in meeting rooms or in the atrium for concerts or plays. But these were all just living and working here. I wondered if we'd have time to explore.

"There." Charles nodded.

A slim woman in a steel gray uniform, trousers, and a jacket with a pale shirt underneath, stood to the side of the bay. Her hair was short, slicked against her head, giving her a severe military look. She was staring at us like she knew us.

"Is she from Galileo?" I said. "Are we all going to have to dress like that?"

"It's not so bad," Ethan said, a little breathlessly—from the higher gravity or because he had a thing for uniforms?

She approached us, her stride predictably clipped and official. Stopping, she looked each of us up and down, slowly and appraisingly, and didn't seem particularly happy with what she saw. I felt like a diagnostic monitor and squirmed.

She donned a perfunctory, official smile. "Charles and Polly Newton? Ethan Achebe? I'm Elinor Ann Stanton, dean of students at Galileo Academy. Welcome to Ride Station. You're the last group to arrive, and we're on a tight schedule, so I hope you'll understand my hurry. If you'll come with me?"

What would happen if I said no? What if I wanted to see more of the station first? The others were already following her, and it was easier to just do what she said than to argue. Although if I ran in the other direction, how long would it take her to find me again . . .

Who was I kidding? Run? I could hardly walk in this gravity. I thought we'd get at least a day to acclimate. But no. We were headed straight to Earth. I wished I'd spent more time on the treadmill.

I hauled my twice-as-heavy bag over my shoulder and set off behind her and the others.

We followed her along the corridor, past other docking bays. The floor gently curved up ahead of us around the cylinder of the station. It almost looked like we were walking uphill, but it didn't feel like it. The station's spin was pressing us into the floor. The optical illusion was kind of fun.

Stanton wasn't much for conversation. Ethan asked her a couple of questions about how many ships were docked at the station and how many other students were waiting to go to Galileo, and her answers were clipped and vague.

We passed five more docking bays. A couple seemed empty, the doors sealed shut, docking tubes stowed, carts empty, and monitors shut down. A couple more were busy, lit up, doorways open, people moving back and forth. I tried to sneak looks down the tubes or at the monitors to see what kind of ships were there, whether they carried passengers or cargo or both. Stanton walked too quickly for me to get a good look of any of them.

She stopped at the sixth bay.

Five kids in the loose, functional jumpsuits typically worn by people who lived on ships or stations were sitting on a steel bench against the wall across from the docking-tube doorway. They stood when Stanton stopped in front of them.

With an authority that didn't invite argument, she said, "All right, students. Gather your things and let's get on board." She turned to the docking tube.

"But we just got here," I blurted. "Don't we even get a chance to look around?" My own accent sounded round and hard compared to hers, even compared to Ethan's. I hadn't realized I had an accent before.

Her smile faltered for a second and she glared lasers at me. The other kids, who'd been picking up the bags slumped on the floor at their feet, froze. There were a lot of shocked gazes looking at me. Charles's thinned lips seemed to be transmitting a message to shut up. But I couldn't.

"There has to be some kind of observation deck," I went on.

"We only got a quick look at Earth on the monitors when the ship was docking. If I'm going to be spending the next couple of years on the place, can't I at least see it?"

"You'll be able to see it on the shuttle monitors, Ms. Newton."

"It's not the same."

She managed to keep up the polite, official façade, but I could imagine her filing away this conversation for later. "Ms. Newton, you're delaying the journey for the others," she said softly, pointedly.

Yeah, I probably should have kept quiet. I wasn't even at the school yet, and I had ruffled feathers of the person in charge. Real smart there. Charles wouldn't even look at me now.

"Why don't we take a look at this shuttle of theirs?" Ethan said good-naturedly. He inched toward the docking tube, gesturing for me to follow. Like I had a choice.

I kept looking at Charles, wanting him to say something clever and derisive, like he always seemed to do when he was talking to me. But he was silent, observant. I fumed.

We joined the others and followed Stanton to the docking tube. I noticed most of the others didn't slouch under the weight of their packs when they slung them over their shoulders. So they were probably station kids, used to the gravity. However, one of them, a willowy guy with black hair and big blue eyes, seemed a little red in the face, and huffing. So he was from low gravity. I took comfort in that. And tried not to slouch. Don't show weakness. Charles might be on to something there.

Right. I could tough this out.

The tube opened into an air lock, which in turn opened into the passenger cabin, which had two dozen padded seats set in reclining positions. This ship wasn't an interplanetary long-hauler or any kind of passenger cruiser. It was an orbital shuttle, designed for hops to and from the planet surface. Functional rather than fancy. Nobody would be on it for more than a couple of hours at a time, after all.

No windows to speak of. Each seat had a monitor on an adjustable arm. That would have to do.

Stanton moved to the back of the cabin and watched us file in, stow bags in cupboards under our seats, and strap in. I hung back, waiting until everyone else was between her and me. One of the crew was stationed near the door, supervising boarding, and I wanted to talk to him.

"Welcome aboard!" he said when I made eye contact. I couldn't tell if he was really that friendly or pretending because it was his job.

"Hi," I said, trying to smile in a way that seemed harmless. "I was wondering, do you think I could maybe get a look at the crew cabin? Just a quick look. You won't even know I'm there. You see, I'm going to be a pilot someday, and I'm really interested—"

His smile inverted into a gee-whiz apologetic frown. "I'm afraid not, the crew cabin is strictly off-limits to anyone but crew."

"I know, but if I promised that I wouldn't be any trouble at all—"

"If it was up to me, I'd say yes, but it's not up to me. I'm sorry." The smile wasn't sincere at all.

"Ms. Newton, is there a problem?" Stanton asked from the back of the cabin with a smile that was looking increasingly fake.

I sighed.

Ethan had left a seat open next to him. Charles also had a seat next to him available. He was in back, where he could spy on everyone. I sat next to Ethan, after stuffing my bag into its cupboard. The effort left me breathless. I fell into the recliner and let my body go limp.

Ethan was grinning. "Isn't this exciting? Europa was nothing like this. I can't wait."

I could.

I might not have gotten a proper observation lounge, but a set of tiny view ports through the front of the cabin gave me a glimpse—my first real, unfiltered glimpse—of Earth. I thought I had known what to expect, and I prepared myself to be blasé about it. I'd seen planets from orbit before. Well, I'd seen Mars, its vast surface and array of shading like paint spilled on a floor. You could see wind storms from orbit, swirling clouds of awe-inspiring chaos. Earth was just a bigger Mars with a few extra colors splashed over it.

But I wasn't ready for the way it glowed.

It came from the clouds. I knew intellectually that the sheets and flowing wisps of white painted over the planet's surface were clouds of water vapor that reflected a great deal of sunlight. If I looked obliquely toward the curved edge of the planet, it seemed to have an aura. The atmosphere here was thick enough to *see*, almost like it was giving off its own light. I had to focus to look past the astonishing cloud layer to the land underneath it. Land and water, a blobby tangle of continents against a deep blue backdrop. The sections of land at least seemed familiar, like maps of Mars, with ridges, valleys, channels, and other rocky features. No visible craters, which made the surface seem awfully smooth. On the other hand, I couldn't picture all that blue being water. I'd seen inside the Colony One storage aquifers, containing more liquid water pressed together than anywhere else on Mars. But this—it covered most of the planet. I tried to put myself in the middle of one of those wide blue swathes, and I couldn't do it. I imagined standing on a smooth, blue plain. Not in the middle of a tank of water.

Then the ship turned, and the view outside the port turned dark. So that was Earth. I thought *strange* and *exotic* when I saw it. But I didn't think *home*. I thought I'd know what it was like to be on Earth, to stand there and be outside, breathing without a mask in a thick atmosphere. It would be like standing in the Colony One atrium, but bigger, right? I wasn't so sure now.

"What do you think?" Ethan asked. He was smiling wide, bright. He had enough enthusiasm about this whole enterprise for both of us. For the whole shuttle.

I shook my head and didn't answer. He was used to looking out view ports and seeing Jupiter. That was big enough that nothing else would ever impress him, probably. He could afford to be happy.

Me, on the other hand—I was sure I was going to be in over my head as soon as the shuttle touched down.

5

We landed at a rural shuttle port on the night side of the planet. Again, we didn't have time to look around; Stanton herded us from the shuttle to a waiting ground bus. We hardly spent any time outside. I might never have left the station. I could have been back on at the colony, sealed up in another metal can.

Except for how tired I was.

Not that I would ever admit it, or show it, or do anything that might hint that I was weak, or scared, even though my heart raced with the work of simply moving my limbs. At least the days here were about the same length they were on Mars. That was something. Maybe I'd actually be able to sleep a normal night's sleep.

I stuck close to Charles. "How are you doing?" I asked him.

"Fine," he said.

"Really? Aren't you feeling it at all?"

He looked at me. "Save your energy. Stop talking."

Well, then. Nice to see he was coping.

I fell asleep on the bus ride to the school. Kind of embarrassing. I was supposed to stay awake, waiting for the ambush. When the vehicle came to a stop, I startled awake, rubbed my face, and pretended I'd been awake the whole time, but I shouldn't have worried. Everyone else was waking up, too. Except Charles, who was gazing around, cool and collected, like he was in charge.

The bus had parked in a spacious garage, and from there a corridor led straight to the dorms. The lights were dimmed, but I had stopped wishing for a better look around. I just wanted to sleep. A good look could wait for morning.

At an intersection in the hallway, a pair of officials in slick gray uniforms just like Stanton's met us. These were residence hall supervisors, and they broke us up into groups to guide us to our rooms spread throughout the residential wing. Charles was in a different group from me. It hadn't occurred to me that Charles and I would be separated. But of course we would, we weren't at home anymore. When his adviser, along with Stanton and the others, walked on without me, I stood rooted in place, staring back at Charles. He glanced over his shoulder, lips pursed, but if he was trying to tell me something, I couldn't guess what. If twins were really supposed to have some kind of psychic link, this proved we weren't real twins. Just a couple of kids who'd happened to be born at the same time.

"Ms. Newton, this way, please," the second adviser called to me.

I slogged after the others toward our corridor.

I learned that this building housed only first-year students. Second-and third-years had their own buildings. We'd spend all three years with the same group of students, so we'd better learn to get along was the implication.

Our rooms on Colony One were small, but they were ours. Here, I'd be sharing with two others, based on the number of beds. Beside each bed was a nightstand and a closet. We had a bathroom with actual running water—the adviser had to show us how to use everything, because we were all from off-Earth. I wondered if all the rooms were split up Earth kids and non-Earth kids? The far wall had windows, but coverings were drawn over them. I still hadn't really seen what Earth's sky looked like. The nightstands had reading lamps, turned on and focused on the beds, and small terminal screens for announcements and wake-up calls. At least I basically recognized everything. Except for the running water. On Mars and on the ship we used dry soap and vacuums.

The terminal screens were all lit up with the overly smiling face of a middle-aged man with brown skin and salt-and-pepper hair in yet another gray uniform. He was standing in a garden in front of a row of very neatly trimmed shrubs. It was like the garden in the Colony One atrium times a thousand. A label called the man Vincent Juno Edgars, the president of the school, and he looked like he was hiding something. When we touched the screens, a message scrolled up welcoming us to Galileo Academy, the finest school in the universe, where we would embark on "the great adventure that will be the rest of your lives."

The closets had our names on them, and the correct luggage was set on the floor next to them. Everything was just so, all in order. It made me itch, thinking of the way everything had been all planned out.

So, here we were. The adviser for this wing, a woman named

Janson with blond hair tied back in a bun, told us to get to bed and get some sleep, because we had an early start in the morning.

"How early?" I'd asked.

She glared. "You'll be awakened."

That sounded ominous.

She left the three of us staring at each other, the sparsely furnished room, and the door, which Janson had shut behind her. These two had been on the shuttle with us from Ride Station. We hadn't had a chance to talk, between traveling and sleeping and Stanton riding herd on us.

"So," I muttered at the others. "Some party. Um. I'm Polly. And you're . . ." Charles would have remembered their names right off. He'd probably hacked a copy of the files of everybody at the school weeks ago.

"Marie," said the one with her hair in a braid, who kept her gaze down. She was already unpacking.

"Ladhi," said the shorter girl with glossy black hair cut shoulder length. "Are you really from Mars?"

She made it sound amazing. "Yeah. And you're . . ."

"Moore Station. Out on the Belt. I've never even *been* on a planet before. I'm kind of flipping out a little." Her eyes were wide; her hands wrung each other. "But you—this must be just normal for you."

"Not really. Mars isn't exactly habitable. You can't leave the colony buildings without life support. And the gravity's way off."

"Oh, the *gravity*. I already hate it."

"They tell me it gets better."

She sat on her bed, letting out a deflating sigh. "I sure hope so."

I sat on my bed, next to hers. I could start unpacking, or I could just collapse and let the gravity pull me into sleep.

From the other side of the room Marie said, "That other guy with the brown hair—he's your brother, right?"

"Yes. Charles," I muttered. I hoped she got that I didn't want to talk about him. Marie nodded thoughtfully.

Ladhi leaned forward. "And the other guy you were with, Ethan. He's really cute."

"Almost as cute as Tenzig," Marie observed, smiling for the first time.

"That's the other guy from Ride Station?" I said. "The tall one?"

"With those blue eyes," Ladhi said with a sigh. "Tenzig Jones. His family runs Aurora Shipping. He's going to be a pilot someday." Her voice got all dreamy.

"*I'm* going to be a pilot someday," I said. "Besides, I'm not really interested. I have a boyfriend back on Mars, actually."

"Oh. And he's okay with this? Being so far away and all."

"Yeah. I mean, we talked it over. It's just the way things are." Actually, I was feeling guilty at how little I'd thought of Beau over the last couple of days. I was sure it was just the trauma of finally getting to Earth. I ought to write him a note telling him I was here, what it was like, and how it couldn't possibly get any worse.

Ladhi kept talking, manic with exhaustion like I was. My ears were buzzing. "My mom really doesn't like it, me being so far away, not seeing me for years maybe. But who could pass up a chance like this?"

I raised my hand. "I'd have been happy to stay on Mars."

"Oh, no," Ladhi said, breathless with awe. "This is the best school anywhere. If you can get through here, you'll be set for life."

"Is that it?" I grumbled. "Doesn't it depend on what you want to do with your life?"

"Well, sure. But you want to succeed, don't you?"

Succeed, according to whom? My *mother*?

I wanted to be a pilot. If being at Galileo made that easier, so be it. But I wasn't convinced that the place was a guarantee to a great life. I put on a good front for her. "Sure."

I hadn't brought very much from Mars: a couple of changes of clothes and my handheld. My boots, and a vial of red-brown sand that made me homesick just looking at it. Mom said they'd have everything here that I needed, and she was right. In our labeled closets we found a whole collection of clothing in exactly our sizes: tailored uniforms with blouses, jackets, slacks; loose-fitting knits for exercising; nightshirts for sleeping; dress shoes and running shoes; and a whole collection of underthings and socks and such. They'd taken scans and measurements from our records and produced it all.

I dressed in the brand-new clothes that felt weird and different—they were made of natural fibers, Marie explained. Cotton. We didn't have cotton on Mars, everything was synthetic. I didn't think I'd have to get used to the clothes, on top of everything else.

In half an hour the lights were off. At least the beds were nicer than on the *Lilia Litviak*. Thick and soft, with plenty of blankets. They were almost as nice as at home. The only reason they weren't as nice was that it wasn't home.

6

In the morning, an alarm rang. Actually, a soft bell that might have been pleasant in any other context chimed from our bedside terminals. As a wake-up call it was kind of oppressive. Especially when followed by Stanton's fake-polite voice announcing that we had a half an hour before we had to line up for breakfast and orientation.

I rolled over and something under my pillow crinkled. Paper. I slapped around above the bed before finding the reading lamp and touching it on.

Polly's eyes only the note read. And how had Charles snuck in here and slipped it under my pillow without waking anyone up? Did I really want to know?

I opened the page and read: *"Let me do all the talking."*

Whatever that meant. Did he think either of us would get much of a chance to talk? I crumpled up the note and tossed it in my closet. I'd look for a recycle unit later.

Marie was already out of bed and getting dressed. I wasn't so eager. As long as I stayed in bed, I wouldn't have to start the day, and I wouldn't have to see what the next few years of my life were going to look like. But as long as I stayed in bed, I was delaying the inevitable. So I hauled myself upright.

Our uniforms were a junior version of what Stanton wore. We'd all look the same, and no one would be able to tell I came from Mars, at least not by what I was wearing. That was probably the point, that we'd all look the same no matter where we came from. Except people would be able to tell anyway as soon as we talked—we all sounded different.

I strapped on my dress shoes, trying to work out their stiff newness, just as Stanton appeared in the doorway. She studied me as I went to join Ladhi and Marie. Her look could have expressed disgust, contempt, or just the fact it was too early in the morning. I couldn't tell.

"Good morning, girls. This way, please," she said, and walked out. We assumed she meant us to follow, and we did so, down the hall and through a set of double doors into a new room. Other clusters of students filed in with us.

It looked like a dining and assembly hall, a wide, lofty space with windows lined along the high ceiling to let in sunlight. I squinted against the brightness and regarded the large space suspiciously. I still couldn't see outside, to see what Earth really looked like.

Those of us from the shuttle joined a swarm of a couple of dozen other students who'd arrived earlier—most of them from Earth. I could spot them pretty easily: they didn't look like they'd been run over by construction equipment in the last day. They were muscular, straight, calm, and smug. The handful of us from offworld—we had to work hard just to breathe.

We all lined up in rows, looking like clones in our uniforms.

I spotted Charles, standing at the end of his row, arms crossed, studious. I hoped to catch his eye, but it seemed like he was trying not to look at me. Like he didn't want to admit he knew me. But he wouldn't be able to deny it. I'd never thought about it before, us being almost twins and looking a lot alike. But here, among all these strangers, I couldn't help but spot it—we both had tall, wiry frames, pale freckled cheeks, narrow noses, and unruly hair the same red-brown as Martian dust. This was going to be just great—we'd be the two weird-looking Martian kids. No way we could hide.

All of us offworlders, the kids from the shuttle yesterday, looked weird—spindly and pale. Even Ethan's dark skin seemed more washed out than the other dark-skinned students. The students from Earth were big, bulky. Monsters. They could beat up us offworlders without breaking a sweat. Snap our delicate, low-gravity bones. We'd have to depend on the civilizing influences of polite society to keep them in check. I'd have said they looked like the weird ones, but we were on Earth, and there were a lot more of them than there were of us. They studied us all with something like contempt. To them, we must have looked like walking, talking skeletons. I started to understand what Lieutenant Clancy had been talking about. The lieutenant had had the build of a station-born person. He'd have known.

We were all eyeing one another, like runners sizing each other up before a race.

Along one wall was a long counter, and behind that had to be a kitchen, based on the warm smells of cooking food coming from it. At least they were going to feed us. Real food, not packaged ship fare. Soon, I hoped, but first, Stanton had a lecture to give.

Her smile was stiff, her gaze appraising. She stood, hands clasped before her, at polite attention. "Welcome, all of you, to Galileo Academy. I know I don't have to explain to you that your presence here makes you part of a prestigious tradition of excellence and accomplishment. Your time at Galileo will be challenging, to say the least, but you would not be here if someone, somewhere, didn't believe you were capable of it." She eyed me then, before her glance darted to Charles. I might have imagined it, her singling us out with an almost unconscious gaze. But to me it seemed to have meaning. The exceptions to the rule, maybe. Her wondering if we could really cut it here.

Janson and the other adviser stepped forward then to list out the rules and procedures, sparing Stanton that chore. Each class had a structured schedule and we must not deviate from it, schedules would be transmitted to our handhelds, clean uniforms were provided in closets, soiled uniforms must be placed in proper laundry receptacles, off-campus communication via handhelds was restricted to the one hour before bedtime recreation-and-study period (the implication being we ought to be studying during recreation period, naturally). Don't leave campus, stick with your classmates, stick to routine, listen to authority figures, and all will be well. Don't slack off, don't disappoint, and don't fail the glorious tradition that is Galileo. I wasn't sure I even understood what tradition was. People had lived on Mars for less than a hundred years, but that was all I knew. Anything that went on longer than that was alien.

By the end I was thinking about how hungry I was and what they would feed us for breakfast. Breakfast on Mars was hydroponic greens, soy protein, juices, and supplements. That had seemed normal. I'd never thought that breakfast could be anything else until we got on the ship, where there'd been fancier foods: pastries, potatoes, fruits, more soy protein, but still the kinds of foods that were easy to make and transport in space, frozen and reconstituted. Before leaving Mars I hadn't thought about how even the food would be different on Earth. I was about to find out what people ate for breakfast on Earth, or at least at Galileo, and I wasn't really looking forward to it. I was still taking supplements, some of which were supposed to adapt us to Earth foods and microbes.

Finally, Stanton and her minions stopped talking and pointed us to the counter, where food was served buffet style in heated servers. I didn't recognize about half of it. Fortunately, I recognized the other half: fruit, potatoes, and cheese. Those were what I piled on my plate.

I was starting to get nervous—even more nervous—because I wasn't sure anymore what would be familiar and what wouldn't. Back on Mars, I could look around and know if something was wrong, know if something looked different. But here, if something looked wrong, like if there was water running from a faucet or if a plate of food didn't smell familiar, how would I know if it was really wrong or just weird? I couldn't pay attention to every single thing every minute of the day.

I was afraid we'd have to sit in our same nice straight rows, but lacking directions to the contrary, people scattered as soon as they had their trays filled. My carefully chosen breakfast in hand, Ladhi and I went to find Ethan and Charles. Maybe we could have our own little offworlder gang. I'd lost sight of Marie, then I spotted her—next to Tenzig Jones, who was at a table on the other side of the room. Well, it was nice that she had a hobby.

Ethan spotted me first and waved. He and Charles had staked out one end of a table. We hurried over and sat across from them.

Charles examined my plate after I set it down. "Good. I was going to warn you not to eat the bacon, it will probably make you sick. We don't have the stomach enzymes to digest it."

"Even with the supplements?" I said.

"Even then."

Bacon. One of the unrecognizable foods set out for us, evidently. I hated that I was a little bit pleased that I'd done something right in Charles's eyes. Not that I'd ever tell him. "What's bacon?" I said.

"Fried pig muscle." He pointed to a wrinkled, dried strip of brown on Ethan's plate. Ethan puckered his mouth and pushed the bacon to the side of his plate, away from the other food.

Um, right. We didn't really have animals on Mars. Not agricultural animals, anyway, although the next phase of colonial development involved importing eggs and hatching chickens, and then building atrium pastures for goats. We had a few cats and dogs as pets that some colonists insisted on bringing, and a few laboratory animals. Our protein came from beans and soy, but on Earth, people still ate animal muscle. Trust Charles to think about it in exactly those terms.

"Why wouldn't they warn us about something like that?" Ethan said. "Limit what we eat until we're used to it, or give us the right digestive aids or something?"

"Yes, why wouldn't they?" Charles said, not looking up from his plate, where he shoveled something that looked like oatmeal into his spoon.

He let that hang there, and we all looked at our breakfasts like they were out to get us.

"Well, I still think it's exciting," Ethan said. Things would be so much easier if some of his attitude would rub off on me.

"I'm not sure," I said. "Everything's so . . . *weird.*"

Ladhi winced. "I'm so nervous, I know I'm going to screw up."

"Just relax," Ethan told her.

Charles frowned. He kept looking around like he expected something to happen. When his gaze finally focused, I looked to see what he'd spotted.

Three of the Earth kids approached our table, closing us in and staring us down. If they looked big from a distance, they looked like giants sitting next to us.

"Welcome to Earth," said the one next to Ethan. He had brown skin, close-cropped hair, and appraising eyes that made me want to look away. He put his elbows on the table and leaned in, like he owned the place. "I'm George Lou Montes. This is Marielle Ella Kent and Elzabeth Lea Rockney."

He said the names like we should have recognized them. I wasn't even sure I could understand him; he had a thick accent, rounded, that made the words run together. I had to listen closely and still wasn't sure I got it. When we all stared blankly at him, he smirked. Like he'd scored a point.

"Do we have to remember all those names?" I said.

"Ethan," Ethan said, extending his hand to shake. Which George didn't, and Ethan let his hand rest on the table.

"Just Ethan?" Marielle asked, and she and Elzabeth bent their heads together and giggled.

Marielle had the most amazing golden hair, tied in a braid over her shoulder, making her look rugged, powerful. Elzabeth was pale, round, curvy, gazing out through half-lidded eyes, like she was always just about to laugh at something. They all filled out their uniforms, which suddenly seemed to hang on the rest of us like sacks.

Ethan continued, unperturbed. "Ethan Achebe. But just call me Ethan. This is Ladhi Bijanai, and Polly and Charles Newton."

"Newton," George said. "Are you really from Mars?" He glanced at us both, gaze narrowed, like he didn't believe it.

"Yes," both Charles and I said at the same time, like a computer with two speakers. We glared at each other.

"That makes you the first Martian students ever at Galileo Academy, isn't that right?"

"That's what we've been told," Charles said.

"Though not surprising, I suppose. As I understand it, the Martian education system just isn't up to standards."

I could punch him. And probably break my hand doing it. Right, then. I could glare at him.

"The standards," Charles said, "are entirely dependent on the desired outcome, or the context in which that education is required. I might question, for example, whether an exclusively Earth-based education would prepare one for surviving a week on a survey expedition across Utopia Planitia. What standards are you referring to, in this case?"

George gave a huff—a laugh or a dismissal or both. "Earth's a little more complicated than your colony, I imagine."

"What do you know about it?" I shot back. "You ever been to Mars?"

"Polly . . ." Charles said in a tone of warning.

Marielle leaned forward next, glancing between me and Charles. "Are you two brother and sister? Really?"

I was about to answer, when Charles said, "We're twins."

"That's so *weird*," Marielle said. "I mean, no family has more than one child these days. It's so, well, *primitive*."

And on Mars, people were encouraged to have all the kids they could manage so we could actually build up a stable and productive population. But I wasn't going to say that when it would only make me sound *more weird*.

I had about lost my appetite. "I don't understand what the problem is. Are you trying to intimidate us? *Scare* us? Bully us into treating you guys like some kind of king of the hill? Seriously?"

Marielle and Elzabeth fell into another giggling fit.

My face flushed, burning almost, even though I had no reason to be upset or embarrassed. They were the ones being idiots. And there wasn't a thing I could say that they wouldn't laugh at. Ladhi had slouched, shrunk in her seat, gaze locked on the tabletop. Ethan was eating toast like nothing was wrong. At least Charles was glaring. But at *me*. What had I done?

"Excuse me," I muttered, extricating myself from the seat, untangling my legs, which seemed to get knotted up in the chair legs and my own uniform pants. I finally managed it and marched out of the room, angry enough to spit.

Colony One was the largest of Mars's four established colony settlements, but it still wasn't big, not by Earth standards, and there weren't very many kids there. A hundred, tops. So we all went to one big school and chose courses based on our interests. We had age brackets but not really class groups. Apart from a handful of designated instructors, other workers and officials around the colony volunteered to teach special courses. By the time most of us got to be teenagers like me and Charles, we'd been all over the colony, we knew just about everyone, we'd learned about basic operations, and we had a pretty good idea what area of study we wanted to go into. I'd had my eye on the astrodrome as long as I could remember.

There wasn't anything wrong with the way we did school, it was just different. And sure, we had cliques and groups and older and younger kids and the rest of it. But this, George and the others . . . something else was going on here.

I needed to be alone, to think. But I didn't have anywhere to go. I didn't know where anything was. All I could do was pace back and forth between the dining hall and the dorm room. Back home I'd escape to the garage, take out my scooter. Or if I couldn't do that because of a dust storm or whatever, I'd go to the atrium and run. Just to get away for a little while.

The thought of running here, three times heavier than I ought to be, made me ill. Even pacing along the corridor made me gasp for breath. This place was awful. Everything about it was awful.

There had to be a way out of this building. So I kept walking.

I found the garage where the bus had let us out last night. Now, in daylight, I could get a good look at it. It was another large room, like the dining hall, with a high ceiling and a row of distant windows to let in light. Daytime revealed a couple of transport buses, like the one that had carried us; some smaller vehicles that could carry three or four people lined up on the far side; and a row of two-wheeled individual transports that seemed useful and intriguing. Most of them looked muscle operated—foot pedals connected to chains and gears that turned rubber-coated wheels. But a couple of others seemed to have motors, like my scooter back home, but with wheels for riding on hard surfaces rather than hover lifts for going over sand. I wondered what I'd have to do to learn how to operate them. Maybe I couldn't run too far right now, but one of those could probably help me work out some frustration.

In the meantime, a door to the outside stood open, and that was all I wanted at the moment. To get *out*.

Across the garage's concrete floor, to the door, and through it, and I was outside.

Air blew at me like a gentle breath from a vent grating. A flat drive led away from the garage, around a curve and out of sight. Away from it on both sides spread a lawn, trimmed grass, bright green—just like the atrium's lawn, I thought smugly.

Then I looked up. And up, and up, at no roof, no ceiling, no dome, nothing holding the air in. Open sky meant no air. I choked, gasped, covered my mouth and held my breath. I didn't have my mask on, what was I doing outside without a mask? But then I remembered this was Earth. Breathable atmosphere. The atrium writ large. Had to remember that. And the sun, just hanging up there, huge, monstrous. I could feel it on my skin, a burning warmth. I could actually feel the UV rays burning me.

A shiver touched my spine, and I forced myself to take a slow, careful breath. Then another. I pressed against the wall of the garage and forced myself to stay there, to feel the sun and breathe the unfiltered air. The lawn, it kept *going.*

Everything was fine, just fine.

I shut my eyes, took several deep breaths, and imagined I was in the atrium back home. The air didn't smell right, of course, and I couldn't have said exactly why it didn't smell right. But it wasn't going to kill me. I'd had all the inoculations. When I opened my eyes again, I could almost stand away from the wall without feeling like I was going to fall down.

So. This was Earth.

"Polly?" Charles stood in the garage doorway, leaning out. "You okay?"

I pointed out to the endless lawn and roofless sky. "Why didn't anyone warn us about this?"

"They did," he said. "You didn't listen." He turned his own gaze up to the endless blue sky, ducking just a bit, as if he expected something to fall on him. "And the warnings don't really help."

I looked over his shoulder into the garage, expecting to see . . . something not good, anyway. "Am I in trouble?"

"Not yet. I told you to let me do the talking."

"Then you should have stood up for us. Why didn't you stand up for us?"

"I didn't need to. The more attention you pay them, the more power you give them. It doesn't matter what they say. We have as much right to be here as they do, and we'll prove it in time without arguing."

I slouched against the wall. This planet was sucking the life out of me. "I don't know how much of this I can take."

"Think about it for once in your life, Polly. These Earth kids—a lot of them have been to school together before, or they've known each other their whole lives through their families. They're Earth's elite, and they're going to use that. Montes's family owns the shuttle that we flew in on—they control forty percent of Earth's suborbital transport. Elzabeth's mother is a representative in the European Union government."

"So? Why does any of that matter?"

"They're used to getting their way. They think this is a game, and they expect to win. You don't want them to win, don't play the game. Understand?"

Stanton arrived then, a frowning automaton. "Mr. Newton, Ms. Newton, this area is off-limits to students without supervision," she said in a kindly voice, like she was talking to toddlers. But her next line sounded like a threat. "Is everything all right?"

I opened my mouth, but Charles talked over me. "We were just taking a walk."

"You should have asked permission or waited for the designated PE period. I won't penalize you now, because I can understand that you may not be familiar with the rules here like the other students are. But from now on, don't go anywhere without permission or supervision." She gestured back to the building's interior, indicating we should go inside.

Dutifully, we marched. Stanton fell in behind us, so I couldn't yell at Charles. Not right away. Back in the dining hall, he found an unoccupied corner of a table, made me sit, and gave me a cup of water. I didn't even realize I was thirsty.

"You see her," I told him. "She thinks we're idiots, too, just because we're not from Earth."

"Don't cause trouble."

"I can't believe you're just taking this."

"They're watching, Polly. Watching, listening. Have you seen the cameras?"

"What?"

"In the upper corners. Just look, don't stare."

I let my gaze wander across the walls, then the ceiling, and there they were, shiny black domes the size of a fist. Surveillance package of some kind, camera, microphone, infrared, who knew what else. We had something like it on Colony One. Mostly, maintenance used them to check on systems.

"They're for security? Maintenance?" I said to him.

"They're watching *us*," he said. "Stanton knew right where to find us."

"What's it mean?"

"We're always being graded, every single minute. Keep that in mind."

"Great," I muttered.

"That's what I'm saying—try not to stand out too much, okay?"

"Charles, have you *looked* at us?"

"All right. Try not to stand out more than necessary."

7

Now that he pointed out the surveillance, I saw the little domes everywhere. Way more than a maintenance crew would need to check on pipes, wiring, and wall integrity. Not that wall integrity mattered here. Back home, cameras watched *things*. Air locks and wiring and pipes, things that needed to be watched closely, or else everybody would die. Here, they were watching *us*. Didn't they trust us?

Our rooms and the dining hall were in the same building, but to get to the classrooms we had to go outside, following concrete walkways that cut across grassy lawns. Once again, the non-Earth kids stood out, because this was supposedly totally normal—but we couldn't handle it. We stood at the threshold like we were getting ready to step off a cliff. I had to hold Ladhi's hand to get her to leave the doorway.

"It's just like an atrium, but really big. Think of it that way," I told her.

"Moore Station doesn't have any atriums, just hydroponics gardens!" She huddled close to me, cringing from the open sky.

I did some research on agoraphobia, an anxiety disorder that sometimes included a fear of open spaces. It was really common for people who grew up on stations or in colonies to experience it when they came to Earth. I didn't have it quite as bad because I was used to being outside on Mars. I just wasn't used to being outside without a suit, and I kept wanting to hold my breath until I could get my breathing mask on.

"Is everything all right, Ms. Bijanai?" Stanton stood aside with her arms folded.

"Ms. Stanton," I answered, being as polite as I possibly could. "I read that there were maybe some supplements, some medications that might help with this kind of situation." I didn't want to use the words "anti-anxiety" or "phobia," because that would make it sound like something was really wrong, that we were broken, and we weren't. We just weren't used to this. Ladhi was shaking.

Stanton offered a pitying, unkind smile. "Those options are available in extreme cases. Is this an extreme case?"

"No, Ms. Stanton," I said quickly, before Ladhi could speak, because I realized this was one of those situations Charles was talking about. One of the times we weren't supposed to show weakness. We were expected to tough it out. If we needed help, then we didn't belong here, and the implication was we didn't belong in the world that came after—including pilot training. "We're just fine."

"Good," she said.

"Just take a deep breath and go," I whispered to Ladhi, and squeezed her hand.

We got through it, and we helped each other. It would get easier, I hoped.

We were scheduled to rotate between classes throughout the day in groups of twelve. Charles and I had the same first class, history. After breakfast, we were all expected to file to class together, like robots. I was the only person grumbling about it.

Galileo Academy's classrooms looked normal enough, even though they were brightly lit with high ceilings, wasting a ton of space. Rows of desks lined up in front a wall-size vid display. But the desks didn't have terminals. They were just flat surfaces with chairs behind them.

"Where are the terminals?" I asked, put out, wondering what the joke was. How were we supposed to look up things? How were we supposed to take notes?

The instructor, standing at the front of the room, cleared his throat and drew our attention.

"All right, students, listen to me." He was a nondescript guy with pale skin and dark hair, heavyset in the way of all Earthers. He was reading from a hand terminal. "Sit when I call your name, starting with the front left-hand side of the room, working across rows." He started reading off names.

We couldn't just sit where we wanted to? Ratty.

"Newton, Polly," he called. The next desk in line was smack in the middle of the room. No escape.

"Where are the desk terminals?" I asked him.

He frowned. "You don't have them. You'll have to put away your handhelds as well. Here at Galileo, you're expected to think on your own."

"What is that—" He'd already turned back to his terminal, reading off the next names. One of the Earth girls giggled.

Charles was eyeing me, and I decided not to do anything—

anything else—that would give him the satisfaction of acting superior at my expense. I'd do what he did: wait, watch, pretend it didn't matter. But no desk terminals seemed really primitive. Wasn't Earth supposed to be all advanced and amazing?

We settled into our places, and I prepared to listen. I was already thinking too hard.

The instructor introduced himself, "I'm Professor Iyan Piotr Broderick. You may call me Professor Broderick. I've transmitted to each of your accounts the texts we'll be covering in class this semester and I expect that you will read them in a timely manner and be prepared to discuss them in class."

If we had desk terminals, or even ports that interfaced with our handhelds, we could look up the information right now.

"Let's get started. We're going to be covering the nineteenth century C.E. forward, with a focus on the political and social dynamics that led to the current climate of nation-conglomerates in loosely associated alliances. Can anyone tell me the names of the first efforts toward a globally recognized political body?"

My hands moved to type at a keypad that wasn't there. I could have looked it up. That was what online databases were for. But five kids put up their hands—including Charles, which didn't surprise me.

Broderick called on one of the Earth kids. Elzabeth. "Yes, Ms. Rockney?"

"The League of Nations first, then the United Nations."

"That's right. Very good. And what prompted their creation?"

Again, hands went up—Charles's first; Broderick didn't call on him, but on another Earth boy.

"The twentieth-century wars," he said.

"More specific, please?"

He deflated, disappointed, and one of the other students said, "World Wars One and Two."

Charles was stewing. His expression didn't change, but the gleam in his eyes got dark. Nobody but me would recognize that he was getting frustrated.

Then I realized: this wasn't just a class; it was a competition.

It went on like that. I didn't know the answers to any of the questions, because why would I? What was I supposed to know about Earth two hundred years ago? On the other hand, I could tell him every single important event that happened on Mars since the Viking probes landed back in the 1970s.

But this wasn't about teaching the answers to things. It was about seeing who in the class was the best and showing everyone else up.

"What about Mars?" I said finally.

Frowning, Professor Broderick glanced at his class roster. "Ms. Newton? We raise our hand in class when we have a question."

We do, do we? Fine. I raised my hand straight.

"Yes, Ms. Newton?"

"What about Mars?" He raised an eyebrow, and I added, "Are we going to be studying Martian history at all in this class? Or any colonization history? I thought that part of what solidified political conglomerates on Earth was the growing number of settlements outside Earth." At least, that was what we talked about in Martian history.

"The outer system is covered in next year's history course."

"Assuming you make it that far," one of the girls hissed. I expected Broderick to reprimand her, but he didn't.

I glared. Then I sat back and kept quiet, because yes, everything at Galileo was going to be like this for the next three years.

We had a break for lunch, which was nice, because I sat quietly, meekly, all the way through history, biology (again, all Earth biology), and astrophysics (mildly more interesting because we had to talk about something other than Earth and I actually knew most of the answers. I still didn't raise my hand, because why bother?). I couldn't sit still forever.

I had time to observe some of the other students, the second- and third-years, as they passed back and forth between their residences and classrooms. They seemed a lot more relaxed, and it was harder to tell the offworlders from the Earth kids. They'd had time to adjust—and it was like Galileo Academy was supposed to turn everyone into Earth kids. Was that why Mom sent us here? It was still weird, thinking that none of them were from Mars. Just us, out of everyone here.

Back in the dining hall, we had sandwiches that actually looked familiar and fruit that didn't. It was long, narrow, and yellow, and I had to watch someone peel the skin off it to figure out how to do it myself. The twelve of us from the astrophysics section ended up at a table together—not by design so much as convenience. Most of the other tables were filled. I'd lost track of Charles. I wasn't sure what class he'd had right before lunch.

Tenzig Jones, who wanted to be a starpilot, too, and Ladhi were in this group. The three of us sat together at one end of the table. The rest of the group were Earthers.

"How are you two holding up?" Tenzig asked. His flat accent

sounded familiar and comforting after listening to that Earth accent all day.

"I'm in so over my head," Ladhi said, and she actually looked like she was tearing up, her eyes glistening. I wanted to hug her.

"It's culture shock, that's all," Tenzig said. "You have to get used to it."

"You've been to Earth before this, didn't you say?" I asked.

"Yeah," he said casually, like of course he'd been to Earth. "Lots of times. I go with my parents on business trips."

"Well, I hope I get used to it soon," Ladhi said.

George, the Earth guy from breakfast, spoke in a fake whisper loud enough to carry. "Embryos don't develop correctly in low gravity," he said with the certainty of his convictions. "Sure, you can inject supplements to increase bone density and muscle mass. People born offworld may *look* human. But there's something about the way the brains form—they never turn out quite right." He brought his finger to his temple and made a spinning motion, the universal hand signal for "wacko." *That* translated just fine.

And that was what everyone in the school was thinking, wondering what we were even doing here. I glared. Even though Charles would have wanted me to ignore him, I had to say something. "Off-planet, fertilization is in vitro and embryos are put in incubators and spun up to full gravity to gestate. We're just the same."

George shook his head, tsking. "That sounds so . . . mechanized. It just isn't the same. But I suppose when you don't have the benefit of being here on Earth, you do what you can to cope."

"We cope just *fine*—"

"Polly—" Ladhi said, her voice low, her hand on my arm.

I shrugged her away. "I'm *fine!*"

"That's exactly what I'm talking about," George said, leaning close as if confiding in his friends. "Brain development is stunted. Leads to poor impulse control."

Like he was some kind of walking disciplinary report. I'd punch him, I really would. Tenzig chuckled, shaking his head. "It'll all come out in the scores, dirtsider."

George smiled wickedly. "Looking forward to it, vacuum head."

The Earthers turned away from us, huddled together in private conversation. The laughter was audible, though.

"That's the trick," Tenzig said, still smiling. "Not to take it personally. It's all a big game."

"I thought games were supposed to be fun," I said.

"Games are for winning," he answered.

"Which would be great if they also weren't for losing."

"I don't think I like it here," Ladhi murmured.

"We just have to stick together," I said, and Tenzig looked like he felt sorry for us.

8

Hi Beau,

It's been rough. I'm trying to give it a chance, I really am. But we've got so much holding us back before we even start. The gravity, for one. The lack of ceilings. I go outside and keep reaching for an air mask, and I have to remind myself that I don't need it here. You just breathe in all this raw unfiltered air. I hate to think what kind of bugs and germs and muck I'm sucking in along with it. We have filtration for a reason, you know? And the rooms are so big, they waste so much space here.

Then there's the Earth kids. So get this, everybody here has three names, and they introduce themselves with all three names like they expect you to remember, when I have trouble remembering even one because they're different. I asked Charles why they're so big on their fancy names, and he said it's tradition. It's what they do because they're proud of themselves and their families. But it's so complicated.

They hate us, they really do. They say things like, if

we—or our parents, or grandparents, or whatever—had been good enough to make it on Earth they never would have left. We're all losers and charity cases. They don't even know what it's like on Mars, or the Moon, or the stations or anything. And they don't care. What's worse, the instructors are pretty much the same way.

I don't see how I'm supposed to learn anything if I have to spend all my time being furious at everyone.

Yours dejectedly,
Polly

PE was the worst because we were automatically at a disadvantage and there wasn't anything we could do about it. George was right: compared to them, by their standards, we were broken. At least we could pick the sport we wanted to do—running, weight training, or a handful of team games played with balls that I couldn't follow without watching very carefully. I picked weight training, because at least there I could stand in one spot. Charles ran because, he explained, he could do it alone. I'd watch, and he'd be the last one in the group running around the school's track—until the others lapped him—and not seem to notice. He kept his face forward, his legs moving, however slowly, and just got the job done.

At least the instructors didn't expect us offworlders to be able to lift as much, run as far, or play as hard as the Earth kids. Not that we even could without bursting our arteries or breaking bones. In another sense, it made it worse. We were segregated. The runners lagged far behind the Earth runners, the non-Earth kids had to play with each other rather than their Earth class-mates, who could accidentally break our bones just by running into us. And I had to stand there lifting tiny little weights no bigger than my own hand. *I'd* have laughed at me. Not that the Earth kids laughed. They didn't have to.

The one classmate who was even worse off than Charles and me and the rest was Boris. He grew up on one of the lunar bases and was used to one-sixth gravity. He'd been through all the same supplement regimes and exercise routines that the rest of us had, but he had so much more catching up to do. He couldn't even manage the hand-size weights. He sure tried, turning red in the face, his whole frame trembling as he lifted it off the floor.

An upperclass student intern was supervising us that day: Franteska—I couldn't remember her other two names—was a third-year with short black hair and a stunningly muscular physique. But then just about everyone on Earth looked stunningly muscular to me. She was an athlete, she informed us repeatedly, proudly, as proof of her qualification to judge us on every little thing. Franteska watched Boris struggling, and I was afraid she was going to give him a hard time, lay out some cutting insult that would make me have to yell at her. And she looked like she wanted to, but she didn't. Instead, she gave a big sigh and told him to put down the hand weights. Instead, she gave him a set of flat disks that she'd pulled off another piece of equipment—not weights but bolts that held the weights in place. *These* he could successfully lift in a standard curl, though he still appeared to be working hard. Boris frowned and wouldn't look at anyone. He never gave up. We all looked out for him, to make sure he had space.

Only way to get through was to get through, but that didn't mean it wasn't hard.

In the evening came dinner, then recreation hour, then lights-out. Every minute of the day was structured and accounted for. If I wanted to record messages for home, I'd have to skip math homework, or do it in half the time. Or skip history reading. Or skip lunch. On weekends, we didn't have class, but we had required extracurricular activities, more study hall, and supplemental PE for offworlders. Biophysical development, they called it. We called it remedial PE. Whoever heard of remedial PE?

Even if we got along great with the Earth kids, we would have stayed separate from them, formed our own cliques, and not made friends among them. It might have made me sad if they didn't drive me crazy every time I tried talking to them.

This was what my life was going to be like, week after week. The Galileo program was three years long—Earth years, at least, which were shorter than Mars years. But it still felt like forever.

The dorm buildings had a couple of big study rooms with good lighting, desks, and terminals, thank goodness, where we were supposed to spend our recreation hours doing homework. Reading for history, a ton—Earth ton, not the lighter Mars ton—of math problems, astrophysics, biology, geography (Earth geography, and I asked if we were going to be studying Mars and was told not until next year, like the history). I never knew where to start when I sat down to study. I usually jumped around. A couple of math problems until it drove me crazy, some history reading, some scribbling on my hand terminal, some more reading. And over and over again. Eventually, somehow, every day, I managed to get it done.

The system was rigged: we didn't grow up knowing basic Earth history like the names of countries that participated in this thing called World War II. Mars didn't even have countries— each colony was an independent business conglomerate. That was how colonists were originally encouraged to settle, they'd get their own country out of it, basically. The stations in the outer system worked like that, too. So Galileo was a contest and a bunch of us arrived here with negative points. Not only that, some of our evaluation was based on how much we participated in class— raised our hands and answered questions—but Professor Broderick, the history instructor, never called on non-Earthers. And yet we just kept going because we didn't have a choice.

Charles buried himself in the work and hardly ever came back into the light. We had a couple of classes together—history and PE—but he hardly ever talked to me. When I tried to talk to him, he gave me a look like I'd interrupted something important. He probably decided that associating with me would hold him back. That was okay. I didn't need him. Ethan, Ladhi, and I stuck close, eating meals together and helping each other with homework. Tenzig and Marie joined in sometimes, along with the other offworlder kids. After the first week or so, most of the Earth kids stopped needling us so badly. Probably because it was way too easy and they got bored with it. And they were swamped with as much homework as the rest of us. They'd have to pick between teasing us or keeping up with astrophysics.

We'd been at Galileo for four weeks, and the routine had become familiar enough that I could believe I'd been doing it forever. Except I still got tired just walking to class, I was still lifting half the weights of my Earther classmates, and I dreamed about rocky brown Martian horizons every night. I missed the smell of canned air from a breathing mask.

One study period, as I sat at one of the tables with a half dozen others and read history on my handheld, I wondered again how the details of international relations on Earth a hundred years ago were relevant to knowing how to fly starships to Jupiter. My mother would tell me I needed to learn this so that I could be well-rounded. So I could understand the way things were now— even Jupiter had been influenced by what had happened on Earth a hundred years ago.

I'd read the same page three times and thought maybe I ought to switch to working on math, when the girl sitting next to me leaned over.

"Hey, you're Polly, right?"

I was so startled I could only stare. She was an Earther, dense and strong. Her hair was black and she wore dangly earrings with her uniform, which wasn't supposed to be allowed. I got the feeling she slipped them off when Stanton was around. "Yeah," I said, blinking. Angelyn, that was her name. I couldn't remember her other two names, though I was sure I'd heard them. I braced for whatever jab she was about to deliver.

"My terminal died and wiped out the whole assignment for history next week. I've got it all loaded back on, but—can you re-mind me, what are we supposed to be reading?"

Was she really just asking me a question? A normal question? "Um . . . the book on twentieth-century African politics. First three chapters."

"Great, thanks," she said, and smiled. A perfectly normal smile. I smiled back. She went back to her seat and we both sat there reading, like nothing had ever been wrong with the universe.

9

Astrophysics was, predictably, my favorite class, and not just because it brought me a little closer to home and didn't make me feel like a boneless weakling. When the instructor, Ms. Chin-sun Lee, asked questions, I usually knew the answers. I even started raising my hand, because it was embarrassing that no one else was doing so. And Ms. Lee called on me, smiling when I gave my answers because I was usually right. She said things like, "Good job, Ms. Newton!" and I might have kind of loved her for it. In her class, the knots finally left my stomach. It was the one class I felt like I could get a tiny bit ahead in the one-up competitions that a lot of class time degenerated into. I'd done escape-velocity calculations before. I knew how orbital mechanics worked. I knew why interplanetary navigation was harder than it looked, because your points were always moving in relation to each other, though I still mucked up the details when I tried to work the equations out on my own. At least predicting the orbits of asteroids was relevant. To me, anyway.

Angelyn—Angelyn Marian Chou, I learned, but she was okay with people calling her just Angelyn—was one Earth student

I could count on not to give me a hard time by reflex. I didn't automatically suspect her when she talked, or wait for her to spring a trap. She was, near as I could tell, honest. Startlingly normal, for an Earther.

I helped her with astrophysics, she helped me with Earth history, and I never felt like she was trying to show off how much smarter she was.

"Polly, how did you get so good at those calculations? I swear I'll never wrap my brain around it."

Orbital mechanics. Mostly, it was formulae involving mass, velocity, gravitational pull, and distance from gravitational masses. Trigonometry and vectors. A lot of numbers to juggle, but once you knew how to calculate them, it was mostly a matter of plugging them into equations. It also helped to be able to picture what was actually going on in the real world. I'd been thinking about what orbital mechanics actually look like since I decided I wanted to be a pilot.

"I don't know," I said, hesitating, not wanting to say too much because letting the wrong bit of information slip meant giving them ammunition.

But Angelyn pressed. "Do they teach this differently on Mars? I can understand why you'd need to know more about astrogation in the colonies—"

"No, it's more just me. I learned a lot of it on my own—" And that didn't look odd at all. A few other people at the study hall looked over, listening in on our conversation, and I blushed because I'd already given too much away. After all, who would voluntarily study M-drive mechanics? "I want to be a pilot,"

I blurted, trying to explain, to make myself seem less weird. Failing.

Tenzig smirked, because of course he did. "Wait a minute. You're here prepping for flight school?"

I wasn't going to lie, and downplaying that would mean betraying my own heart. I wouldn't do that, not even to avoid the confrontation. "Yes."

Not just that, and I would never say it out loud, but I also wanted to go farther than anyone else had ever gone before. I wanted to be one of the people who didn't fly just interplanetary but *interstellar*. They were building the big multi-M-drive ships now that would make that happen. I'd be just finishing up school by the time the first missions to Alpha Centauri were ready to go. I would be part of that. I never said it out loud because I couldn't bear it if people made fun of me for it. People like Charles.

Tenzig shook his head, chuckling like this was hilarious. The others looked back and forth between us. Maybe waiting to see who would throw the first punch. I could probably deck him without breaking my hand.

"You really think you can get into flight school just because you want to?" Tenzig said.

"Not just because I want to. I'm good enough to do it. I'll pass any entrance exam they throw at me."

His expression sank into pity. "You need more than that. You need connections. Why do you think I'm here? When they only have a few spots, and lots of people who can pass the tests, who do you think they're going to pick?"

"They'll pick the best people they can."

"You just don't get it, do you? If they have to pick between you and me, who are they going to pick?"

I curled my lip. "I'll arm wrestle you for it."

"My grandfather pioneered the Moon Belt shipping routes. My parents are responsible for carrying most of the ore mined in the Belt to the manufacturing platforms. If my mother called admissions at the school, what are they going to tell her?"

"Hello?" I said. Someone stifled a laugh, I didn't catch who.

"I'm sorry to be the one to tell you this, but you don't have any pull with these people."

On paper, I was just as good as him. No, better. "My mother is director of operations of Mars Colony One. My grandfather was one of the charter colonists," I said, my voice sticking on the words, because I felt like I was using them as a weapon. Or maybe a crutch. I wanted to do this on my own, not depend on my family for getting me through this. On Mars, no one cared who my mother was, I had to pull my own weight.

"You think that means anything to anyone here?"

"Martian greenhouses feed your Belt miners," I said lamely.

"Flight school admissions don't care about that, only what you can do for Earth."

We could throw out counterpunches over and over, and it wouldn't do any good. Did I expect him to suddenly say, "Oh, yes, you're right, how could I have been so ignorant"? No, he wasn't going to do that. But I kept arguing anyway. Charles would have walked away by now.

"I think—" I had been about to call him a couple of names but realized I probably couldn't even insult him right. I'd use some weird Martian insult, like *Dusthead* or *You're full of sew-*

age, and he'd just laugh at me. I tried again. "I think we'll find out which of us is right, in the end."

Then I walked away.

Six weeks in. My skin itched. I was tired of second-guessing every word that came out of my mouth. The longer I stayed, the thicker and weirder my Martian accent sounded. I had to get out of here. I had to do something. Back on Mars, I'd take out a scooter. I wouldn't even go very far, just run it around the colony a couple of times. That was all. I wanted to do that here. I *had* to do it, or I'd go crazy.

I asked around to find out about those cycles in the garage, what class I would have to take or club I would have to sign up for to learn how to ride one. Nobody knew. Nobody would admit they were there. I even did the responsible thing and went up to Stanton herself one morning at breakfast and asked.

"Ms. Stanton?" I said, as politely and demurely as I could. "You know those cycles in the garage? What are they for?"

I had noticed by now that when she was annoyed, she got even more polite. "They belong to the groundskeeping staff, for inspecting the perimeter of the grounds."

"So there's no way I could take a lesson on one, or check one out?"

Her smile grew even more stiff. "Of course not."

"There's no class I could take, or request for PE—"

"Not at all," she enunciated, and I took the hint.

That didn't mean I thought she was *right*.

Doing some research online during study hour, I found the

manuals for the motorcycles. When the library-monitor program that kept tabs on us asked what I wanted them for, I gave some excuse about working on a physics problem, and it authorized my looking at them.

I had a couple of problems from the start: I'd need a keycard to activate the cycles, and I'd have to dodge the surveillance cameras.

I wasn't the best hacker in the universe. If I had to guess who was, I'd say Charles. At least, he'd gotten himself into most of Colony One's computer systems by the time we'd both started school. He didn't mess around with anything important. He just wanted to see if he could, "Just in case," he always said. He and Mom kept up a polite fiction about it—she knew he could do it, and therefore all the department heads and officials at Colony One knew he could do it, but they all pretended that they didn't know, just as long as Charles left everything the way he found it, which he did, because he knew they knew and were letting him alone.

But I wasn't going to ask him for help. Not in a million years. Any hacking I did, I had to use my own know-how and hope it was enough. Which meant not poking too hard. Which meant not trying to do anything crazy like actually shut down the security cameras in the garage. I did, however, find a maintenance program that would temporarily shut off the cameras in that part of the dorm while it tested the electrical system. That would give me about half an hour without anyone tracking me.

All I had to do then was figure out how to steal a keycard, fake a keycard, or learn how to bypass the security lock on a motorcycle.

At PE the next day, Angelyn and I spotted each other on weights. I'd bench-press while she made sure I didn't crush myself with the measely ten kilos I'd loaded, and then I'd do the same for her—thirty-five kilos. I felt like a pity case—she could lift three times as much as I could. But she didn't seem to mind. I even asked her about it, why she would want to lift weights with me when she could help someone who was more at her level. She blushed and confessed that she wanted an easy day of it, and spotting for me seemed the way to do it. "But I wouldn't have done it if I didn't actually want to hang out with you," she added quickly.

Hey, at least she was honest. And that gave me a chance to talk to her when it was her turn to lie back and lift.

"So, do you ride motorbikes?" I hoped that wasn't too suspicious.

She wrinkled her nose, easily hefting the weights in a set of repetitions. "Not really. Once on vacation on St. Thomas we rode aqua jets, but it's not really the same thing. Going that fast seems a little bit scary to me."

"Oh, but it's not, I had a scooter back on Mars, and it's amazing, the way the whole world just whips on past . . . anyway. Have you seen the cycles in the garage?"

"The garage? No, I haven't been in there since we got here."

"Well, they've got these electric cycles. Stanton says they're for the groundskeepers—"

Her eyes widened. "You didn't actually talk to Stanton about it, did you?"

"Well, yeah, I wanted to know, I figured I ought to ask."

"You just keep pushing, don't you?"

I frowned. "I never know I'm doing it until I've already done it." There were all these rules that no one had bothered to write down, like that you weren't supposed to ask questions because it made you look weak.

Angelyn frowned back. "You're trying to figure out how you can take one of those bikes out, aren't you?"

"What makes you say that?" I said, but I wasn't at all convincing.

She shook her head. "You're going to get in so much trouble."

"Only if they catch me."

She looked at me like I was crazy. But she also looked a little bit thoughtful. Intrigued, maybe. Because what if I really could get away with it?

"You'd need a keycard," she said. "If the bikes are part of the groundskeepers motor pool, they probably keep the cards right there in the garage. That's what they do at my parents' place, anyway."

I had to think about that for a minute, that her parents had a place big enough to have its own groundskeepers. But I could process that later. Right now, I had a plan.

"Interesting," I replied, as if it were just an observation.

Student supervisor Franteska stalked over to us, arms crossed, glaring like some military drill sergeant. "Less talking, more lifting, *girls*."

I matched her glare as she stalked off and didn't even care if she liked me or not.

Angelyn seemed worried. "Polly, whatever you do, be careful, okay?"

"Always," I said. "Can you help me put another two kilos on this?"

10

I figured if I went extra early in the morning, I'd be okay. I'd stay out for fifteen, twenty minutes, tops, and be back in time for breakfast before anyone missed me.

That night, I set the alarm on my hand terminal and slipped it under my pillow. I shouldn't have bothered, because I hardly slept anyway, I was so worried about making sure I shut off the alarm before it woke anyone. If Ladhi knew what I was planning, she'd freak out, and Marie would roll her eyes and think I was being immature, if not actually report me. I kept waking up all night long, so I finally shut off the alarm entirely. My heart was thudding, my head was fuzzy, but that only made the adventure more exciting. This was way more interesting than the artificial, slow-cooker drudgery the school had been pounding at us.

Quickly, I slipped on my exercise clothes. I stuck a cap on my head, pulling it down so the brim shadowed my face. I'd set the maintenance program to cut off power to the cameras for a half an hour, starting right about now, but just in case my hack didn't work and the cameras spotted me anyway, I hoped I'd be hard to identify. I shouldn't even look like a student.

Doors recorded every exit and entry and who made it. I used the same maintenance program to trick the doors between the room and the garage into thinking I was a repair operator passing through, and not a student. I hope it worked.

I ducked through the door and into the corridor outside the room, looking over my shoulder to see if the noise had woken my roommates. They didn't so much as flinch—so far so good. I continued down the hallway like I belonged there, striding confidently. If everything was going as planned, the cameras weren't even recording me.

I reached the garage, and one last door—the larger overhead door leading outside. I keyed in the code and waited for a heart-stopping minute until the door slid upward with a sigh. The sky outside was a dull cottony gray of predawn. A slight breeze blew, carrying a chill. Angelyn and the others said sky like this meant rain was on the way, and wouldn't that be something to see? Nothing like the dusty winds of Mars.

Now all that was left was the cycle.

I'd studied these things up and down: chemical-battery operated, solar recharge, carbon-fiber struts and frame, rubber tires. Most of the controls were on the handlebars for easy reach, with an instrument panel in the middle showing speed, direction, and power output. And they did in fact have an activation key. I hunted around for it, and wonder of wonders, Angelyn was right: the activation keys were in a cupboard on the wall. It wasn't even locked. On top of that, the keys were helpfully labeled with numbers that matched the cycles' ID plates. It was like someone wanted me to borrow one.

In another cupboard I found helmets, took one that fit, and was ready to go. Looking over the cycles, I picked the one that seemed like the zippiest, released its brakes, and wheeled it to the open garage door. The driveway stretched ahead, curving along the mist-touched lawn, an undeniable invitation. The path was flat, paved, and smooth, obviously designed for someone to go very fast on it. I already felt better. I could sense all the stress of the last few weeks blowing away on an artificial breeze.

I straddled the cycle and double-checked the controls—my fingers around the brake lever, thumb on the accelerator button. Just fifteen minutes, I reminded myself. Once around the building and back, just like at home. No one would ever know.

The electric motor hummed; I felt it more than heard it, a vibration rumbling up through my legs. I took a moment to get used to the sound, the feel. The front wheel turned on its fork for steering. The seat bounced a little on shock absorbers. I had to get used to the balance, which was a lot different from the scooters at home. These had rubber tires on the ground rather than hover lifts, which couldn't fall over. But apart from that, this would be familiar.

Finally, a grin on my face, I put the cycle in gear and revved the motor.

I wobbled a bit. I wasn't proud of that, but no one was looking, and the way my blood was rushing I was lucky I didn't fall over. After coasting a few meters, I got my balance and turned up the speed. A few more meters like that, a bit more acceleration, I was really cruising. And it was marvelous. I wore the helmet, but nothing on my face—no goggles, no breathing mask. The wind hit me, skidding across my face, making my eyes tear up.

The land slipped past. I was *doing* something. *Going* somewhere. Forward movement. I couldn't even feel the gravity anymore. I was flying. I laughed out loud.

I could have just kept going. Down the road, off school grounds. The solar recharger on the cycle's battery meant I wasn't going to run out of fuel. I wanted to see the ocean. That would probably shake me up even more than the open, breathable sky. If I was going to spend all this time on Earth, I ought to actually see some of it, right?

It would have been so easy to keep on going.

But I didn't. I was good. Sensible. Even Charles would have admired how responsible I was being when I got to the edge of the school grounds, marked by two tall steel pillars and an automated security checkpoint. I slowed and stopped, putting my foot down to help brace the cycle upright. The pillars probably had a motion-sensitive beam across the way, tracking whoever entered and left. Through the gates, the flat black road and trimmed lawn continued, then curved around a forested hill. I couldn't go past it. I considered riding another fifty meters or so until I could see around the hill, but I'd already been out longer than I should have been. So I turned around, opened the power, and sped back to the garage, enjoying a last few moments of freedom.

I'd left the garage door open behind me. I probably shouldn't have done that.

My plan was to ride the cycle into the garage, park it exactly where I'd found it, close all the doors, put away helmet and key, sneak back to my room by the time my hack on the surveillance cameras expired, and no one would know I'd done anything. Except Charles, if he noticed, would ask why I was so giddy happy.

But that didn't happen, because Stanton and three others in Galileo security uniforms were standing in front of the open garage, blocking my way in. I turned sharply, not really sure where I thought I was going, just wanting to get away. Maybe I thought I could run. I should have just put on the brakes and faced them. But I turned, yanking the handlebars, and the cycle's tires slid out from under me. I crashed to the pavement, skidding another two meters before stopping. The ground scoured my clothes and skin. That really hurt.

I lay there for a moment, the right side of my body burning, the cycle's front wheel spinning next to my head. The motor had cut out, at least. I tried to move, discovered I could, because the pain was all on the surface. Nothing broken. But maybe I should have pretended to be concussed so that they'd carry me to the infirmary and I wouldn't have to talk to anyone. When I looked up, Stanton and the others were staring down at me.

"Are you all right?" she asked in a flat tone.

"Um. Ow?" I said.

The guys in security uniforms lifted the cycle upright, and I slowly pushed off the ground. Stanton didn't offer to help, of course. The right side of my clothes was shredded. The skin on my arm and leg under them weren't much better, scraped raw and red, and embedded with grime. It was tender now, but it was really going to hurt in an hour or so.

"Can you explain yourself, Ms. Newton?" she said. I didn't say anything, because the answer, essentially, was no, I couldn't explain myself. I didn't think I had to—it seemed self-evident: I'd taken a motorbike out for a ride.

"Go to the infirmary, get cleaned up. I'll meet you there to discuss repercussions."

Maybe they'd send me home. I hadn't thought about that and felt suddenly hopeful.

Gravity had returned full force. It took forever for me to bend my bruised limbs and get myself to my feet. Stanton watched the whole time. In lighter gravity, I wouldn't have smeared on the pavement quite so hard. It wasn't fair.

The infirmary was part of the dorm complex, down another corridor. The nurse there wasn't much more sympathetic than Stanton. After peeling out of my clothes—what was left of them—I put on standard hospital scrubs. Then I sat while the nurse washed the cuts and scrapes on my arms and legs, and doused them with an antiseptic spray. That *really* hurt, but I clenched my teeth, kept my mouth shut, and blinked back tears. I didn't want to give anyone the satisfaction of seeing me cry when it was my own damn fault.

The moment the nurse finished wrapping the cuts in an antiseptic gauze, Stanton appeared, gaze focused like laser beams. She didn't get close, didn't get in my face. Just stood there regarding me from the edge of the exam room. I felt like a bug in a petri dish.

"Feeling better, Ms. Newton?" she said.

"I'm fine, thanks."

A long pause followed. I could feel my own heart beating, faster than normal, nervous.

"May I ask: How did you sabotage the security protocols?"

I picked at the gauze on my arm. "I didn't *sabotage* them, I just . . . worked around them."

"All right. How did you *work around* them?"

They could find out how I did it by going over the computer network maintenance logs. They'd probably already done it. This wasn't about finding out how I did it; it was about getting me to admit I'd done it. I talked faster than I was thinking, as if I could just say the right thing to make her understand. "It wasn't that big a deal. I just went through the maintenance program to temporarily shut down power to the cameras. Didn't touch security at all."

She blinked at that, startled, as if that had never occurred to her. Which meant they'd lock that hack down and I'd never be able to use it again.

"Ms. Newton. You do understand that the security is here for your own protection. This isn't a prison."

A little voice in my head, one that sounded suspiciously like Charles, told me to lower my gaze and say, "Yes, Ms. Stanton, I understand."

Really, I'd already won. I'd gone for my ride. I'd gotten out. Despite falling and getting scraped up and Stanton glaring at me, I felt better. I'd escaped gravity, however briefly. Now it was just a matter of whether or not I'd be kicked out of Galileo entirely.

"What did you hope to accomplish, Ms. Newton?"

"I just wanted to go for a ride."

"Organized PE isn't enough for you, is that it?"

"This is different, I just—" I shook my head, because she wouldn't understand. Shut my mouth and didn't try to explain.

"I'm afraid this episode can't go unremarked," Stanton said.

"You'll be put on restrictions for a month. Private study hall. Additional work in every class. You will not be allowed to raise your hand in class. You'll be watched, Ms. Newton, so don't think you'll be able to repeat your little expedition. Breakfast is in an hour. Go to your room, wash up and get changed, and join your classmates in the dining hall. Understood?"

I glared, trying to return the laser gaze, but she'd had a lot more practice at it than I had.

11

If I'd acted a little more hurt—if I really had gotten a concussion, maybe, instead of just having to pick dirt out of my skin—I probably could have stayed in bed all day. Maybe next time.

When I entered the dining hall, everyone went quiet and stared at me. Who knew what kind of rumors were flying about me? I didn't want to find out, but I didn't see how I could avoid it. I scanned the tables, and found Ethan, Ladhi, Marie, Tenzig—and Charles. He nodded at an empty chair next to his. Chin up and shoulders straight, I went to the counter, picked up my tray of food, and joined the rest of the offworld freaks.

As soon as I sat down, conversation started again in a wave of hushed whispers. I could guess what every single person in the room was talking about.

"Oh, my gosh, Polly, what happened?" Ladhi studied me and my gauze bandages with wide eyes and gaping mouth. "When we got up and you weren't in bed—we thought you'd died or something!"

"If she'd died she would have still been in bed," Marie said. "We figured you ran away."

"No. I just took one of the cycles out for a ride, that's all," I said casually, shrugging off the episode.

"Wow, you really did it," Ethan said. "Are you okay?"

"Oh, yeah, I just got a little scraped up." I'd have to be careful not to wince every time I moved . . . I glanced at Charles, waiting for him to say something snide, but he was entirely focused on his food.

"So how much trouble are you in?" Tenzig said.

"I don't know. Stanton was pretty unhappy."

"How could you tell?" Ladhi asked. "She always looks so . . . so *pristine*."

"Oh, I could tell."

"You fell, didn't you?" Tenzig said. "Pretty much everyone falls the first time they take out a cycle."

"Have you ever ridden one?" I said.

"Yeah. They're a lot of fun, but you really have to know what you're doing. You should have asked me for advice."

"I did *fine*," I said. "And you're right, they are a lot of fun."

"This is really going to mess up your record, though," he added. "Flight school doesn't much like reprimands."

I hadn't thought of that. Of course, I hadn't intended on getting caught. Best not to think about it.

Breakfast ended, and everyone filed out to go to classes. Charles stayed at the table, though, and I lingered, waiting until we were alone.

"So," he said, "what really happened?"

"I had to get out. I had to go for a ride, so I did."

"You hacked security on the doors?"

"No, I hacked maintenance to cut power on the cameras. But

I had to tell Stanton about it so it probably won't work again. You know, if you were getting ideas."

"I'm almost impressed."

"Gosh. Thanks." I smirked.

"Polly, this isn't Mars. You can't just . . . carry on like that. In case you haven't noticed, they don't trust us here. They don't trust anyone."

"I wasn't hurting anything," I argued, and he frowned at the bandages on my arm. I added, "Much. I wasn't hurting anyone *else*."

"That's not the point," he said. "What are they going to do to you?"

"I'm grounded. Extra study halls, extra work, extra monitoring, and no social time. I thought Stanton was going to send me home," I said, then sighed. "If I do something even crazier next time, maybe she'll send me home."

"Don't do that," Charles said.

"Why not? I hate it here."

"Because if they send you home, I'll be here by myself. At least with each other, neither one of us is the only kid from Mars."

There was that, I supposed.

"I'm sorry," I said. "I'll try to fit in from now on."

"Don't do that," he said. "Just . . . try to be more *subtle*."

"Subtle as a Martian dust storm, that's me," I said.

He might have actually twitched a smile at that.

Life under restrictions was about the same as before, only even more annoying. No one to talk to at study hall. Having to sit through class without saying a word. Extra PE. The good side of all the extra work was I slept very well at night.

The worst part, though, was my mother sending a message full of dire warnings and disappointment. Stanton must have reported on me about the stunt, and now Mom was convinced I was going to flunk out and destroy my chances for any kind of successful future. It freaked me out a little, when I kept thinking getting kicked out meant going back to Mars and my old life.

My old life. Right.

I was two weeks into restrictions when I got a video from Beau. Not an e-mail, a whole video, which I was excited about at first because I'd get to see him and hear his voice on the screen of my handheld. But right away I knew something was wrong because he couldn't look straight at the camera. His gaze sort of drifted all the way around it, to the ceiling, then the floor, then over his shoulder as if something were following him, even though he was only sitting at the desk in his room. His hair was rumpled. I knew exactly what it would feel like if I touched it—rough, warm, a little greasy.

"Um. Hi, Polly. How's it going?" He'd never sounded so nervous before. So reluctant. Maybe someone was standing to the side, holding a gun to his head. "So, yeah. Things are okay here, I guess." He glanced offscreen and pressed his lips together before continuing, and the knot in my stomach tightened.

"Oh, just spit it out, why don't you!" I shouted at the screen, because I knew what was coming.

He mumbled some more. "There's . . . we really need to talk.

Or I need tell you something, I guess. We can't really talk." His nervous chuckle sounded stupid. "Yeah. Um."

Then a voice hissed at him from out of sight. *"Just tell her!"*

That sounded just like Victory Mason. Prettiest girl in class back on Mars. And she'd stolen my boyfriend. Because I was two hundred million kilometers away and couldn't do a damn thing about it.

Beau finally said, "I'm really sorry, but . . . I think we should both be open to seeing other people. I mean, we knew it probably wasn't going to work out, with you being so far away and everything."

No, we hadn't known that. We'd sworn undying loyalty. Or rather, I had.

"You're a really good person, Polly. It's not you—"

"Oh, don't say it," I muttered.

"—it's me. And we'll still be friends, I know it. But, yeah. It's just not fair to you, you being on Earth and probably meeting all these great guys. You should enjoy yourself. Yeah, that's it. Um—I'm really sorry."

And the picture cut out. The screen went to black, and I spent a long time staring at it, not knowing what to think. I thought about playing the vid again, studying every nuance—every time his gaze had swung to the left, offscreen, he must have been looking at Victory, who'd been egging him on the whole time. He could have just not broken up with me and I'd never have known, and I wouldn't feel like such dirt now. Ignorance would have been better.

Really, I should have been happy that Victory made him tell

me. He could have just gone out with her and I'd never know. In the end, I'd rather know.

I thought about playing the message again, but instead I deleted it. I would never talk to Beau again.

I was glad of the restricted study hall then, being in my own cubicle where no one could see me. Where I didn't have to talk to anyone, tell anyone why I was staring at my handheld like I wanted to kill it. I really could have smashed it to pieces at the moment, except for being numb. I couldn't move, I realized. The more I thought of it, the more I thought it wasn't even Beau I missed. Would miss. He said, "It's not you, it's me," but really it was me, wasn't it?

Because I wasn't worth waiting for.

I had to sit for another fifteen minutes before I could go back to the dorm for lights-out. I wanted to do anything other than sit here. I wanted to run, scream, fly, anything. But none of it would help. So I went numb.

Then, finally, it was time to go, all of us filing back to our dorm rooms.

Charles sidled up to me. "What's wrong?"

"I don't want to talk about it."

"Beau finally broke up with you, didn't he?"

I looked at him. "I hate you, Charles."

"He's not worth it. You can do much better than him."

"I don't *want* better. He was my *boyfriend*. I like him." At least I used to. I frowned hard to keep my stinging eyes from tearing up.

"I heard a new Earth saying. 'There's always more fish in the sea.'"

"What's that supposed to mean?"

"It means . . . there's always more fish in the sea." He turned the corridor to his wing of the dorm. And I . . . I didn't know how I was going to sleep.

I didn't care about the restrictions anymore because the constraints and isolation reflected my mood. If I didn't have a chance to talk to anyone, that was just fine. I didn't want to talk to anyone.

Other kids screwed up and got put on restrictions. George got caught sneaking out of the dorm after dark. One of the older students had hidden tobacco-based drugs—cigarettes—in his locker. Angelyn had to explain cigarettes to me, and I was baffled, because it was another example of how people on Earth wasted their air. Trying to smoke tobacco at Colony One would get you deported, because it would ruin the air-filtration system for the whole settlement.

Compared to things like that, my stunt with the bike started looking kind of cool. People didn't give me quite such weird looks.

Sometimes, walking back and forth between the dorm, classes, and meals, my friends would walk with me to keep me company. That was how I finally figured out I kind of had friends here. Usually, it was Ethan, Angelyn, or Ladhi. Charles never did, and that was okay. But I was shocked one day after astrophysics on the way to lunch, when Tenzig trotted up to me and walked alongside. Suspicious, I looked at him sidelong. He was studying me. I waited for him to say something, kind of hoping that he would get tired of staring at me and walk away.

"I could help you, you know," Tenzig said finally. "That stunt with the cycle—that took guts, if nothing else. You might actually make a pretty good pilot."

If nothing else—like brains and common sense? As far as I was concerned, I was already a pretty good pilot. I just hadn't had a chance to fly anything bigger than a scooter. Yet.

"Help me how?" I said.

"Like I told you—I have connections. I could put a good word in for you."

"You think I can't do it on my own?"

"I'm just trying to help, that's all."

"What are you going to expect in return?"

"You're suspicious. Can't I just be a nice guy?"

"Gosh, why start now?"

"You're kind of a hoot, Polly. Maybe I want to help because I like you."

I blushed in spite of myself. I didn't want to blush, or have him looking at me like he really did like me. He seemed amused, but I was afraid he was laughing at me. I could have kept the argument up for hours, and he would have just kept smiling like that.

"How about if I need help I'll let you know?" I said.

"That's a deal."

There went that blush again.

While we picked up our trays of food, Ladhi pulled me aside and hissed, "What did Tenzig want?"

"He was just giving me a hard time," I said.

"The way he was standing? No way."

"I didn't really notice how he was standing," I said, but I was blushing again and angry at myself for it.

"Don't tell me you didn't notice how close he was standing to you."

"I can't say that I did."

"He was standing *very* close. I think he likes you."

"No way. He thinks I'm weird."

"Maybe that's why he likes you."

"He should chase after Marie, the way she's been hanging all over him."

"That's just it—he doesn't *have* to chase her."

"I don't get it. I don't get any of it."

"You should at least enjoy it. The attention, I mean."

All the attention I'd gotten so far had been horrific. Why would I go looking for *more*? And why couldn't I stop blushing?

12

A week later came our first field trip. Field trips, I understood. We had field trips on Mars, to visit the early exploratory rovers, left exactly where they'd stopped when their batteries ran out and their missions ended, and to study local geology. A field trip on Earth couldn't be that different, right? I thought I might be left behind—I was on the last week of my restrictions—but it turned out this was meant to be an educational experience. I couldn't *possibly* miss out on an educational experience. So I got to go. Or *had* to go, depending on your point of view.

Autumn had come to Earth's northern hemisphere. Autumn here was nothing like autumn at Colony One. Colony One, in Mars's northern hemisphere, had long springs and blustery summers that were only a little less cold than winters. Fall and winter got cold enough that most maintenance and science crews didn't go out unless they absolutely had to, but at least they were shorter, because of Mars's eccentric orbit. Apparently Earth had a lot of variations in weather and climate, but it went way beyond wind and temperature. Precipitation changed, depending on where you were and what season it was. Mars didn't have any precipitation at all, no matter where you were or what time of year it was. I had to admit, I may not have liked Earth all that much, but liquid water falling from the sky? When I finally got to see it, it was crazy interesting, like a garden sprinkler big enough to cover everything you could see. The ground turned mushy, and the air smelled clean. Earth's atmosphere wasn't just thicker, it seemed *alive*. And then I found out that when the temperature got cold enough, the rain would freeze and turn into snow. Like the polar caps of Mars falling piece by piece. I saw pictures—snow-covered land looked like a temporary ice cap painted over everything. And then it just melted away.

I'd never get used to any of this.

We were making this trip before too much rain and snow interfered. It was our first trip off campus since arriving at the school, and we could have gone anywhere—a random museum, drive around the block, hole in the ground—and I'd have been happy.

But we were going to the western coast. We were going to see the ocean.

Stanton and a couple of instructors acting as chaperones herded us onto a suborbital flight to a town called Monterey—this would be my first look at a real Earth town. I'd already gotten used to the idea of settlements that sprawled above the ground instead of under it; I understood the concept pretty well. What I hadn't expected when I saw the paved streets, rows of buildings made of wood and concrete, was how fragile it all looked. Like a brisk wind would come in and knock it all down. And yes, the place had been here for hundreds of years.

The ground transport—the bus—that took us to the coast was a lot like the one we rode when we first came to Earth, which gave me a weird sense of repetition, like I'd done all this before. Just like that bus, these windows were tinted, and I didn't know if they were trying to keep us from looking out, or to keep the rest of the world from looking in. Maybe Earth kids rode in closed-in boxes all the time, because none of them seemed bothered by moving without knowing where they were going.

The bus gave us a comfortable ride. I could hardly feel us turning around curves and climbing up and down hills. But we were, though I could catch only a hint of the landscape outside. It *felt* like traveling up and down hills on Mars.

After we stopped, the biology instructor, Mr. Han, stood and lectured us for ten minutes about what we'd see and what we should be looking for—birds, shells, and seaweed that had been washed onto the sand by the water, animals that might be living in the sand itself, like insects or crustaceans. If we were very lucky, he said, we might see sea lions. Mr. Han was one of those excitable instructors who made everything sound like the most amazing thing in the world. He was so emotional about the sea lions he almost made me want to see one, except I knew from reading how big they were, and that they were predators with very sharp teeth, and I wasn't sure anything that big and powerful should have a mind of its own. Didn't large Earth predators occasionally eat people?

Finally, Mr. Han stopped talking, the door opened, and we filed out to see it all for ourselves.

I didn't know what to expect. I didn't know that I expected anything. I thought—assumed—that I'd be shocked. Overwhelmed by the sight of something I'd never seen and couldn't possibly imagine. I had expected to be astonished. But the first thing that hit me was a brisk breeze that tangled in my hair. It was fresh and wet and smelled a little like a greenhouse compost pile—damp, decayed. It didn't smell bad, but it didn't smell like anything at Galileo.

We were in a flat, paved lot, and Mr. Han gestured us to a path that led over a hillock covered with matted weeds and grass. We lined up out of habit and filed over the hillock and to the sand.

The flat sheet of blue-gray water stretched to the horizon, turning to haze where it met the sky. It looked like the desert: a vast rippling stretch of sameness. Intellectually I knew it wasn't. But that was what I thought of. I'd watched sand move across the desert like that, flowing and surging in a storm. I had to remind myself that this was water, and that I had never seen so much water in one place.

A wide stretch of pale yellowish sand sloped down to the water, and that looked familiar, except where the water stretched and crawled over it, the waves coming in and out, reaching and splashing. The sand it left behind was soaked and rubbed smooth. The shore went on in both directions as far as I could see, curving around in the distance to a dark, rocky cliff.

The students scattered, jogging along the beach in both directions, except those of us from offworld. We stood at the edge of the beach, staring. Not saying a word, not even noticing what the others were doing. Just staring.

"Are you kids all right?" Han asked, looking down the row of us.

"Yes, sir," Charles was the one to answer, finally. "Just taking it all in."

"Well, you'd better get to work, we'll only be here an hour before we move on." He wandered off to go supervise or whatever.

"What are supposed to do again?" Ladhi asked breathlessly. "I forgot."

"Come on, let's get this over with," Tenzig said, stomping away to cover up the fact he'd been astonished with the rest of us, instead of blasé about the panorama. He stomped so hard he slipped in the sand and had to put his arms out to keep his balance.

"Mr. I've Done It All isn't so used to walking on sand, is he?" I said.

"And you are?" Marie said.

"Yeah," I said. "I actually am." This was coarser than the sand on Mars, worn down by water rather than pulverized by wind. Martian sand was mostly dust and rock, but it was slippery, just like this. I could walk on it just fine, and proved it, stepping carefully, knees bent to counteract slippage. Ladhi, who'd never even been on a moon before she came to Earth, looked terrified. I held my hand to her. "Come on, it'll be okay."

She took hold of my hand and we walked toward the water together.

After a few minutes, Ladhi—and everyone else—got used to the sand and the startling sight of endless water, and we worked on our assignments: hunting for shells and bugs and watching the slender gray-winged birds that soared overhead. They seemed to be watching us as much as we watched them, tilting their heads and looking down with strangely knowing eyes. Birds—the planet was absolutely littered with them. Like trees and grass and bugs and everything else. The Earth kids seemed to take it all for granted. They weren't even looking.

"Do you want to go in?"

I blinked and shook myself awake. I'd been staring at the water, hypnotized, for who knew how long. Angelyn was looking back at me, amused.

"What?" I said stupidly. "What do you mean, go in?"

"Swim. You can swim, can't you?"

I said, "Why would someone who grew up on Mars know how to swim?"

She laughed, but it was good-natured, her eyes alight. "I don't know, maybe you have swimming pools?"

"We have to filter every ounce of water we use. I can't see anyone just . . . jumping into a bunch of it."

"We'll wade, then. Just up to our ankles. You can't come to the ocean and not go in!"

She sat in the sand right there, pulled off her shoes and socks, and rolled up her trouser legs. Farther down the beach, a few others had already waded into the water, laughing as the waves tucked and lapped around their legs.

What the heck. This was supposed to be an adventure, wasn't it? We left our shoes and socks behind.

The sand under my feet was cold, sending goose bumps up my legs. The wind got in under the cuffs of my pants. It felt . . . freeing. I wasn't used to being open to the elements like this. The sandy winds of Mars could scour flesh off bone. On Mars, you respected wind. Here—this was like a game.

I squished my toes in the wet sand, digging little holes, feeling the grit. Angelyn was already ahead, splashing in tongues of water washing back to the sea.

"Come on! Just go for it!" She ran farther on, until the water was ankle deep.

When the water approached, I almost ran, because it looked like it was attacking, that whole inexorable mass of it coming for me. Heart thudding, I stood my ground, and the edge of a spent wave ran over my feet, rubbing like silk, wrapping around my ankles.

"It's *cold*!" I said, hissing. Angelyn laughed and jumped, sending water spraying.

I just stood there. So. I was standing in the ocean, my feet wet, and getting cold. Strange. Watching the waves, I tried to predict and dodge them before the water could rise past my ankles, but they always surprised me, surging unexpectedly, flowing on top of each other, sending me dancing away to keep from getting drenched.

Angelyn was standing up to her knees now, holding her pants legs up to keep them from getting wet. Not that it worked, because the cuffs were damp with spray. The way she was grinning, it seemed to be part of the point.

The churning waves generated a pale, frothy foam that collected on the sand and around my feet. I crouched to touch it, and it collapsed around my fingers. Another press of water, crisp and icy, splashed against my hand. Curious, I touched my finger to my tongue. It wasn't just salty—everyone said the ocean was salty. It was also slimy and bitter, full of tastes I couldn't name.

The ocean, I decided, was like the deserts of Mars or the vacuum of space. It could swallow you up and no one would ever find you. I decided I'd keep my distance.

We had our checklist of things we were supposed to look for, and images to take with our handhelds. I kept having to look at the sample images to be sure I was finding the right things. The idea of finding anything larger than microscopic creatures just running around was so weird. After finding a crab—what was supposedly a little one, as big as my thumb—with its claws, shell, and flat black eyes, my skin itched. The things could be anywhere, buried in the sand under my feet, crawling along behind me.

We got a ten-minute warning to finish our work. Angelyn and I found our shoes and dusted off our feet the best we could. The wet sand stuck to my skin like glue. I rinsed off as much as I could in the water, watching Angelyn for how to do it, but I just got more sand on me, and when I tried to brush it off I got it all over my hands and arms.

Angelyn just laughed. She seemed to love it. "Yeah, you never really get it all off until you get in the shower."

"Great," I muttered.

Back at the bus, beyond the grass-covered dunes, Ladhi stood shivering, hugging herself. "This place is disgusting," she said. "I'm never going to get all the sand off me. I can feel it in my *hair*." She scrubbed her fingers in her hair for emphasis.

"On Mars they vacuum you before you come in out of the air lock, to get all the sand off."

"I could use a good vacuuming."

Mr. Han asked us to transmit our images and reports for grading. I was pretty sure I hadn't been able to tell a gull from a sandpiper. Sure, this was all nice, pretty, and educational, and I would always remember sticking my feet in an ocean full of water. But I wondered if the point of all this was to demonstrate yet again that us offworlders didn't know anything about Earth.

That night, we stayed in a borrowed dormitory at a nearby university, and the next day we headed to Yosemite Park for what Stanton called a "self-esteem and confidence-building workshop." I didn't even know what that meant, so I took a chance and asked Angelyn.

"It'll probably be some obstacle course or game or something," she said.

"So glorified PE."

"A little. But better—a different kind of PE. It'll be fun."

I huffed, skeptical.

It was worse than I could have possibly imagined.

First, Yosemite Park. If the ocean was overwhelming, this place was even more so. The ocean went on forever, but at least it all looked the same. Yosemite had trees, forests, rocks, mountains, cliffs, meadows, rivers—all in the same place. We got out of the bus and I saw trees—an endless blanket of them. Just like the ones Ethan was so excited about, and sure enough, in the bus he had his face pasted to the window and could barely sit still. I had read about forests. I knew what they were—lots of trees together. I had seen trees—the atriums at home had them. So I should have known what to expect. But I didn't. Hundreds of trees. Millions of them. There wasn't a roof, so they kept growing, so high I couldn't see their tops.

If I scoured away all the vegetation, the cliffs and valleys here would have looked like the ancient river-cut valleys on Mars. But here, the river was still cutting through the valley. More moving water.

I hated the way this planet kept startling me.

"Close your mouth, Polly," Charles said, walking past me, following the rest of the class as we left the bus. The instructor—somebody new, a Mr. Kristoff Anthony Keller, who was a local guide for the park—led us from the bus down a dirt trail that passed through part of the forest, winding in between towering pine trees. I reached out and scraped my hand across the bark. They didn't even feel like atrium trees. These were rough, scarred, damaged, and probably had bugs crawling all over them, invisibly. Birds and other animals rustled in the branches.

The path left the trees and entered a meadow, a wide swath of grass like the lawns at Galileo except these were wild—uncut and smelling of dry sunlight. I never thought about sunlight having a smell before. Several piles of equipment lay before us: backpacks, tarp-wrapped bundles, coils of rope. Some of it looked like survival gear.

Then we learned what the "workshop" was going to involve.

Stanton and Keller split us up into groups and assigned each group to one of the piles of gear. Charles and I had somehow ended up in the same group, probably because all the offworlders had been shuffled off together, once again separated from the Earth kids because, as Stanton explained, they didn't want to push us too hard. Everyone understood that we couldn't handle the exertion.

That was getting really old. We'd had time to adapt by now and managed to keep up with the Earthers, usually. Not that we looked it—we still all looked like skinny little twigs, but never mind.

So here we were: Charles, Ladhi, Ethan, Tenzig, Marie, Boris, and me.

"I shouldn't even be in this group," Tenzig muttered, staring longingly at the group next to us, which included George, Angelyn, and Elzabeth. "I've spent enough time on Earth my bone density is practically normal."

"I'm sure you'll manage somehow," Ethan said.

I picked through the gear: backpacks, a stove, a bundle of freeze-dried food, a GPS unit, thermal blankets, some rope and tarps. Survival gear. This seriously looked like the most normal collection of objects I'd seen since getting to Earth. We had everything here we used on Mars except breathing masks and air canisters—which we wouldn't need here, of course.

Keller explained what we were going to be doing with the equipment: spending the night outside. We'd hike on a predetermined route, follow directions, find our camp, prepare our food, conserve our water, and return in the morning. This was an exercise in cooperation and confidence building.

"When this is all done, you'll feel like you can conquer the world!" Keller announced happily. He was younger than Stanton and much more exuberant. He wasn't here to mold us into perfect Galileo students; he was here to get us as excited as possible. Which made me suspicious. He had to be hiding something.

Stanton gazed on blandly.

"As if I'd want to conquer the world," Charles said flatly, and the instructor gave him a nervous sidelong look.

Keller sounded way too chipper. Like he was getting ready to start an experiment. Which he kind of was. "All right, you'll have to pick someone in your group to be in charge of the map and GPS. The rest of you divide up your gear, pack it up, and get ready to move out."

Kids in the other groups started moving on either side of us, and someone laughed—probably thinking this was *fun*. In our group, we just stood there looking at one another, wondering who was going to start.

"Well?" I said to Charles, "aren't you going to demand to be in charge of the GPS since you think you're the only one who could possibly be smart enough to use it right?"

"What makes you think I'd do that?" he said. "It's not like we can get lost—the instructors will be monitoring us the entire time. They've given us a path to follow. There are no real stakes here, so I don't care what we do."

"I'd rather we didn't embarrass ourselves," Tenzig said.

Charles donned a thin, sly smile. "And there's the part of the exercise they didn't tell us about."

I huffed in frustration. Couldn't he get through anything without being all smug?

"Would anyone mind if I took charge?" Ethan said, and I had to admire him for stepping up.

"I probably have a lot more navigation experience than you," Tenzig said, reaching into the pile for the handheld GPS unit. "Why don't I take it?"

"Fine," Ethan said. But I thought I'd rather have Ethan telling us where to go than Tenzig. I'd just have to keep in mind what Charles said: none of this really mattered, did it?

I dived into the gear and started sorting it into reasonable-size batches to go into the packs. If we each took one heavy thing—tent, stove, water—and one light thing—food, stove fuel, ropes—we should do all right.

"What do you think you're doing?" Tenzig demanded, watching me.

"I'm packing. What does it look like I'm doing?"

"You're doing it wrong is what you're doing."

"No, I'm not." I'd done overnight expeditions on Mars, I knew how to pack.

"We're not going to be able to carry it all," he said.

"Yes, we are, if we take it easy."

"I'm not letting the rest of you slow me down—"

"Look, you're in charge of the GPS, why don't you let the rest of us handle the packing?" I said, staring up at him.

"Everything all right here?" Keller asked. His smile never wavered.

"Fine," we all muttered at him.

He helped us secure the gear in the packs and showed us how the packs were supposed to fit, which helped a lot. The packs had frames that balanced the weight, so we'd be able to carry more than we thought we could, even with Earth gravity. He explained the directions, pointing out the start of the six-kilometer-long trail we were meant to follow. Many trails branched out from here, I saw, meaning none of us could really get lost. Our campsite would be at the end of the trail. We'd spend the night there, pack up in the morning, and be back by lunch. And probably be ready to murder somebody.

The other groups started out before we did, but that was okay. Charles may have been right, this might have been a competition, but I was betting the winners wouldn't be judged by how fast they did things. I wanted to get this *right*.

Somehow, the seven of us hauled our packs onto our backs, stashed individual water canteens where we could reach them, and prepared to set off into the wilderness.

"Aren't there animals out here that can kill us?" Ladhi said to Keller as he was waving us off. "Like bears and dogs and stuff?"

"They won't bother you here," he answered. "Trust me!"

We started walking, reached the trail, and within minutes we could no longer see the meadow behind us, or hear anything but birds and our own breathing.

"He was supposed to say no," Ladhi said, frowning.

13

We walked. The packed-dirt trail went through the edge of some woods, winding around trees and rocks. Every now and then, the forest opened up to places where the hillside was bare rock with fallen boulders strewn through the trees. Active geology at work. Even I recognized the signs, and the familiarity with formations I'd seen on Mars was comforting. The trees lined a meadow in a valley, and across the open grass, the steep wall of a cliff rose up. Just like a cliff on Mars. Except for all the trees, of course. Something kept whistling in the branches above us. Tiny little birds, hopping around, zipping between branches. I only caught glimpses of them.

"How can they expect us to sleep outside?" Ladhi said. She kept glancing up, like she expected the sky, or trees, or rock, or anything, to fall down on us. "That's inhumane. Isn't there some kind of law about that? About cruel and unusual punishment?"

"Technically, by enrolling in Galileo we agreed to any Galileo-related activities. Including this," Charles observed. "The courts would consider it consensual."

"What would happen if we refused to play along?" Boris wondered. Dripping sweat cut stripes through the dust on his face and neck.

"Black marks on your record," Tenzig said. "They could probably even boot you out." The station kid was making a good show of pretending the exertion in heavy gravity didn't bother him, but he was sweating as much as the rest of us, and his steps weren't any faster.

Ethan sighed, slapping his arm. "Ow. What was that? Oh hell, was that alive?" He was staring at a tiny red smear on his palm.

"Bugs," Tenzig said.

"Insects," Charles added. "Parasitic. They feed on human blood."

Flinching, Ethan made a retching noise and scrubbed his hand off on his pants.

"Oh, *gross!*" Ladhi said. "I thought that instructor said nothing out here would attack us!"

"He probably didn't think insects were worth mentioning," Charles said.

I'd seen clouds of the little freaks—a hundred black specks that hovered off the trail, like antigravity dust. Life—this planet was swarming with it and I wasn't sure I liked it. It made everything so *grubby*. On Mars, we knew exactly where the life was and could be confident that it would swarm only in petri dishes.

"They don't really eat blood, do they?" Ladhi said, checking her arms, patting her shirt, eyes wide and horrified.

"It's probably best not to think about it too much," I said. That was what I was doing—not thinking about it. I just had to remember that people had been living on this planet for tens of thousands of years, and humanity had somehow been able to survive bloodsucking insects during that time. Mostly. Charles had wisely not mentioned the diseases they might be carrying, which was something else I'd read about and was trying to ignore. Sure, space would kill you given half a chance, but nobody talked about the millions of ways *Earth* was constantly trying to kill people.

We'd been given lotion to spread over our skin to protect against UV radiation. This shouldn't have been too scary, since on Mars we had to wear entire environmental suits to protect against radiation. But it was a reminder that as much as people liked to think it, Earth wasn't totally safe. It was just a different kind of dangerous.

"I'm really sorry, guys, but I need to take a break," Ethan said, sinking onto a rock in a small clearing.

None of us argued. The trouble with stopping was how hard it was to get started again. My legs ached, from my feet rubbing in my boots to the burn in my muscles. It was easy enough to fold up and sit on the ground, right where I stopped.

We sat on rocks and dirt, too tired to talk, taking sips from our canteens. The air felt so hot I had trouble breathing. I didn't think air could get this hot without killing us all. And yet here we were, miserable and alive.

Ethan splashed water from his canteen onto his face, which seemed like a great idea.

But Charles said, "Careful with that. We have to make the water last until tomorrow."

"Oh. Yeah. Sorry." Ethan put the cap on his canteen, which he put back in its slot on his pack.

This wasn't a test of cooperation or a confidence-building

exercise. It was a test of sheer endurance. How long could we last before screaming for someone to come and take us back home?

"Maybe we could just sit here until tomorrow," Ladhi said. "How would they know?"

"They're tracking us," Tenzig said. "I bet they come check on us if they see our GPS unit stops for more than a few minutes before we get to the camp."

"And how many black marks would that get you?" Charles said. Tenzig scowled.

The sense that this was all a game increased when we reached our destination. The narrow trail curved around a hill, and the forest opened into a wide, flat space cleared of rocks and debris. It looked like it had been prepared for us.

"According to the GPS, this is it," Tenzig announced, which we'd all pretty much figured out for ourselves.

We'd gotten here just in time. The sun was setting, the shadows darkening. Being in a valley with mountains around us, we were losing light quickly. We had flashlights, but it would be best if we could get everything set up before the sky got completely dark.

We were too tired to argue about how to set up. Ethan and Ladhi got the stove up and running. Tenzig, Marie, and I managed to put up our shelter, a sheet of lightweight fabric held up with poles and ropes. Charles and Boris sorted the food and arranged something resembling dinner. Each of us laid out our own bedroll. Charles discovered a container of insect repellant in our mini first-aid kit. We used just about all of it on ourselves and around the perimeter of the site. It had a sharp, mediciney stink to it, but I figured that was a good thing—if it stank, surely the bugs would stay away.

The food was some raw stuff—fruit, nuts, chocolate—and some freeze-dried stew stuff that we added water to and cooked over the stove. I didn't taste it so much as feel it—the hot food felt incredibly good after the long, sweaty day, warming my stomach, then my whole insides. We nibbled for a while, cleaned up, put everything away, and turned the setting on the stove from cook to heat. As hot and sweaty as we'd been during the day, the air had turned chilly after dark. We were glad for the blankets.

The five of us set our bedrolls in a circle around the stove, wrapped ourselves in blankets, then . . . just sat there. It felt early. As exhausted as we clearly were—Tenzig wasn't even arguing with anyone—we didn't seem to want to sleep. So we talked.

"I don't know how I'm ever going sleep," Ladhi said. "There's things out here waiting to eat us. I just know it."

"They probably cleared out any animals before they brought us in," Ethan said reassuringly.

"Human beings weren't meant to sleep outside," I said. "If we were meant to sleep outside, why did we evolve into living in houses? Forget colonizing the solar system, roofs are one of humanity's greatest achievements."

"Hey, turn off the stove for a minute," Charles said.

Ladhi complained, "No, it's cold out!"

"Just for a few minutes, I want to see something." He was looking up into the night sky visible above the clearing.

Ethan turned off the stove, and the orange heating element faded.

We'd all been staring at the light, so we needed a few moments for our vision to get used to complete darkness. When the outlines of the trees and mountains around us took on definition, Charles pointed up.

"Look," he said.

We looked up and saw the stars. Millions of sharp and sparkling lights on a black backdrop. Nothing between us and the universe.

I saw a line of three stars close together and my breath caught. Orion's Belt—was that Orion?

"It's the same constellations we have," I murmured.

"Of course it is. A couple hundred million kilometers doesn't mean much next to light-years," Charles said.

"I know that, I just wasn't . . . I dunno. Expecting it."

"There—we don't see that at home." He pointed to a reddish spot close to the horizon. "That's Mars, I'm pretty sure."

I wasn't used to hearing Charles sound uncertain about anything, but I could understand why he might. Hard to believe that tiny, inconsequential spot was an entire planet—our home. Rationally, we knew it was. Emotionally, it was hard to take in. The spot of light was so tiny. So far away. But it was also pretty—bright and twinkling, it stood out from all the other lights around it.

"Can we see Jupiter?" Ethan asked.

"Given the time of year and location, I think . . . there." Charles pointed to a strong buttery light in a different part of the sky.

"Oh, wow," Ethan breathed. "I've seen Earth from Jupiter through a telescope. It looks just like that, just a twinkling dot. But it's blue. You can tell it's blue."

How did people on this planet, thousands of years ago, ever figure out those bright lights were planets and not stars? Because they really did look different. Different colors. And if we watched them every night, they would move differently across the sky. The stars held their places for tens of thousands of years. The planets moved week by week.

I started talking out loud, not even realizing I was, like my mind was moving so fast it just wanted to *go*. "They're like spots on a map. They're places, and I want to go. See them up close, for real, not just as spots of light in the sky. I can't stand being *grounded* like this."

"I want to go home," Ladhi said, sighing. We wouldn't be able to see Moore Station without a telescope. Too small, not reflective enough. But she was looking in a certain section of sky, like she knew it was there, tens of millions of kilometers away.

I looked across our little stove to Charles, whose face was mostly shadow, a faint outline of light marking his chin and cheek. Just then he looked up at me, caught my gaze. Nodded, just a little.

"It's going to be okay," he murmured. Was that for me or for him?

I must have slept, because I woke up. Several times, in fact, drifting off and starting awake, feeling disoriented every time. My feet were sore, my legs stiff when I moved them. I dreamed about having sore feet and never really seemed to fully regain consciousness. The air felt colder every time I opened my eyes. And wetter, like I could stick out my tongue and take a sip of the dampness. I pulled the blanket tighter around my shoulders and curled up against the chill.

Finally, when I started awake again and looked past the edge of the shelter, the sky was light. Well, lighter. A foggy gray instead of dark, and the stars had vanished. I heard noises—chirping, peeping. There didn't seem much point in trying to go back to sleep. I hauled myself up to sitting. Ethan was already awake and next to the stove, which he'd turned up to heat what looked like water.

"Morning," he said, glancing at me, smiling. "There's coffee mix with the food supplies. Want some?"

I muttered sure, or thought I did, and scratched my hair, which felt grubby and tangled. I'd never felt so sweaty, dirty, and gross in my whole life. And we had to do the whole hike over again today.

Birds were chirping and flitting all over the place. There must have been hundreds of them, which was disconcerting, because I couldn't see them; they were hidden in the foliage. Like everything else on this planet, waiting to turn around and bite me.

The coffee wasn't bad. Tasted pretty good, actually, and convinced me that I really was awake. By the time the smell of it spread through the shelter, the others were awake, scrubbing hands over faces. There was a latrine nearby—a wooden shed with a chemical composting toilet, which sort of ruined the effect of being in wilderness. Breakfast was energy bars and dried fruit, and even those tasted good after the cold night.

"What do you know," Tenzig said during the short meal. "We survived the night."

"There really weren't too many horrible things that could happen to us in just one night," Charles said. "Not this close to civilization."

"You call this civilization?" Ladhi said, scratching her head, picking out tangles in her hair, which was longer than mine. I could brush mine with my fingers. She might have to chop hers off after this. "I think there's something living in my hair."

My head starting itching even more after that. I didn't want to think about it.

Somehow, we'd survived our night in the wilderness with nothing worse to show for it than a few blisters, bug bites, sunburns, and muscle strain, which seemed like more than enough damage for one trip. I didn't know if I had any more confidence than when I'd started, but I did have the satisfaction of knowing I could play Stanton's stupid little games.

Packing to go back was a pain. Nothing seemed to fold down as small as it had been when we started, none of it fit back in the packs as neatly as it had yesterday. We kept stuffing the packs, restuffing, and still gear poked out at awkward angles. We had to let the stove cool off, which meant we finally got everything put in some kind of reasonable order, and there it was, sitting all by itself in the middle of the clearing. So we had to start over *again*.

But we managed, got our packs on and were ready to go. Tenzig consulted the map and GPS—more to feel like he was doing something official than because we really needed directions when the trail was right in front of us. Really, how hard could it be? And didn't we all feel better about ourselves now? Doing this on Mars, *that* would have been a challenge.

Mom could have started a fancy school on Mars instead of making us come here.

The air was getting warm again, and the sun had climbed.

Though it seemed to be burning my skin, the heat didn't get any deeper. My bones were still cold and my muscles still hurt.

"We'd better step it up, people," Tenzig said over his shoulder. "They're expecting us back in an hour."

We were walking single file down the trail, and we all glared at him.

"They'll wait," I said.

"They'll think we can't hack it," he shot back.

I grumbled, "The way I look at it, they stick a bunch of off-worlders in the middle of a jungle—"

"Forest," Charles said.

"Whatever—told them to go all survivalist with equipment they've never used before and minimal instructions. I figure if we show up at all without calling for help, we proved we can hack it."

"He wants to get back before the other groups do," Charles said. "This is a race for him."

Ladhi looked back and forth between them. "Is it? Is it supposed to be a race?"

"No," I said. "We'll get back when we get back and it doesn't matter."

We walked for another half hour, feet dragging, scuffing in the dirt. The sun wasn't quite as hot when we were under the trees, but during an open stretch, it beat down. No one had thought to put hats in our collection of gear.

Somebody's laughter rang through the trees.

I looked around, couldn't see anything. It might have been birdsong. Then it came again, along with the sound of voices, an easygoing chatter.

"What's that?" Ladhi stopped and stared, fearful, as if wild animals would announce themselves with loud voices.

The noises came closer, until Charles said, "It's the competition."

We stopped and waited. Sure enough, a group of students came around the curve in the trail behind us. George, Elzabeth, Angelyn, Bently, and Tamra. All Earth kids. Not anyone I particularly wanted to see at the moment.

"Wow, look at this," George said to the rest of his group. "Where'd you people come from?"

"We've been here the whole time," I said. "Where'd you come from?"

"This is our trail," Elzabeth said.

"If I may," Charles said, moving forward, and I wanted to stomp on his foot or something because I was sure he was about to say something insufferable. "Your trail followed a loop, didn't it? You started at a different trail that circles around, passes through our camp, and ends up back at base. While we went straight out and straight back." He looked around at the rest of us. "I imagine their route was about twice as long as ours."

George laughed. "So you guys got the wimpy kiddy route? That's super rich."

My face burned, and I didn't know if it was because I was embarrassed, angry that they were laughing, or angry at the instructors for going easy on us. I could have hiked the long trail, I knew I could have.

"It's not like they gave us a choice," I said.

"Oh, I know. They're just taking good care of you."

"Yeah, you just laugh it up," Tenzig said, as if he were the one doing the teasing.

"If you'll excuse us," George said, making a show of shouldering past us, leading the others down the trail. They really were walking faster than us, as if the hike took no effort at all. Angelyn threw us a smile.

"How do you like that?" Ethan said.

"Come on," Tenzig said, marching faster.

I just stared. "What do you think you're doing?"

"We can keep up with them," he said, his voice echoing from ahead.

"No, we can't!" Ladhi said.

"It's not worth the trouble," I added.

"You losers stay behind if you want," he said, continuing on, huffing for breath.

"We're not going to lose points for being late," Ethan said. "But we'll lose points for not sticking together."

"I'm not walking that fast," Ladhi said.

I sighed. "Let's just go. We'll catch up eventually."

We hiked on at the same pace we'd been going. As long as we could still hear voices ahead, we couldn't be doing too badly. If Tenzig was smart, he'd hang back right at the end so we all showed up at base together. Then he could have it both ways.

The trail was familiar this time, at least. We'd passed these trees, rocks, curves before. We didn't have to check the GPS. Just keep slogging. No matter how tired we were, we'd get to rest at the end of it. It would all be over.

Someone ahead screamed.

A chaos of noise followed. Voices shouting, another scream, a clatter of rocks.

I ran, not stopping when Charles yelled my name.

Around the next curve was a place on the trail where a rocky slope led down to a meadow. Now I could see the geology of it: constant slides cleared the trees here as rocks broke off from the cliffs above and tumbled down the precipice. Rocks I understood, and they behaved on Earth just the way they did on Mars.

The group of Earthers had been caught in one of these rockslides. Even now, pebbles and fist-size stones were tumbling after the couple of boulders that had broken off and crashed on top of them in a bit of terrible timing. The air was hazy with dust.

Most of them had fallen to crouches on the trail and were starting to get back on their feet, brushing off dust, looking around. I ran into Tenzig, who had stopped at the edge of the clearing.

The scream sounded again—from below. I looked.

Angelyn had fallen from the trail and now held on about four meters down, lying flat against the slope, clinging to a rock. If she let go, she'd keep going, scraping against the rocks another thirty meters down with nothing to stop her fall. Dirt and pebbles dislodged around her, knocking into her, loosening her grip. She kicked her legs, digging her feet into the dirt to try to get a better hold, but the movement only made her anchor more unstable. She even still had her pack on; it was dragging her down.

I dropped my pack off my shoulders and looked for rope. Ladhi—she had one of the ropes on her packs. Charles had the other. Where were they? Just as I turned to call to them, they came running up on the trail behind us. They stopped to take in the situation like I had, eyes wide.

Ladhi's rope was strapped to the outside of her pack. I yanked it out from the strap, then went to Charles—he'd already taken the other rope out of his back. Uncoiling the first rope, I held one end and gave the other end to Charles.

"Hold this," I said, and grabbed the second rope out of his hand.

"Polly—" he began, but I was already over the edge of the trail, on my butt and skidding toward Angelyn.

14

This probably wasn't the smartest thing I could have done. The smartest thing would have been to send an emergency signal from our GPS unit. Maybe someone else was doing that. All I could think about was getting to Angelyn, because even if someone was calling, help might not get here in time.

I didn't slide down the rock right above her—I was sending down a rain of pebbles and didn't want to hit her. I held tight to the rope—I could tell Charles was keeping it anchored on the other end, maintaining tension.

"Hang on!" I called. Angelyn was lying still now, aware that every movement threatened her grip. She looked up at me, lips pursed, gaze pleading.

I was almost at her level and the dirt under me was slipping—I didn't know if I was going to be able to stop. I dug in my heels, and the rope jerked in my hands. I held on and came to rest— Charles was holding on to me. With the few extra meters of rope I'd left dangling, I knotted a loop around myself, under my shoulders. As long as the knot held, and Charles didn't drop the other end, I'd be fine, I wouldn't fall.

"You okay?" I asked Angelyn.

"Scratched up," she said. She was covered in dust, and several cuts on her arm were bleeding. But she was aware and talking, and that was good.

"Can you get this around you?" I slipped the second rope off my shoulders and lowered it to her. Slowly, moving a centimeter at a time, she raised an arm and reached—and slipped. The dirt under her shifted, sliding in a piece and carrying her with it on a conveyor belt of pebbles and debris. She let out a scream and lay flat, attempting to stop herself.

I lunged, skidding as I dived for her. Rocks dug into my arms, but that didn't matter. Stretching, I hoped for a few more centimeters. The rope pinched around my chest. Her hand seemed to keep falling away from me.

And then I had it. My hand closed around her wrist, and her opposite hand swung over to grip mine, a reflexive grab for safety. We clung to each other.

"I've got you, it's okay," I gasped. She whimpered.

The rope around me pulled tight and squeezed the breath from me. I hung there, gasping against the pressure. Angelyn's weight pulled at my arms; they felt like they were stretching, tearing out of my shoulder sockets.

But the rope held. We didn't slide any farther.

"Can you get your pack off?" I said.

"But I'll lose it—"

"Who cares? It's dragging you down."

Next to her, I could help her unlatch the straps and pull them over her shoulders and still keep hold of her. I shouldn't have worried—she wasn't going to let go.

Finally, after some tugging, the straps released and the pack fell away, bouncing down the slope, falling over an edge, and dropping hard into the trees below. That could have been Angelyn. She stared after it, maybe thinking the same thing.

"Don't look down," I said. I had to remember to follow my own advice on that one.

I still had the second rope looped around my arm, and I worked one end loose and snaked it to Angelyn. We needed an anchor, so if we lost our grips she wouldn't fall again. Together, we worked it around her middle and tied it tight, and I tied the other end around myself, looping it with the first rope. So we were both safe. Now, we just had to climb back to the trail.

I looked up—we'd come an awful long way down. The row of faces leaning over to stare down at us seemed very small.

"Can you climb?" I gasped, catching my breath, trying to ignore the tightness in my chest. We kept hold of each other, holding hands—the ropes were just for emergency. We could help each other up.

"Don't know," she gasped back.

I dug my feet in, trying to get a purchase, but the dirt slid out from under me. I scrambled up a few centimeters then slid back down again. My rope was still taut, at least. We were hanging on.

"Polly!"

I craned my neck back; Ethan was shouting. "We're going to pull you up!"

He and a couple of the others were already hanging onto the rope; they'd pulled it around the trunk of a tree to brace and give them more leverage. I didn't see Charles. I didn't have a hand to wave back with—one was holding on to Angelyn, the other the rope, and I found I didn't want to let go.

"Okay!" I shouted back and hoped he heard. Turning to Angelyn, I said, "Ready?"

We tightened our grips on each other and kept hold of our ropes.

The rope clenched around my rib cage. Somebody—several somebodies—were pulling. This time when I dug my feet into the ground under me, dirt slid out but I didn't slip. We started inching up the slope.

Angelyn got her feet under her, so we were both able to help, staggering up the incline while the others pulled. It seemed to take forever. My hands were soaked with sweat and kept slipping. So were Angelyn's. She finally had to let go of me and hang onto the rope, which she could get a better grip on.

I had blisters on my hands, bruises on my chest, scratches along my arms. Angelyn wasn't much better. But slowly, we climbed. As Ethan and George and the others hauled, we braced our feet on the disintegrating incline. And then hands were reaching for me, grabbing my shirt, the rope around my chest, Angelyn and her rope, and they pulled us to safety. My legs were boneless; I collapsed, lying flat, gasping for breath, wondering if I'd ever be able to breathe normally again. Angelyn sprawled next to me. Reaching out to touch my hand, she smiled. So did I.

Through the tangle of legs and crouching bodies, I finally spotted Charles. He was sitting far back from the edge. The other end of the rope was wrapped around his chest several times. He was still holding the trailing part of it in hands that were scraped raw, like mine.

An air car arrived shortly after that.

Tenzig had hit the emergency call on the GPS unit as soon as I went over the edge. When the rescuers found out that nobody was in danger of dying, they landed the car, settling in a clearing a ways back on the trail because there wasn't room on the ledge above the slope. If we had been seriously hurt, they would have dropped the rescue team straight on top of us. As exciting as that might have been to watch, I was happy we didn't see it. It would have meant I'd screwed up and needed rescuing myself. That would have been embarrassing. As it was, I was just tired.

Angelyn's Earth friends quickly surrounded her, murmuring over her, hugging her. One of them put a blanket over her shoulders. Somebody—Ethan—handed me a bottle of water. I smiled in thanks. I was breathing hard. It might have been panic.

Two uniformed rangers, one of them carrying a medical kit, appeared on the trail and settled next to us. We were pretty obviously the victims here.

"Don't forget to look at Charles." I pointed to my brother, who'd dropped the rope but still held his hands loose and limp. Clearly, they hurt.

One of the rangers said, "Both of you just relax, you may be experiencing shock, so make sure you keep breathing . . ."

Angelyn caught my gaze and smiled. "Thanks," she said.

"No problem. You'd have done the same for me."

"No, you'd have found a way to climb back up all on your own," she said.

I laughed it off, because she was looking at me like I was some kind of superstar, and I didn't like it. Now I wasn't just the kid from Mars, I was the kid from Mars who did crazy stunts. Somebody else would have helped Angelyn. Anybody would have.

The park instructor, Keller, was there, and for all his suspicious enthusiasm he seemed pretty competent here, effectively gathering the rest of the students together and making sure they were all right. Farther back on the trail, observing, her arms crossed, was Stanton. She didn't look happy. I suppose not. Imagine having to report to Angelyn's prestigiously important parents that their daughter had smashed onto the valley floor during a confidence-building exercise.

The medical guy checked us all out, put antibiotic ointment on our cuts and scrapes—George and Tenzig also had burns on their hands from pulling on the rope. But we were all declared healthy and fit to travel. A couple more air cars arrived to carry us back to the bus. So we didn't have to walk back. But was it weird that I was a little disappointed that I didn't get to finish the trek on my own two feet?

By the time we got back to the base meadow, the other groups had returned already, had their gear collected, and were ready to go. They looked on in awe as we disembarked the emergency air car. We were going to have to explain all this a million times, weren't we?

I didn't want to talk to anyone. My arms hurt. Breathing hurt.

Finally, we were on the buses and headed back to the shuttleport, and from there back to Galileo. I expected to sleep the whole time.

I was shocked when Charles sat next to me on the bus. I stared at him, but he just looked straight ahead, not saying anything. Both of us had white gauze on our hands, which made us look kind of alien. More alien, rather.

"Aren't you going to tell me that was stupid?" I asked him, once we'd started moving and he still showed no sign of interacting with me. "That I should have waited and come up with a better plan?"

"You didn't know if we had time for a better plan," he said. "You did what you thought was right."

"But was I?"

"Obviously. We all survived, didn't we?"

"But—" I slouched. "Are you *sure*? There had to be a better way."

"That's the shock talking, Polly."

"I'm not in shock."

"A dangerous experience, extreme physical exertion, of course you're in shock."

"I wasn't *really* in danger—"

"Sometimes I think it would take a nuclear explosion to do you in, as much trouble as you get out of," he said.

"That almost sounds like a compliment."

"I'm mostly thinking about how to use that trait to our best advantage."

That sounded ominous.

After a few more minutes, he asked, "What do you think happened?"

"Rockslide. You saw the way that section of trail was open—that area had a lot of rockfall. Happens all the time."

"But this time it just happens to fall right when a group of students is walking under it," he said, and I couldn't tell if he was asking a question or thinking out loud.

"Erosion," I said. "Coincidence."

"You think they would have had us hiking up there if they knew that rock was about to fall? You don't think they check that sort of thing?"

"What are you saying?" I was speaking in a hushed tone—we both were. "Someone pushed that rock down on purpose?"

"I didn't say that," he said.

Leave it to Charles to turn a simple accident into a big production. "This isn't some kind of puzzle for you to solve. It's just an accident."

"You're probably right," he said, straightforward, like nothing was wrong. "Don't worry about it."

Easy for him to say.

15

Back at Galileo, Stanton escorted Angelyn and me to the infirmary. My second visit there in a matter of weeks. I wondered if
that was a record? I kept telling her I was okay, I felt fine, I hadn't
gotten hurt, I was just banged up a little. My ribs hurt when I
breathed, but they'd get better. She muttered something about
stress and made us stay. We sat on chairs next to each other until
the nurse arrived. Charles somehow avoided accompanying
us, even with his torn-up hands. I didn't know how.

Angelyn still held a thermal blanket wrapped around her
shoulders. She hadn't said much, and even now her head was
bowed. She was shivering, just a little.

"Hey," I prompted, "you okay?"

She straightened, as if I had woken her up from a nap. "Ms.
Stanton says I might still be in shock. That's why she wants the
nurse to look at us."

I didn't feel like I was in shock. Sure, I'd been scared—the
whole thing was kind of a rush, really. Lots of adrenaline. But I
wasn't sick. Angelyn still looked as pale as she had when she was
clinging to the slope. "That was pretty hairy stuff. When I saw

you halfway down that rockslide—oh, my *gosh*, I thought I was going to throw up." I laughed—not because we'd been in danger, but because we'd survived. I remembered the thrill, when I knew I had hold of her, and she wasn't going to fall. "But it's okay. We were smart, we got out of it. We're okay."

She hugged herself tighter. "I almost died. I've never been that close . . . to almost *dying*. I've never even thought about it before. Now I can't stop thinking about it."

I looked at her. "You weren't going to die. Maybe get smashed up pretty bad . . ." Probably best not to go there. "Besides, you can't think about it all the time. I mean, if you *really* think about it, everybody's that close to dying all the time. Our bus could have gone off a cliff, the suborbital could have crashed, some weird disease could sweep through the residence halls—"

"No," she said, shaking her head. "None of that could happen, all the safety protocols, everything's so *safe*. You don't *have* to think about it."

"You can fall and die spontaneously at any time, really. There was this guy who worked with my mom, back on Mars. One day, he just fell over. Died right there, without a sign or anything. Turns out it was a brain aneurysm. A blood vessel just blew up and killed him. He'd had yearly checkups and they'd never caught it. Thing is, something like that could happen anytime, to anyone—"

"Polly, can you just be quiet, please?"

I slouched and shut up. Thing was, I hadn't really thought about it before, either. The way I grew up, the way everyone on Mars grew up—we were taught that the planet would kill us if we weren't careful. An air lock could blow, the power systems could fail. If the colony buildings depressurized, if we went outside without enough oxygen, if the heating system went out—there were so many ways you could die on Mars, you didn't think about it or you'd never get anything done. That was what I'd been trying to tell Angelyn. But it came out wrong.

It meant you always knew where the emergency breathers were. You were always ready to react.

The nurse arrived. Same one as last time, and she rolled her eyes a little bit when she saw me. I must have looked okay—surly and glaring, actually—because she went to Angelyn first, took her temperature and blood pressure, checked her bandaged cuts and scrapes, and announced that she needed to stay under observation overnight. Angelyn actually looked relieved, like she felt better with someone watching over her.

I got my temperature and blood pressure taken, then was poked and prodded, which made my chest hurt even worse. The nurse frowned. Then made me stand behind a bone scanner.

"Cracked ribs," she said.

"What does that mean?" I said.

"You'll need to rest."

So I had to stay in the infirmary overnight, too. She also prescribed extra calcium supplements. Apparently, my non-Earth bones were so weak they'd taken damage from the pressure on the rope, and I was lucky they hadn't all broken and collapsed my lungs and killed me. The nurse asked what made me think I could tie a rope around my middle and climb up the side of a mountain? I answered, Because it *worked*?

The overnight nurse stayed in her office, leaving Angelyn

and me on our beds in the infirmary, with the lights out, only a glow coming in from the hallway.

I had to admit, lying flat on my back, perfectly still, felt kind of good. I still hurt when I breathed. Cracked ribs, right.

"Polly? Are you awake?" Angelyn whispered from her bed.

I blinked, startled; I'd been almost asleep. "Yeah."

"I just want to say thank you. You saved my life. So thank you."

Saved her life—sounded very momentous. Huge, really, and in a way, scarier than falling. I didn't want to be responsible for something so important. I'd helped her because I could, because that was what you did—helped people. At the colony, we couldn't survive without working together.

"I'm really glad you're okay," I whispered back.

I heard her shuffle as she arranged her blanket, rolled over, and settled in to sleep.

Now, I was awake, totally, and all I could think about was the pressing ache across my ribs when I breathed. I couldn't believe how much had happened over the last two days; it all seemed hazy now. Like it had happened in some video about someone else. Angelyn hadn't really fallen, and I hadn't really saved her. The rockslide hadn't really happened.

But it had. Against all odds, it had.

The next morning, I demanded to be set free, cracked ribs or not. I didn't have a concussion, I wasn't bleeding, I didn't want to be here anymore. The place smelled like a hospital and my stomach was turning. I promised the nurse I'd rest, and I got a note in my file excusing me from PE for the next two weeks. Angelyn was still asleep. She'd be fine, but the nurse would let her stay as long as she needed to.

Another note from Mom arrived on my handheld. Once again, Stanton must have reported what had happened immediately. Was she sending my mom reports every week? Every *day*? Why did that give me chills? The note wasn't long, just saying that she was glad I was all right, and that she was proud of me for "stepping up" when someone needed help. Again, I felt baffled. Why wouldn't I? Wouldn't anyone?

I went to the dining hall for breakfast.

As soon as I entered the room, people looked at me, even more than normal. Even worse than after the motorcycle incident. Their heads bent together as they whispered. I blushed. I didn't really want to know what they were saying. Ladhi and Ethan were sitting together, and I joined them. Charles wasn't here.

"Hey, it's the big hero!" Ethan said in greeting.

I scowled. "Is that what everyone's saying?"

Ladhi stared. "Polly, of course they are. I was there, I saw the whole thing—it was amazing. *You* were amazing!"

"It was . . . I just . . ." I slouched and stared at my toast. "I didn't do it to be amazing. I didn't even really think about it."

"It still makes you a hero," Ethan said. "Maybe even more of a hero."

"Is Angelyn okay?" Ladhi asked. "No one's seen her."

"She's still in the infirmary," I said. "She was in shock." My shock seemed to be delayed—I was starting to feel twitchy. "Did any of that seem weird to you guys?"

"Which part of it?" Ethan said. "Because the whole trip seemed pretty weird to me."

"If there was even the slimmest chance of an accident happening, do you think they'd have had us out there?"

"I suppose there's always a chance of an accident. Transport breaking down, building catching on fire."

"Maybe the whole thing was only supposed to *look* dangerous. Like it was all a setup to see how we'd react."

Ethan shook his head. "Accidents happen, that's all it is."

Before I could reply, a hush fell over the dining hall. Angelyn had entered the room and went to the kitchen for her tray of food. She must have decided she'd had enough of the infirmary, too. Everyone was staring at her like they'd stared at me. She looked okay—the color had come back into her face, she was clean, her hair washed and done up in a braid. A big gauze bandage covered her elbow where she'd cut it on a rock. It looked incongruous with her otherwise neat appearance.

She scanned the tables, and when her gaze found me, her eyes lit up. She came over to join us, and I shifted to make room.

"Hey, how're you feeling?" I said.

"Better. It's hard to believe it even happened now. Seems like a dream." Her smile was pensive.

"Oh, my gosh," Ladhi said, pointing at the bandage. "How bad did you get hurt?"

Angelyn shrugged, blushed. She'd probably been hoping no one would notice. "A few scrapes. It itches a little." Ladhi seemed very impressed. "I think Polly got hurt worse than I did—cracked ribs, the nurse said."

"Oh, my gosh," Ladhi repeated. "And you didn't even say anything."

"I get out of PE for two weeks," I said.

"And she just shrugs it off," Angelyn said.

We ate, then it was time to go to class. As we were cleaning up and shoving our trays back through the window to the kitchen, Angelyn stayed close to me.

She bent her head, lowering her voice to tell a secret. "The psychologist thinks I should go out again. Hiking, rock climbing, something. Overcome my fears or something like that. I wanted to ask you—will you go with me?"

"Yeah, sure," I said.

"Good," she said. "Thanks."

I should have said no. I'd passed that test, I'd proved myself, I didn't want to go through that again. But I said yes without thinking, just like I threw myself off that trail without thinking. Because we had to help each other. Despite all the competition, we did.

Well, most of us had to help each other. On my way out of the room, after dropping off my tray, Tenzig sauntered up to me, walking with me into the hallway.

"What do you want?" I said, more surly than was probably necessary.

"What you did yesterday? Totally slick," Tenzig said. His smile seemed genuine, like he was really impressed, but with him it was hard to tell. "Rescuing someone like Angelyn? That'll erase any black marks on your record. Good job."

"I didn't do it to erase any black marks," I shot back. "I did it because I could—anyone could have done it."

"Don't bet on it. A lot of people just don't have the guts for it," he said, and I scowled. "Polly, don't look so sour. I'm serious. Piloting programs love that sort of thing. It shows you have what it takes."

"I already know I have what it takes."

"Yeah, and now they will, too. I was wrong—you won't need my help at all." He stuck out his hand for me to shake.

I had to wonder what the joke was. In his world, I didn't have enough status or pull to be able to get him anything, so why would he be nice to me? Then again maybe, just maybe, he was being nice. I took a chance and shook his hand. His grip against mine was warm and sure, not too loose, not too tight—not trying to start some kind of contest.

Then, instead of letting go, he pulled himself close, leaned in casual-like, and kissed me on the cheek. Not a big kiss. Just a light press of dry lips on skin that sent a spark flying to my scalp.

He turned and walked away, head bowed, expression hidden, as if the whole thing had been spontaneous and innocent and he was afraid of what I was going to think. What *did* I think? I touched my face; I could still feel where he'd kissed me, and smell the soap on his skin.

I wondered: What was *that*?

16

"What are you wearing to the banquet?" Angelyn asked me at breakfast about three weeks after the hiking accident and a couple of weeks before said banquet.

The banquet. Everyone had been talking about it for days. Around the end of the year, the school held a big party for students and their families—Earth families, who didn't have to travel a couple hundred million kilometers to get here—to celebrate the winter holiday and the halfway point in the year. Apparently, it was a big deal.

I shrugged. "This, I guess."

"Oh, no. You can't wear that."

I looked down at my school uniform. "What else am I supposed to wear?"

"You wear that every day. This has to be special. Didn't you bring anything nice from home?"

"I could only bring what I could carry. Weight restrictions. I've got a couple of shirts and a pair of pants. What do you mean by *nice*?"

"A dress. Party clothes. Something snappy."

I didn't even know what that meant. I stared blankly at her.

"You don't have *anything*?" she said.

"It's at the school. I figure my uniform ought to be fine."

"No one else will be wearing their uniforms. Seriously Polly, we really need to go shopping."

I didn't know how to do that. I kept looking at her like she was speaking a different language, and she sighed, exasperated. "Sit by me at study period tonight and we'll start looking."

So that evening instead of studying for biology I sat with Angelyn and looked at dresses on her handheld. The craziest outfits, every color I could imagine and then some, skintight with flounces and ruffles on shoulders, hips, and hems. Shining and sparkling fabric. The whole idea seemed to be to turn people into decorated artwork, because I couldn't imagine actually functioning in a gown like that. Angelyn scrolled through dozens of them and sighed at every one.

"See anything you like?" she asked.

"I don't know." I wrinkled my nose. I didn't even know what I was supposed to like. "What are you wearing?"

Her eyes got wide and shining as she punched up a new file and showed me a picture. The gown was . . . beautiful. I couldn't even say why it was beautiful, I could just tell that it would make Angelyn look gorgeous and slinky and very grown-up. It was midnight blue and made of some fabric that rippled and shimmered across the model's body, clinging to curves and falling away like water. Its neckline scooped almost to her breasts, and thin straps left her arms bare. Some kind of electronics made spots of light glow and swirl on the skirt, like actual stars. I imagined Angelyn in that dress, with her hair done up like the model's, in curls that fell in waves over her shoulders. She wouldn't look like Angelyn anymore.

I wasn't sure I even had curves. Not like that, anyway. "Wow. I've never seen a dress like that."

"Don't you have parties on Mars?"

"Of course we do. But everybody just wears their regular clothes." Importing fancy stuff like this got expensive, especially when there wasn't much use for it. I'd sound boring, trying to explain that to Angelyn, so I just let it go.

"We'll find you something, don't worry. What's your favorite color?"

Red, I decided. Dark Martian red. Angelyn started searching. She looked me up and down and announced that with my willowy frame I'd look good in something fitted and slinky, with a long skirt. I took her word for it and made a mental note to look up if "willowy" was good or bad.

We narrowed down the choices. She showed me picture after picture and asked me if I liked it or not, and I went with my gut feeling because what else could I do?

Finally, we found one. It had a skirt that flowed, long sleeves, and embroidered swirls on the neckline. It was rust red, like Mars at sunset. Angelyn said it would bring out the color in my complexion. I had never thought much about my complexion until I came to Earth.

Then all we had to do was enter in my measurement scans, pay for it, and have it delivered. It was that easy. Almost.

"There's a problem," I said when we got to that part. "I don't know if I have any money."

"What do you mean, you don't know if you have money?"

"I know my mother has money—she had to, to send us here. But I don't know if *I* have any. You know?"

"She didn't give you an allowance? Like spending money?"

"I think she figured I'd be at school all the time and wouldn't need any. The school provides just about everything, and there really isn't a whole lot on Mars to spend money *on*." This was all getting exasperating. I sighed. "Can I get back to you?"

"The dress isn't going anywhere. Not until you order it, anyway."

Angelyn had done this before. Lots of times. She must have had closets full of nice clothes stashed somewhere. I couldn't even imagine that. It seemed . . . excessive. On Mars, those bright fantastical colors would be covered by brown dust in seconds.

I spent a day gathering intelligence. Recon. Surreptitiously, like I was just curious and not desperate for information. Ethan had a suit he planned on wearing; his family had ordered it and had it sent to him, knowing he'd be going to fancy parties. I didn't ask Tenzig—I'd started blushing whenever we ended up in the same room—but I expected that he had a suit like Ethan's. I kept stealing glances at Tenzig, wondering what he was up to. He always seemed to be watching me, which was kind of creepy, but kind of . . . not. He started sitting next to me at lunch, even. It meant one of two things: my status after rescuing Angelyn had gotten so great that he thought sitting next to me made him look good, or else he liked me, which felt weird.

Marie had stopped talking to me, which made time back in the room awkward. That didn't surprise me, but it made me sad.

I was absolutely relieved that Ladhi and Ethan kept sitting with me at lunch. I wished I could find a way to tell them how much I appreciated that, without sounding awkward or weird.

Finally, I messaged Mom about the dress.

Dear Mom:

I've got a problem. There's a banquet coming up—it's supposed to be a big party thing, everyone's really excited, and apparently everyone gets dressed up in super-nice clothes. Like skirts and dresses and suits things. I've never worn a skirt, but I guess I'm supposed to. One of the girls here—a friend, Angelyn—said she'd help me buy a dress. But I don't know how much money to spend. I've never really had to worry about stuff like that, you know? So, I wondered—do you have some money you could give me to buy a nice dress? Otherwise I'll just wear my school uniform. Thanks.

Oh—school's fine, and Charles is fine. I know he probably hasn't written you. But he hasn't taken over the school. Yet.

Your Daughter, Polly.

P.S. I don't know what Charles is wearing to the banquet. He probably has it all figured out on his own.

Mom answered my note the next day. She must have sent a reply as soon as she got my message. A day was pretty much absolutely the soonest my message could be transmitted to Mars and have her message get back to me. It gave me an idea how important this whole banquet with nice clothes thing was.

Dear Polly:

Your banquet sounds marvelous! Of course you need a nice dress for it. This is one of the reasons I wanted you to go to Earth—you'd never have such an experience on Mars. I've opened an account on Earth for just such purposes, for you and your brother. The access codes are attached—it's set to your and Charles's biomarks. Don't worry about amount or expense. Just listen to your friend's advice and have a good time. Snap some pictures for me, if you think of it!

It's so nice to hear you're making friends and getting along so nicely on Earth.

Love, Mom

She'd never sounded so excited about anything. It made me nervous.

Ladhi, it turned out, already had a nice dress. She'd brought it with her, in fact. Belt stations apparently had more parties than Mars did. She showed me the outfit, and it was gorgeous—a light, filmy fabric that wouldn't have added much to her weight allowance. It draped around her in some complicated pattern that made her look so much better than the school uniforms, showing off her graceful limbs and coloring.

Which was the point, I realized. None of us really looked *good* in our school uniforms. I hadn't thought about it in those terms before. But I still thought I looked pretty good in my Mars clothes—they made me look like I came from Mars. I almost changed my mind about what to wear, but I'd already ordered the dress.

Marie had a dress, of course. All the offworld girls but me had known to get dresses. Mars was the only place that didn't have a tradition of formal clothing. I had to think about that.

Last of all, in study hall fifteen minutes before lights-out, I cornered Charles.

"What are you wearing to the banquet?" I asked him.

"It's a surprise."

"Oh. Because Mom sent us money to buy nice clothes. Apparently, we need nice clothes."

"Yes," Charles said. "She's had investment accounts on Earth for years, that's how she's paying for tuition here."

"Oh." I hadn't even thought about how long Mom must have been planning this, to collect all that money. "So, do you need money?"

"No. I've got it all worked out," he said. "What are you wearing?"

"Angelyn helped me find something."

"That'll be interesting," he said, with that superior arc in his brow he always got.

"What?"

"Nothing."

I grumbled. "So when were you going to tell me that we needed a costume for this banquet thing?"

"I did you the credit of assuming that you'd figure it out on your own. And I was right."

"Charles. We're the only kids from Mars in this whole ratty school, don't you think we should have each other's backs?"

"If I offered my help—if I walked right up to you and told you that you needed help and I was the one who had the answers—would you even listen to me?"

"I'd probably wonder what you were up to," I said. In fact, I might do exactly the opposite of whatever he suggested, just to keep from falling into the trap he'd set. Except he probably knew that was what I'd do, so doing the opposite would be exactly what he wanted me to do . . . That was the trouble with Charles. No matter what, I couldn't win.

"Exactly. You ought to just keep on doing what you've been doing. You're obviously functioning well enough."

"What about you?"

"I'm shocked that you would even take the time to care."

"You are my brother."

"I'm fine. Really. You don't have to worry about me."

"And you don't have to worry about me," I said. "Everything's fine."

"Right. Of course it is."

The night of the banquet arrived. I'd assumed we'd be in the dining hall—sure, it'd be dressed up and polished. They might even be able to get rid of the constant boiled-vegetable smell. But no: we had fancy invitations, printed on real paper, informing us that the banquet would be held in the school's main administrative building. Most of us had never even been there. That was where Stanton had her offices. Where the people who ran the school worked. Apparently they also had a banquet hall.

"It's for wining and dining the school's patrons and sponsors," Angelyn explained. "Rich parents and things. Makes them feel special."

"That seems excessive," I said.

"It's how it goes."

Angelyn came to our room to get ready. I needed all the help I could get. Marie humphed at us and stormed off to one of her friends' rooms. Every girls' room in the dorm, and a couple of the guys' rooms, had turned into a chaotic mess of makeup, shimmery fabric, and enthusiastic squealing. I'd never seen anything like it. It was a tornado made of clothes.

Ladhi, Angelyn, and I wriggled into our dresses and helped each other with hair and makeup. They looked great. Angelyn's slinky blue gown looked just as amazing as I imagined it would. She wore high heels that made her seem like a statue, a piece of finely carved artwork. And her hair—she brushed it out loose, and she'd done something to it so it lay in dark ripples down her back. She was self-conscious about the wide scar on her elbow from where she'd been scraped up in the fall. The concealer she put on it didn't hide the pink very well.

"As soon as we get a break in school, I'm going to have surgery to get rid of it," she muttered.

"It's a badge of honor," I told her. "Show it off." I was one to talk. I still ached around my chest if I got tired, but I tried not to show it.

But Angelyn washed off the makeup and let the scar go.

Ladhi was magical, in purple silk that seemed to drape around her body, molding to her shoulders and hips. Gold earrings dangled, and she wore intricate sandals that laced around her feet. I had no idea how I looked. I didn't look like myself, for sure. And those sandals—I'd let Angelyn pick out a pair to go with my dress, because they all looked horrifying to me. My feet would be practically naked. And what if I had to run in those? Angelyn and Ladhi just kept telling me everything would be okay.

I was wearing the dress. It had arrived in a box just a few days ago, and I'd pulled it out like it was going to bite me. It looked . . . well, I'd never seen anything like it. Not clingy like Angelyn's or airy like Ladhi's, it flared out in the skirt, flowing like ripples in sand, and the wide neckline framed my face and neck. It was made of a shimmery red fabric that changed shades in the light, depending on how I moved. It looked even better in person than it had on the screen. It made me look older, sophisticated. Angelyn studied me a minute, then ran back to her room. She came back with a length of fabric, a filmy black shawl that she draped around my elbows and let fall behind me. I looked almost elegant.

She also did something to my hair that made it fluff out and shine, like it was another perfect accessory. I looked older and taller—which meant I stood well above both Angelyn and Ladhi. A mutant. But an elegant mutant.

"Wow, look at us," Ladhi said, as we stood side by side in front of the square bathroom mirror. We looked like we should have been in some kind of video. I was actually getting excited about it all.

We joined a stream of students walking from the dorms to the banquet at the admin hall. Just after dusk, the sky had darkened, gray clouds against deep blue. The concrete path was lit with solar lamps set along the sides, about a foot high. It was like we were walking on a trail of light. The girls had gone all out, with fancy gowns, hair styles, and glittering jewelry. I was glad I'd listened to Angelyn. For once I actually felt like I belonged. The guys wore suits, tailored jackets and trousers, with colored shirts, and ties. They looked slick and polished—strange, almost, after seeing everyone in plain uniforms week after week.

I wondered what Charles looked like. I couldn't find him.

The admin building was at the edge of the Galileo compound. It didn't look much different from any of the other buildings—a straightforward block, minimalist and efficient. The rows of small windows were all dark except for a few on the ground floor, which glowed with soft, dim light.

The path of lamps steered us to a side entrance, where double doors stood open, leading to a short hallway that opened into a massive room. Bigger than the vehicle garage at Colony One. Bigger than anything. Three stories of nothing rose above us. I just stood there looking up, and up, my jaw hanging open. This whole night was make-believe.

The room was decorated like something out of a video, again. Miniature fountains in the corners, multifaceted lights that glittered like crystals suspended from the ceiling, mountains of flowers in vases or molded into arcs and spirals made to look like they'd grown that way. They were cut—I checked, they didn't have roots, just stems stuck in water. They'd all be dead in a few days. This room had more flowers than entire greenhouses on Mars, and they were all dying. It seemed a little sad.

Once inside, people started pairing off. Two girls who every-body knew liked each other grabbed hands and bent their heads together, giggling. Their eyes lit up, and they were clearly having a great time. Elzabeth and George arrived arm in arm like some kind of king and queen of the universe. Marie tagged along with a group of offworld students, including Tenzig. He scanned the room as if looking for me, smiling wide when he saw me. I smiled back, but nervously. My beautiful gown suddenly felt tight.

I looked for Ethan, couldn't find him, so turned to go find Angelyn, lingering near the wall nearby.

"Can I ask a question?" I asked her.

"Of course," she said.

"Are we supposed to be here, you know, *with* someone?"

She got a sour look on her face. "It's not a requirement."

"But . . ."

Her smile was sad. "Be nice, wouldn't it?"

"Is there someone you wanted to be here with?" I asked care-fully.

"You know that upperclassman? The one who helps run the track activities at PE?"

"Yeah," I said. "He's cute." He was. Earth guy, fastest runner at the school, with floppy hair and a nice smile.

"And he'll never look at a first-year like me."

"You never know," I said hopefully.

She paled, worse even than when she was hanging on the side of a mountain. "What about you?" she asked, changing the subject. "You have your eye on anyone?"

My brain flailed. "Not really."

"Tenzig keeps watching you. Maybe you should ask him to dance."

"Maybe I should look for my brother and make sure he's not plotting total destruction."

Tables around the edges of the room held food. More different kinds of food than I'd ever seen before. I couldn't even identify a lot of it. The vegetables I got, even though they were sliced into elegant little sticks with ruffled edges. There were bowls of things to dip the vegetables in. There were lumps of something on toothpicks. There was a cake—happily, I wasn't going to have to get anyone to explain cake to me. We had round, fluffy, mooshy sweet things on Mars, because humanity couldn't exist without dessert. I had to extrapolate from there to what I was seeing on display at the Galileo winter banquet. Because it must have been a cake, but it was taller than I was. It had multiple cakes stacked together and painted different colors. It didn't even look edible.

The rest of the hall was filled with round tables covered with white tablecloths, fancy place settings, and candles. Real candles with open flames. I even touched the first one to be sure—the teardrop of flame wavered and flared as I passed my hand over it, and the brief sharp heat of it stung my finger. I resisted an urge to find a fire extinguisher and put them all out—it would have been my first impulse at home. Open flame and artificial atmospheres didn't go well together.

They were so casual about the air here.

I folded my arms, hugging myself, and took it all in.

"It does seem excessive, doesn't it?" Charles had slipped in to stand beside me. He was wearing his Martian outfit: tan shirt, beige trousers, brown jacket with a Colony One patch on the sleeve, boots. He'd polished the boots, and the jacket had been washed and pressed. I had to admit, the outfit looked pretty good. Like a uniform, almost. He also seemed older, broader through the chest than I'd ever noticed before. He might have been one of the tallest guys in the room.

People in their formal costumes did double takes when they walked past him, looking over their shoulders, like they weren't sure they were really seeing him. Nobody could mistake him for anything other than what he was: a Martian. He stood with his shoulders square, hands tucked behind his back, and didn't seem to notice the attention.

I felt very small standing next to him. I kind of wished I'd worn my Colony One jacket and trousers, too. But I squared my shoulders, uncrossed my arms, and carried on.

"Yeah," I said. "Did you see, they've got open flames?" I pointed to the candle on the nearest table.

"And running water. A flagrant display of excess resources."

"Is that what this is all about?" It suddenly hit me: were the fancy clothes and jewelry, the money this cost all for show? A display of waste because they could, including the three stories of empty air above us, which on Mars would have been filled with floors, rooms, equipment, or oxygen-generating vegetation?

"Not *all*," Charles said. "But mostly, I think."

"Huh." I looked around with new eyes, mentally putting price tags on everything. Yeah, somebody was showing off here. The school wanted to impress the parents and investors, and the students were all trying to impress one another.

"It's kind of small," Angelyn said. She had stopped beside me and was also looking around, but her gaze was narrow, appraising, skeptical: she had seen better. "I guess there's only so much you can do at a school. My parents have thrown some really epic parties."

"What for?" I blurted.

Angelyn looked at me with that expression people got when I'd said something strange and alien. "Because it's fun," she said.

Fun? I wondered. All that effort, preparation, expense, anxiety—and it was supposed to be fun?

I must have looked astonished, because she said, "Do you really not have parties on Mars?"

"We do," I said, defensive. "We have concerts and birthdays and holidays and everything. It's usually just getting together in one of the atrium gardens and hanging out and eating."

"Then it's the same thing," she said, smiling. "Relax and enjoy yourself."

Right. I felt like I was accelerating into an asteroid field.

When Ethan spotted us, he came over to say hello. He must have arrived earlier and had been here the whole time, clustered with another group of students and talking. He looked happy to see me.

"Wow, Polly, you look great!" He looked me up and down, and I wanted to cross my arms and hide. The whole point was for people to look at me, right? And suddenly my hair itched and my dress felt crooked. I wanted to fidget. But I smiled. With my friends around me, the place didn't feel so alien.

"Thanks," I managed to get out before I completely folded in on myself. "So do you."

He was wearing a steel gray suit with a red waistcoat, which made him look tall, confident, and rich. Ethan Achebe of the Zeusian Mining Enterprise Achebes. It all made sense. He was here as a symbol for his whole family.

And Charles and I were a symbol of Mars. What the heck did people see when they looked at us? The rugged young man in the alien brown uniform and the girl who looked like a dust-filled sunset?

"Charles, why didn't you dress up?" Ethan asked.

"This is dressed up, on Mars," he said. Ethan waited for further explanation, but Charles remained silent. He wasn't going to explain himself.

We all looked grown-up. It was like we were getting glimpses of the people we'd be in ten years. Daunting.

"Oh, my parents are here!" Angelyn exclaimed, and ran off.

I looked to see where she went: a man and woman, obviously her parents. She had the man's refined chin and nose and the woman's long legs and dark hair. They were dressed just as spectacularly as she was, him in a tailored black suit and her in a shimmering dark dress.

Two parents. And to think, Mom handled both me and Charles all by herself. Charles had planted himself like a guard at the edge of the room, watching everything. Ethan and I were suddenly by ourselves, side by side. And that was okay, I decided.

"You have any family here?" Ethan asked.

"No. At least not that I know of. When my grandfather left for Mars, he pretty much cut all his ties to Earth. How about you?"

"I've got a cousin who runs the trading office here on Earth. She's supposed to be here. I've never met her. But you know, family's family. I'm sure she's great. And my parents will want her to check up on me."

If we had any family on Earth, none of us knew about it. Grandpa Newton abandoned everything, changed his name, and helped found Colony One. We just had Mom back on Mars, and an anonymous, medically selected sperm donor for a father. I had never felt the lack of a biological family. On Mars, we were all family, in a way. This whole biology thing seemed . . . contrived. We'd beaten biology just by living on Mars at all. But the connections seemed very important here.

Ethan's cousin found him, then. Wearing silky trousers and a tailored jacket in bright colors, she was short, stocky, and vibrant, with brown skin and a wide smile. She didn't look anything like Ethan, who stood tall, dark, and spindly beside her. That didn't seem to matter; she hugged him and gushed over him all the same.

Catering staff in spiffy suits seemed to be running the whole thing. Stage-managing it, even. After a stretch of time in which everyone got drinks and we all stood around talking and complimenting one another, we were guided to assigned seats at the tables. Charles and I were placed at a table with Angelyn and her parents, a serious-looking couple, and an Earth student I didn't know well and his parents.

I wasn't sure, but Charles and I might have been the only students here who didn't have an adult relative with us. Even Boris from the Moon had Earth family looking out for him. It made me feel like we'd sneaked in, and as soon as someone discovered us, we'd get thrown out.

The families with enough money to send their kids to Galileo were dynasties. The names were important, representing decades or centuries of wealth and power. *That* was the connection, not so much the biology. Again, I felt like a fluke, because all people knew about me was that I was from Mars. I was here representing an entire planet. Maybe Charles had the right idea—if we were going to be aliens anyway, we might as well act like it.

"How does it feel, being the first Martians to attend Galileo?" Angelyn's mother, Ms. Chou, asked in that beaming way that meant she was expecting a polite answer.

I didn't know what answer she expected, so all I could do was say what I thought. "It's weird. Mars is Mars, it's different, but people expect us to get everything about Earth, you know? I'd like to see you guys come to Colony One and try to understand everything. Ow—" I blurted, then clamped my mouth shut to stay quiet. Charles had dug his heel into my foot under the table.

"It's an honor," he said evenly, as if reading from a script. He probably was. He'd probably memorized a whole list of reasonable responses to standard questions. He always thought of these things. "We're happy to represent Mars among the best students throughout the solar system. We only hope we can live up to such high expectations."

"I wouldn't worry about that," Angelyn said, beaming. "I think Charles may be the smartest person here. And Polly . . . well, I told you all about Polly. She's fearless."

My face went as red as my dress. I wanted to blurt out that it was nothing. I hadn't done anything special, I'd just done the reasonable thing, the logical thing. I was just Polly—the weird Martian kid.

Charles rested his heel on my foot again, threatening to do harm. So I kept my mouth shut and smiled shyly.

Mr. Chou said, "Your mother is Martha Newton, isn't she? Director of operations at Colony One?"

I blinked, surprised. "Yeah. You know her?"

"Only by reputation," he said. "She's quite influential, isn't she?"

"I don't know—" This time when Charles tried to step on my foot, I yanked it out of the way.

My brother sat back in his chair, hands steepled together, kind of sinister. "Polly and I aren't really old enough to be involved in her work, so I couldn't say. Do you have a lot of dealings with Mars, Mr. Chou?"

"The company I work for deals in hydroponics-equipment manufacturing and development. It's always been my hope that we could develop closer ties with Mars, both politically and economically. Colony One has become one of our chief competitors."

"You'd like to buy out the manufacturing interests on Colony One, you mean," Charles said, and Mr. Chou was left staring, his smile frozen.

"That's a bit of an exaggeration, son," he finally answered, with a stifled chuckle. Charles just kept staring, until the older man dropped his gaze.

Ms. Chou said casually, gesturing with her empty fork, "We hear so many rumors here about what's really going on all the way out there, with no way to check, because we only have the information that the governing board—people like your mother—deems fit to tell the rest of the system. It's just so interesting, I think—hearing about it firsthand."

"I'm sure you get plenty of independently reported information," Charles said. "You're just hoping we'll let something slip."

"Wait a minute," I said. "Are you trying to get us to talk about Mom to give you some kind of inside information?"

"I'm just trying to make polite conversation," she said. Her glare, matched with a sweet smile, was cutting, like she'd won a point.

"Anyone want dessert?" Angelyn said, gesturing vaguely over her shoulder at the table full of cake. She was glaring at her parents—and at me. If she could have reached me under the table, she probably would have kicked me, too.

"Yes," I said, and we both scooted our chairs out and made a dash for it.

By the time we'd reached the cake, she was frowning. "I'm sorry. They said they wanted to meet you, and I thought it was because of what happened at Yosemite, so I asked for us all to sit together. I didn't know they'd grill you about Martian politics."

"Not that I even know anything about Martian politics," I said. "But Charles seemed to enjoy it. I'm sorry he's so . . . so . . ." I couldn't event think of what he was.

"We're supposed to be having *fun*," she muttered.

"Charles *is*," I said. "Didn't you notice?"

The whole banquet production had two purposes, I decided. One was to have conversations like Charles and the Chous had just had, where they tried to one-up each other or get information without seeming like they were trying to do so. The other was to show everyone else what a good time you could have. Everybody laughed a little too hard, and the smiles were a little too fake.

But I did have a good time—eating. I tried at least one of everything I couldn't identify that wasn't meat. I ate way too much.

Then the music started.

"Oh, there's going to be dancing!" Angelyn said, her eyes lighting up. "Do I even dare ask Harald?" Harald—the upperclass guy she liked. She was looking at him across the room. All the upperclass students looked so much more comfortable here. I didn't think I'd ever get that way. Assuming I managed not to get kicked out.

The band was live—more than a dozen musicians, which made it bigger than any band I'd ever heard. We had live music and musicians on Mars. Concerts in the atrium. Quieter, usually.

The sound filled the banquet hall. It was almost too loud—I'd have to shout to talk. By this time, the adults had all collected on one side of the room and seemed to be gossiping. About politics, money, each other—us. I hadn't realized what a big deal Galileo was until I saw how pleased everyone seemed about being here and showing off.

The band played something old-fashioned and jazzy. As Angelyn said, it was music you could dance to. I would have preferred something classical, that I could sit and listen to, like we did at home. I was tired, and the thought of dancing in Earth gravity made my bones feel like lead. But I wasn't going to be the first one to leave. I could hear it all now: those Martian kids, so antisocial, so *strange*.

They were probably saying that anyway.

A lot of people were dancing now. Angelyn was still watching

Harald, her brow furrowed. He glanced this way once—and smiled at her. I nudged her and said, "Be fearless." That seemed to settle it for her. Straightening her shoulders, she walked over to him. I didn't hear what she said to him, but he smiled wider, and a minute later they walked together to the middle of the floor. I could see in seconds they were both good at dancing, and Angelyn never looked away from him.

I was left holding a glass of punch and watching, and I didn't even mind. Ethan drifted over, his hands locked behind his back, and I expected some pithy observation about how great everything was. But he pointed over his shoulder to the dancing.

"Polly. You want to?"

I didn't know how to dance, but I didn't say that. "How can you have the energy for it after all this?"

"I'm sure I'll be beat tomorrow. But for now, why not have fun?" He was smiling, not having to fake enjoying himself. Good for him.

"Ethan, I don't think I can even—"

Then Tenzig came over from the side, like he was trying to sneak up on me, but not very hard. He looked Ethan up and down, then focused on me. His smile seemed sly.

"Are you going to dance, Polly?"

Ethan was giving him a strange look, and I felt suddenly queasy. "I was just trying to decide."

"Come on. Let's go." He tipped his head, a suave gesture.

I looked back and forth between them. Ethan's brow was raised, hopeful. Tenzig held his hand out, demanding.

This was a simple problem. I ought to be able to figure this out. Why couldn't I figure this out? It was just dancing. Say yes to one of them, or no to both. But why did they even have to ask? Either one of them? At the same time? Or I could walk away.

I couldn't figure it out. So I set down my glass of punch and left. Walked right in between them, marching away to the far wall, past the dessert tables and to the door. I could leave the whole party. I didn't need to be here. No one would miss me.

Stanton was standing by the main door, the one we'd come in. She wasn't in her usual gray uniform, but her black gown, floor length with long sleeves, might as well have been a uniform. She was scanning the crowd with a pleased, inward smile, like she had orchestrated a complicated plan and was watching it unfold flawlessly. I wondered what kind of report about all this she was going to be sending to people like my mother. It made me want to do something like tip over the punch bowl, just to be contrary. But I didn't want to spend another six weeks on restrictions.

I wasn't going to try sneaking past her. There had to be another way out of this cave.

"Polly, what's wrong?"

I jumped, flinching like someone had set off an alarm behind me. I was going *insane*. It was just Ladhi, looking wide-eyed and earnest.

"I thought this whole thing was supposed to be fun," I muttered.

"Oh, my gosh, it is! I danced with Boris! Did you see us?"

I glared. How dare she be more socially well-adjusted than me. "I'm not interested in dancing. I don't know why everyone else is."

"Doesn't anyone go dancing on Mars?"

"Yes, of course people dance on Mars, but not—" Not like this, with all the social rules and nice dresses and people saying things they didn't mean or that meant something other than what they were saying, and impossible decisions like what to do when two guys asked you to dance at the same time. I crossed my arms and looked away. "I'm just in a bad mood."

Her brow furrowed; she looked at a loss. I felt bad for snapping at her. But not bad enough to say anything about it.

"Well," she said, shrugging a little, "can I help?"

"I think I just need to be alone for a little while."

She hesitated, then wandered back to the dance floor, Boris, and whatever.

The hall had plenty of corners for me to hide in, and that was what I planned on doing—sulking until the party broke up and I could go back to the dorm without anyone noticing. Really no point to the fancy clothes after all, was there? Well, now I knew.

I must have been standing there fifteen minutes, staring at nothing in particular, when I heard my name. "Polly?"

Tenzig approached, holding two glasses, head tilted in query. He'd followed me.

I glared. "I'm not interested in dancing."

"You really should try it. But for now I just wanted to see if you'd like a drink. Or something." He held out one of the fancy punch glasses, filled with purplish drink.

"You're being awfully nice all of a sudden."

"I don't know what gave you the idea that I'm not a perfectly nice guy."

"Because you're kind of a jerk."

He ducked his head, hiding a smile. "Come on. You just have to get to know me."

If I didn't know better, he seemed like he actually was trying to be nice. I took the glass he offered and drank a sip. Just fruity punch. No itching powder or hot sauce or poison or anything. I drank another sip.

"Thanks," I said. "You know, you should ask Marie to dance. She really likes you."

"But I want to dance with *you*. I wasn't trying to scare you or put you on the spot or anything back there."

"I wasn't scared," I said.

He brightened. "Prove it. Come dance. Really, there's nothing to it."

It was half-dare, half-earnest request. Now, when it was just the two of us, I couldn't find a reason to walk away. "All right, then. If you say so."

He stuck his elbow toward me, and I knew what to do with it because I'd seen couples walking around like this all evening. I set the punch glass on a nearby table, tucked my hand in the crook of his elbow, and together we walked to the open space of the dance floor just as the band started a new song.

We had music and dancing on Mars—of course we did. I even recognized the tune, something that got played over and over because it was familiar. But I'd never danced the way I'd seen couples here dancing, two by two, as if it meant something. Not even with Beau. We'd held hands at concerts, that was it. Courtship rituals of the common Earth human. What did I think I was doing?

But Tenzig knew what he was doing, just like he always did, and he put my left hand on his right shoulder, his right hand on my left hip. Clasping our free hands, we were locked in formation.

"Just move along with the beat," he said. "Follow my lead."

I was so nervous I had a hard time even listening to the music. Again, I wondered when the fun was supposed to start. Though Tenzig seemed to be having a fine old time—his smile was warm, and he never looked away from me. Disconcerting, really. Especially the way his attention made me flush. My *toes* flushed, feeling warm and tingly inside my sandals—which it turned out, made even my feet feel sexy.

Okay, maybe this was a little bit fun.

I felt awkward, but he didn't seem to mind. Just smiled wider, steadying me with his hand on my hip. I grasped his opposite hand and used it to brace myself. Probably didn't look like much, not like the elegant couples who must have been doing this their whole lives. But that didn't seem to matter.

Maybe I'd get used to all this after all. Earth gravity, the way the skirt hung off my hips and kicked around my knees, the way everyone around here seemed to care so much about not just what you did but how you did it. Courtship rituals. It was a game and I just had to learn to play by the rules, like Charles said. That was all.

Tenzig yelped, a screech of shock. At least, it sounded like shock, and pain. He sure faked it pretty well, because I couldn't tell what had gone wrong. At the same time, he pushed himself away from me and glared.

"*Ow!* That's my feet you're stepping on! You're so . . . so clumsy! You can't even *function* in full gravity, can you?" With a final glare, he stalked off to the punch table, where a group of his friends clustered. His Earth friends.

Leaving me there in the middle of the floor with a wide circle of people surrounding me, staring at me. Somebody giggled. I didn't see who. The music never stopped.

"I . . . I didn't—" My voice choked, my eyes stung. Had I stepped on him without noticing? I didn't think so. I wouldn't put it past me. But I *hadn't*. I knew I hadn't.

"I didn't step on him," I said softly, for all the good it did.

Heads together, murmuring at each other, people turned back to the drinks, the food, the music. But they continued stealing glances at me over their shoulders. I could only imagine what they were saying about me. Bowing my head, I picked at the fabric of my skirt and walked out. Straight past Stanton this time. I didn't care if she was standing guard. I didn't care about anything. She let me go, following me with her granite gaze.

17

It had all been a setup. He hadn't wanted to dance with me. The whole time, he wanted to stomp me into the floor in front of the whole school. Well, he succeeded. I should have danced with Ethan from the start.

The air felt cold through the thin fabric of my dress, and my skin broke out in goose bumps. I suddenly wished for an environment suit, so I could hide better. I hugged myself, shivering, and my teeth started to chatter. I let them chatter because it kept me from crying, and how stupid was it, crying over something like this?

I was determined not to run. Step by step, I walked back to the residence hall, my feet pounding on the concrete sidewalk in the awkward sandals that Angelyn made me wear. What idiot came up with the idea of walking on tiny little heels in high gravity? Finally, I reached the dorm building and keyed myself into the room. All I wanted to do was curl up in bed and stay there. Forever. I didn't even care about changing clothes first. I didn't care about messing up the nice dress. This stupid dress that I'd spent so much time worrying about. That I'd gone and asked my mother for. That I'd actually cared about.

Reaching my bed at last, I sat down with a huff and slumped, too tired and numb to do anything. If I sat here long enough, maybe I'd melt and never have to talk to anyone again. A folded sheet of paper lay under the pillow. The white corner of it stood out against the gray blanket. I picked it up, unfolded it.

A letter from Charles, handwritten in neat block letters on the back of his invitation to the banquet. How did he *do* that?

IT'S JUST A GAME. YOU WIN ROUNDS, YOU LOSE THEM. THE TRICK IS NOT LETTING ON WHEN YOU THINK YOU'VE LOST. MOVE ON TO THE NEXT ROUND.

It could have meant anything, and for all I knew it was part of the same comedy routine that the whole evening had turned into. He was playing a joke on me, and just because I couldn't see it didn't mean he wasn't laughing.

I looked down at myself, at the dress I'd thought was so beautiful, the sparkly shoes, the slinky fabric and curves. Now it looked like a costume, something I didn't have any business wearing. Everyone in that room had probably thought so, too. Had they all been looking at me and laughing?

I unfastened and peeled off the dress, then went into the shower, spending a long time under the spray, turning it up as hot as it would go before shutting it off. That was one thing Earth had going for it that I'd gotten used to quick: long, hot showers. A truly excessive waste of water, but I could see why people liked it: it made my muscles melt. I felt better. When I got back to the bedroom, the place was still empty. Everyone else was still at the party, dancing. Having more fun than I was. I went to bed, curling up and covering my head with the blanket.

The others came back maybe an hour later. I heard giggling down the corridor, then the door opened.

"She's in bed," Marie whispered. I froze, my breathing shallow, refusing to move or make a sound, to give anything away.

"Polly?" Ladhi said, her voice hushed. "Are you okay? Are you awake?"

I didn't say anything, listening to them come in, talking as they tried to keep their voices to whispers. They talked about the food, drinks, music, how nice everything was. Who danced with whom and who looked like they were serious. Through it all, I pretended to sleep. I didn't want to talk to anyone.

I must have fallen asleep very, very late, after the lights switched off and Ladhi and Marie stopped giggling and carrying on. But that just meant I had to wake up when the lights came on. Just because we partied the night before didn't mean we weren't expected to keep to the schedule today, which meant getting up, eating breakfast, and going to PE and study hall. I don't know how Stanton and the rest of the tyrants expected us to get anything done today.

Not that I wanted to get up at all. But I couldn't stay under the covers all day. My bladder wouldn't let me.

I made sure to get up before everyone else, hurrying to dress and finish in the bathroom. Maybe I could get to breakfast before anyone else was awake to stare at me. Maybe I could just . . . lock myself in a closet for the rest of the year.

No such luck, of course. When I got to the dining hall, people were already there, a handful of brave—awake—souls. I froze at the door, looking at them all.

Charles was there. He looked up from his food, met my gaze, then looked down again. Which meant he wanted to talk.

I couldn't tell if everyone else was stealing glances at me, too. I should be used to it by now.

Taking a deep breath, I walked up to the window to get a tray of food, then made my way to Charles's table to sit across from him. I stared at him; he kept eating.

"Well?" I said finally.

"I was going to ask you that."

I stirred roasted potatoes with my fork. "I didn't step on his feet."

"I know you didn't," I said. "I saw the whole thing."

"You did?" A witness. Vindication. I thought about it for a minute. "Why were you watching me?"

He glanced at me sidelong, but otherwise his expression didn't change. "Just looking out for you." He said it deadpan, like it didn't mean anything.

We ate for a time, Charles hardly looking up and me continuing to study him for a hint of what he was thinking. I still couldn't tell.

"So why'd he do it?" I said. "Why'd he lie?"

"To embarrass you. Draw attention to you. Bad attention, to take away from what you did at Yosemite. Win some kind of coup. Status point."

I thought about Charles's note, about this being a game. "Did you know he was going to do that? Is that why you left the note?"

He sat back and shrugged. "I had a feeling he was going to try something with one of us. He probably decided he wouldn't get enough of a reaction out of me, so he went after you."

In the clear light of morning, I'd started to wish I'd had even more of a reaction. I wished I'd had my punch glass in hand, so I could have poured it all over him. Or I could have just, you know, punched him. "So he just wanted to make me look bad and him look . . . what? Clever? Is it just because we're from Mars?" I sighed and squished my food with the fork. If Tenzig showed up anytime soon, I might just throw the whole tray at him.

"The question is, what are you going to do about it?" Charles said.

I wanted to strangle Tenzig. Grab his head and dunk it in the punch bowl until he drowned. Drop him off the top of the building. Then I remembered . . . don't let on when you think you've lost. Move on.

"Nothing," I said. "I'm not going to do anything."

The corner of Charles's lips flickered up in the briefest of smiles.

"So. Do you think we should tell Mom that Angelyn's dad was asking about her?" I asked.

"I'm sure she's already aware of the Chous' interest."

"Really?"

"He wouldn't have asked if he didn't already know about her and her agenda. He was trying to find out something personal. Some kind of weakness. It's like you said, he was fishing, he may not even have known for what."

Ladhi came in, then Angelyn, and they both gave me worried, sidelong glances as they picked up their trays and came to sit by me, tentatively, like I might bite their heads off. And I might have, but like Charles said, I had to let it go.

"Are you okay?" Ladhi asked, wincing as if afraid of the answer.

"I'm fine," I said, and it was true. "Angry, but fine."

"Competition is one thing," Angelyn said, biting. She sounded just as angry as me, which was comforting. "But people ought to be able to look good without tearing other people down. That defeats the whole purpose."

A hush passed over the room, and I knew what it was about without even looking up. Tenzig had arrived. People were watching him, and me, waiting to see what we would do, if Tenzig would rub it in by continuing the name-calling, or by gloating some other way, and if I would try to get back at him.

What I did was turn to Angelyn and grin, saying, "I saw you dancing with Harald."

Angelyn blushed, and Ladhi jumped in, figuring out exactly what I was trying to do, telling her how sexy they looked, and pretty soon we were giggling and carrying on enough to make Charles roll his eyes at us. But we didn't pay any attention to Tenzig.

I heard Tenzig laugh even harder on the other side of the room, as if even that was part of the competition. I didn't care. And I felt better.

Right up until Ethan came into the dining hall. I hadn't even said good night to him last night, and he was one of my real friends in this place. I apparently had forgotten that. I caught his eye and waved to him to make sure he came to our table. We always sat together, of course. I just worried that he might have thought things had changed. I didn't want them to change, not like that.

"Hi," he said, slipping into place as the others scooted to make room.

"Hi," I said back. Still blushing.

"So," he said, picking at his food. I think he might even have been blushing, too, but his dark skin hid it better. "You have a good time last night?"

I shrugged. "I've seen better parties."

"Yeah," he said, chuckling. "Me, too."

I kind of wanted to drag him off to speak privately, but I didn't want to wait. I might forget what I wanted to say, or I might change my mind about saying it. And if these really were my friends, it didn't matter.

I set down my fork. "Ethan, when you asked me to dance, I should have said yes. I'm sorry."

He hesitated, like he had to think about it a minute before he smiled. But he did smile. "I'm sure you were just confused about these strange customs that you Martians aren't used to."

Sighing dramatically, I nodded. "Earth people just make everything so hard."

"It's tradition," Angelyn said defensively, but with a wry smile to make it okay. "It's tradition to make things complicated."

I said, "Someday, you're all going to come to Mars. I'll show you around. We'll go camping. With breathing masks, the way you're supposed to." And we all laughed. Except Charles, who seemed to be studying us like we were some kind of anthropology project.

Maybe, just maybe, everything would be all right.

On our way to class, I ran into Tenzig. Or he ran into me, on purpose. Not that it mattered. He had some quip or insult all ready to deliver. Maybe he would offer to give me dancing lessons. He kept talking about how he wanted to help me out, right?

"Hey Polly. About last night—"

Or maybe, could he possibly be trying to apologize?

"—if you want me to teach you how to dance the right way, I could help you with that. I keep trying to help you and you keep snubbing me—"

No, no apology there.

"Tenzig," I said, "you must really be worried about getting into a piloting program if this is the kind of sewage you have to pull to get noticed."

He stopped cold, staring at me in disbelief as I walked on.

Yeah, by the end of that day I was feeling pretty good.

18

As if the first field trip hadn't been traumatic enough, we had to do it all over again. Personally, I thought Stanton and her crew were crazy. This whole school was crazy. This whole planet. Then I thought they probably knew it and just didn't care.

The Earth kids were all very excited about the trip to the Manhattan Cultural Preserve. I got the impression this was going to be different from the town of Monterey.

Angelyn explained. "It's a city. Well, it's an island and a city. An island with a city on it. It used to be the financial and political center of . . . of *everything*. The first United Nations headquarters is there. But it's also got *amazing* shopping—real shopping, not online. And parks, theaters, restaurants, museums—the whole thing's a museum, really. No one lives there anymore who isn't part of the staff. It's like a living history thing."

I had no idea what to expect after that. Mars wasn't part of the United Nations. I kept wanting to ask how any of this was relevant.

"I think we should go to one of the Moon colonies," I said. "So you all can see how the other half lives."

She wrinkled her nose. "I've never been in zero g. I'd hate to go weightless and find out I'm one of those people who get sick from it."

"They can give you medication for that."

Once again, Stanton and her crew piled us in to a suborbital, and away we went.

I watched out the window as we approached, and the area below disconcerted me almost as much as the wilderness around Yosemite had. I'd wanted to see what a giant aboveground city looked like—this was it. While I thought I understood the concept, I hadn't quite understood the size of it. The land below us was solid city as far as I could see. Kilometer after kilometer of buildings made of concrete and steel, glinting glass, endless grids of streets. I'd done the reading. At its height, this island—a narrow corner of land, really—had had a population of over twelve million people. I couldn't even imagine that. There weren't that many people in the whole world—at least, not if the world was Mars. I kept wondering how many people could live crammed together like that. Apparently, some cities on Earth had even more people than that right now. And it was considered normal. I shivered thinking of it.

We landed at a port outside the city and took a maglev to the island, preserved behind flood walls that kept back the waters of the rivers and harbor. The ocean—a different ocean from the one we'd seen on the last trip, because Earth just had that many oceans—was beyond the harbor, but it all still looked like unbelievably vast stretches of water to me. The train traveled a tunnel that went under the river, and that tunnel was the most at home I'd felt since coming to Earth. Underground, sheltered, safe. I wondered why people on Earth would spread upward, building towers hundreds of meters tall, instead of digging underground. Especially considering the gravity situation. I would have thought underground would be easier. Not as far to fall as from those tall buildings. But apparently they liked that sunshine thing. Wimps.

Once we arrived inside the cultural preserve, we took a bus, and an instructor—a specialist who lived on the island and spent all his time doing tours like this—lectured about the history, the buildings, and all this stuff that was supposed to be very important.

We stopped in front of a massive, ornate building with columns, domes, and rows of windows, where we did a lot of walking and looking at things. A *lot* of walking.

Mars had museums. We had *Spirit* and *Opportunity*, *Viking* and *Curiosity*, all resting under their own little domes to protect them from wind and dust, with bronze plaques mounted on them telling when they'd landed and why they were important. I'd been to the prefab habitat that had been chucked straight from Earth, where the original colonists had lived until the first tunnels of Colony One were finished. So it wasn't like I didn't know what museums were, or what I was in for this trip.

Manhattan was different. The island was a location frozen in time on purpose and preserved as a memorial to the way things used to be. Every building we went to was a museum, filled with art or preserved animals or old furniture or a million other things. Clutter, basically.

I had never really thought of history, because human history on Mars started with those monuments of old robots. I'd never thought about anything that came before because there wasn't any evidence of it. We didn't have clutter because no one had brought anything that wasn't necessary, and we hadn't been there long enough to accumulate it. Here, that's *all* there was—scraps of what had come before, and before that, and before that, on and on forever. The guide kept talking about it all like it was *my* past, like I should feel some connection to it. But I didn't. They showed us marble statues and I wanted to yell at them that Mars didn't even have marble, or limestone, and I had never seen either one before in my life, and they should stop talking at me like I should know how amazing it was.

I started thinking that maybe my grandfather and the other colonists had come to Mars because it wasn't littered with so much *stuff*.

Eventually we arrived at the main art museum at the edge of the immense park that filled a big chunk of the island. The guide shepherded us around and lectured about various artifacts that were supposed to be important. I mostly tried to figure out why the big slabs of blue tiles with a yellow animal thingy painted on deserved a whole lecture of their own while the gigantic room-size statues of some other animals with the heads of people didn't.

I finally nudged Angelyn. "Can I ask a really stupid question?"

"Sure."

"Those aren't really real, are they? There isn't some kind of creature running around in the wilds of Earth with human faces and beards like that."

"Um, no. It's symbolic."

"Oh. Of what?"

She shrugged. "Some kind of myth or religion or something."

". . . one of the great cities of early civilization, giving rise to the legend of the Hanging Gardens of Babylon . . ."

I thought maybe I should be takings notes, then I figured I could just look it all up later.

The museum was basically a lot of pictures of things, done in a lot of styles, from the last five thousand years, from all over Earth. Five thousand years was a long time, I knew that. I knew I ought to be impressed by the pots and stone carvings and the drawings and sculptures that had survived all that time so we could look at them now. I was supposed to be paying attention to the pictures they showed or the stories they told. I was supposed to be learning how they were made and what that said about society or technology or whatever. I might have cared at some level. But I kept catching myself staring into space.

Then I had an idea. A good and bad idea at the same time.

A surprisingly large amount of the art had to do with horses. I knew what horses were, I'd read about them, seen pictures. They had a huge role in human history before the invention of the steam- and internal-combustion engines. But I had a hard time imagining them. When someone said "horse," I saw a picture from an encyclopedia. Not a real horse. But the instructor talked about horses like he assumed everyone had seen one, discussing the way the painting technique caught the sheen of the coat and the individual hairs. But I'd never seen a horse, and looking at some of the sculptures and pictures I'd have assumed horses had perfectly smooth, plasticky bodies. He said something about the animal's eyes flashing, as if it were alive. And I couldn't help but think, *What, the eyes light up?*

I wanted to see a horse for myself. A real one. Not some piece of horse-related art that was important for what it said about culture or technological progress. A real live, breathing, eyes-flashing horse.

As a matter of reconnaissance I had actually done some research on my own. I had to know something about the enemy terrain if I was going to conquer it. Or at least not get defeated by it. And it turned out that Manhattan had horses, right here in the very same park the museum was located in. I decided to find one.

The guide wound down the lecture on the blue-tile Babylonian thing, gazing up at the piece with awe, obviously expecting us all to do likewise. I knew what would happen next: he'd wave us on, leading us to the next room and the next treasure of Earth to be admired. I hung back, walking a little slower. Let everyone get ahead of me, which wasn't hard; I pretended to admire the other artifacts in the room, pursing my lips, nodding. Shuffling my steps, I let the rest of the group round the corner, and their footsteps on the floor grew fainter.

And then they were gone. I slipped back the way we'd come. Just casually walking, not running, because that would be suspicious. I sort of looked around, as if I was noting the exhibits, nodding at them thoughtfully. Only one of the uniformed museum staff members who seemed to stalk the place randomly stopped me.

"Are you lost?" the man asked.

I barely slowed down to answer. "Oh, no, I just got separated from my group but I think they're in the next wing," I said, pointing. I totally knew what I was doing and had every right to be here.

"All right," the staffer said, waving me on. "Have a nice afternoon." He didn't even blink at my Martian accent. Did Manhattan get a lot of Martian tourists?

A minute later, I was out the front door and down the steps. I had escaped. Wasn't so hard after all. And now I had a city to explore.

I went around the building and into Central Park.

It reminded me a little too much of Yosemite. Too many trees blocking the sky, rocks and vegetation piled everywhere. But Yosemite, right in the middle of a city? Earth had it all. I supposed that was the point.

The park had a few wide main paths, cut across with lots of small footpaths and trails that looped around. They didn't go anywhere—that wasn't the point. They were just for walking, around and around. The whole point was to be outside. I still felt naked without my breathing mask. What if the air ran out? However much my brain knew it wouldn't, my gut wasn't so sure.

The horses would be on the wide paths. Mostly, they pulled carriages, though people rode some of them in saddles. I had no idea what that would look like in person. But maybe I'd find out. I picked a direction and started walking.

I was trying to figure out the difference between Central Park and Yosemite, why one was considered a "park" and one was "wilderness," when they both had trees, grasses, rocks, birds—nature, in other words. Nature that wasn't rocks and wind and microorganisms, anyway. The fact that one was surrounded by a city and the other wasn't couldn't be the only thing.

It must have been the people. The park had a lot of people around—mostly school groups like the Galileo students, obvious clumps of tourists, other tour groups wandering around. They were all easy to spot—herds of milling people led by alert-looking guides in the official Manhattan tourism vests, who constantly pointed and talked. Everyone was taking pictures with their handhelds.

Before too long, someone was going to stop me and ask me why I wasn't part of a group or taking pictures. So I walked like I had someplace to be and I knew exactly where I was going.

The park was enclosed—I couldn't possibly get lost, which was good. However, I could walk in circles all day long without realizing how long I'd been doing it or how far I'd gone. I tried to pay attention to landmarks, so I'd know if I started walking in circles. I couldn't get rid of the feeling that I was getting lost. I could always check the map on my handheld, I told myself, even though that would make me a wimp. Surely I'd find a horse eventually, and I wouldn't get lost doing it.

Benches sat along the path every dozen meters or so. Finally, I sat in one, admitting my feet were tired. My legs were tired. My lungs were tired. This whole planet made me tired. I should have been used to it by now. Maybe if I sat in one place, a horse would come to me. Maybe I should have thought of that earlier.

I slumped on the bench, grumbly and angry at myself, when it happened. The horse came to me.

I heard it first, a clomping noise I didn't recognize. But it caught my attention—it sounded strange, unnatural. Rhythmic. So I looked. And there it was, pulling a carriage, just like in some of those pictures.

A person sat in the front part of the carriage, holding straps that apparently steered the horse. But I hardly noticed them. I just saw the horse. Even at a distance, the animal looked big—as tall as the cart it pulled. It could fill a room—a small room, but still. And it just got bigger as it approached. Its four legs moved in sequence, a steady beat. Its color was a golden brown, almost like some of the rocks on Mars at sunrise, glinting color when light hit it through the trees. Its head bobbed; its fibrous tail, so long it almost touched the ground, swished. And if its dark eyes didn't flash, they did shine, and I could tell it saw me, because its ears flicked toward me when I stood up.

It was just so big, I couldn't figure out how anyone had decided that sitting on one or making it pull a carriage or anything was a good idea. I didn't realize I was moving toward it until the driver tugged gently on the straps, and the animal stopped beside me.

I was looking straight at its shoulder, where the powerful neck met the round body. It smelled weird—warm, earthy, organic. Straps wrapped around its head, chest, body, attaching the carriage to it. The horse didn't look uncomfortable, but I wondered what it would look like without all the harness, running all on its own. I could feel body heat coming off it.

"Would you like to pet him?" I glanced up, startled, and the driver, a brown-skinned woman with long black hair, smiled at me. "Go ahead and touch him, on the neck there. His name is Bunny."

I'd just wanted to see a horse. I hadn't thought this was possible. Raising my hand, flattening it, I almost couldn't bring myself to touch the animal. But it stood so calmly, it hardly seemed real. My heart raced.

I touched it, briefly, and took my hand away. I thought maybe the thing would jump, and my muscles tensed, ready to run. But it only flicked its ears again, like they were some kind of radio dish, picking up every little noise. I touched it again, resting my whole hand against it, then rubbing down its neck. I didn't expect the animal to feel so soft. My fingers tingled with the coat's softness, and the solidness of the body underneath. And it was warm, like an engine.

"You've never seen a horse before, have you?" the driver asked.

I glanced at her. "No—I'm from Mars."

"You've really come a long way, then."

I just kept petting that horse's neck, over and over again, marveling at the warm, solid, shivery skin. The horse didn't seem to mind. My grin felt wide and silly, but the driver seemed to be used to people being silly around her horse. Bunny the horse.

Bunny turned his head, just a little, to look back at me with his large side-set eye. I flinched back, not sure what it was doing—but it just shook its head and huffed through wide nostrils. As if I had any doubt that it was alive, really alive.

"Polly! Polly Newton!"

Stanton was calling from down the path, hands cupped around her mouth. Even at this distance I could tell she was glaring at me, furious. Oh, well, I knew this couldn't last forever. I knew I'd get caught. Not getting caught wasn't the point—the point was, how long could I go before I got caught?

I'd done what I wanted. I'd seen a horse, and it had been amazing.

"I think I have to go," I said to the driver, my smile sheepish. "Thank you—thank you very much. Bye, Bunny."

"No problem. And welcome to Earth."

She waited for me to step away, then clicked her tongue and

murmured a word, and the horse walked on. The steady clomping of its big horny feet sounded friendly now.

I went back toward Stanton to face the inevitable. She waited
for me, because why should she make any more effort than absolutely necessary? Fine by me.

"Hi," I said, smiling like nothing was wrong, and stopping
when I got to her.

"You left the group," she said, and waited.

"Um, yeah. But it's not like you couldn't find me," I said.
"What with security cameras everywhere."

"Would you like to explain why you left the group?"

Not really . . . I had so many potential reasons I could give her,
after all. "I thought seeing a real-live horse would be more educational than just seeing a lot of pictures of them. And since I
didn't see Central Park or a zoo or anything on the schedule,
I . . . I took some initiative. An independent study project."

Her expression—anger, suppressed—didn't change. I hadn't
thought my rationalization would actually work. But it sure
sounded good. I didn't let my expression change, blinking back
at her innocently.

"Come along, Newton," she said, and turned, and marched
away. I followed, scuffing my feet.

My hands still smelled like the horse's warm coat.

19

When we left the park, Stanton put me in the very first seat on the bus and made me stay there while she collected everyone else from the museum. When the rest of the group filed onto the bus and saw me, they stared at me and bent heads together, whispering. Again. Apparently, I'd caused a bit of a sensation. Again. Make that a bit of a panic this time. I'd disappeared, I'd gotten lost, I'd fallen down a hole and was hurt or dead and no one would ever see me again. It was Angelyn's fall all over again, and our field trips were cursed. Or at least I was cursed, and people squeezed as far away from me as they could when they walked past, like they didn't want to get cursed by association.

Charles, however, didn't care about stuff like that and slid into the seat next to mine.

He kept looking straight ahead when he said, "So, what did you?"

"I escaped," I said, crossing my arms.

"Not very well, obviously."

"I wasn't trying to escape *permanently*. I just wanted to see a horse."

"Did you?"

"Yeah."

"So mission successful."

"Yeah." He didn't say anything else. Just looked straight ahead while everyone behind us talked and chattered and rustled. I couldn't figure out what he was thinking, if anything. Twin telepathy failed, yet again. He didn't even seem to feel my stare boring into him.

Stanton put me on restrictions for the rest of the trip. I would stay at the hotel assigned to us, or on the bus, but I would not be participating in any activities with the rest of the group. Everyone else was going to see a play tonight—Manhattan was historically known for theatrical productions. I would not. I couldn't say I was all that disappointed. I'd have done it all over again for the chance to run my hands down the horse's neck.

When we got back to our hotel, Ethan pulled me aside in the lobby. I was about to get angry because I thought he was going to be all pitying and sympathetic, looking at me like I was crazy. Or dangerous. That was the weird thing, the way people looked at me like ducking out for the sole purpose to seeing a real-live horse was somehow dangerous. Upending the social order or something. Whatever. But Ethan didn't do that.

"I'm sorry you can't come to the show tonight," he said. And he really did seem sad, or disappointed, or something.

I shrugged. "It's okay. You guys can tell me about it later. Not a big deal, really."

"Well, it kind of is." He pressed his lips together and his dark eyes glanced away. Something was wrong, but I didn't know what, so I waited for him to just say it. "I guess . . . I was kind of hoping this could be like a date. I know a field trip can't really be a date. But . . . well. I figured I'd ask anyway."

I had to look up at him, he was so tall, even though he seemed kind of slouching and chagrined at the moment. Sheepish, I think was the word. I had tried so hard to not care about the play, and now all of the sudden, when it wasn't going to a play for school but going on a date with Ethan, it sounded so much more fun.

And why couldn't anything on Earth work out the way it was supposed to?

"Yeah," I said, smiling. Grinning, maybe. Kind of silly-feeling. "I'd like to go on a date. I mean, if I wasn't grounded again. But yeah."

I took a chance. Another chance. You'd think I'd be cured of that by now. But I took his hand and squeezed. We stood there for a moment, hand in hand, just looking at each other. And it felt . . . nice.

"Um. Great," he said, then after another long moment he glanced over his shoulder. "I suppose I don't have to go to the play—"

"No, it's okay, you should go," I said. "You don't want to miss out on all that culture and learning and privilege-to-be-here stuff. Go get ready, I'll be here when you get back."

He smiled, gave my hand another squeeze, and went off to the elevators and rooms.

I still had my handheld. I could read or watch a vid from the comfort of my bed. Or soak my near-blistered feet. Higher gravity even made blisters worse.

Before leaving with the rest of the group for the play, Charles managed to slip a note in the room I was sharing with Ladhi.

POLLY'S EYES ONLY

Keep an eye on the lobby for me. Think of it as anthropology, and pretend that you like anthropology. There'll be a quiz later.

Why did he have to be so *hyper*?

Technically, I was supposed to stay in my room, but Stanton didn't say *specifically* I was supposed to stay in my room and not wander to the hotel lobby. Mostly, she implied it, but she also didn't leave any chaperones behind to supervise me. She should know better by now than to trust my good graces. The hotel had security vids, and presumably she'd told building security staff not to let me out of their sight. If it was me doing the restricting, I've have put security locks on the doors and elevators and disabled my key code from getting me through anything. Would Stanton have thought of that? Even without Charles's note prompting me, I decided to test her, just to see for myself.

My room was unlocked. The lift door let me pass. I didn't have to show my ID pass or anything. The trick was just like back at the museum: keep walking like I was allowed to be here and wasn't doing anything wrong. Chin up, all the way.

The doors to the lift slid open and I entered the lobby, with its wide granite floors, potted plants, and intimidating furniture. We'd been informed that the whole thing was made to look like a fancy historical hotel from two hundred years ago in a living history kind of display. The only difference was the automated services at the front desk instead of the uniformed workers there would have been in the old days. The real wood, the big plush furniture—all exactly the kind of thing you'd expect to see on Earth.

I wondered if I could just keep walking, across the lobby and right out the front door, waving to the doorman as I went. That was part of the living history: a uniformed doorman in a big coat with shining brass buttons. He'd spoken to us about the building's history when we arrived. Stanton might have told him not to let me go, but what was he going to do? He might yell at me, but I was pretty sure he wouldn't grab me or tackle me or anything. People around here didn't seem to go for that sort of thing.

I had decided to go ahead and try it, just to see what happened, when I noticed that the doorman wasn't there. I hesitated by the wall near the elevators, because instead of the doorman, George was standing near the front door next to a broad-shouldered man in a long coat, someone I'd never seen before. His arms were crossed, squeezed tight, and he glowered. The doorman was nowhere in sight.

Maybe Stanton had set guards to make sure I didn't escape. Maybe George was one of the guards, but if that were the case, George would have looked happier. And I couldn't imagine him agreeing to miss the evening's field trip. It was all very confusing. The man had a comm piece in his ear and watched out the glass by the front door. Then he nodded.

Another man in a long coat came in through the door, took hold of George's shoulder, and the two men sandwiched him between them as they rushed out the front door. The second long-coated man held something low against George's back. Shock gun? Ballistic pistol?

Otherwise, they just looked like three people walking out into the night. Nobody would look at them twice. Maybe they were his bodyguards.

No, they weren't.

I ran to the front desk and started tapping at the concierge screen. Help, where was the help button? Or the security button? I couldn't find anything relevant; all the buttons were about choosing a room and getting food delivered.

I went back to the front desk help screen, opened an audio search box, and said, "I'd like to report some suspicious activity. A kidnapping, I think."

Words appeared on the screen: "Describe the suspicious activity."

"I told you, a kidnapping, two men dragged out one of the students. They didn't look like they belonged."

More words: "Situation described does not match known parameters."

Of course this sort of thing wasn't normal and didn't happen every day, but shouldn't there be some kind of category for "not normal"? I growled at the screen, and it showed me an error message with a request to please repeat my statement. This was stupid.

I pulled out my handheld and pinged Charles. His handheld probably wasn't even on. He didn't answer, but I sent a message: "Something's happened to George."

As proof of how worried I really was, I tried Stanton next. I had to look up her code, because I hadn't thought I'd ever want to call her for anything. Again, no answer. They were at the theater, they wouldn't be getting calls. I could leave a million messages and it wouldn't do any good, because this was happening *right now.*

Nobody was around; the lobby was empty.

I tried the front desk screen again. "How do I activate the fire alarm?"

The screen replied: "Is there a fire at your location?"

"Yes!"

A klaxon rang out, loud and throbbing, rattling my bones and filling the whole building. Well, that ought to get someone's attention. Nozzles popped out of the ceiling, spraying fire-retardant foam. A white mist filled the air and covered the floor, the front desk, the furniture.

I crouched by the desk, but that didn't keep me from getting soaked. Small price, right?

The lobby filled with people pretty quick after that. Guests from other tour groups looking startled and half asleep at the same time, people in hotel-staff uniforms, and a bunch of people in security uniforms came in through the front door. Half of them ducked back into hallways and offices when the foam sprayed them. A couple of people screamed, maybe on general principle. A bunch of people asked where the fire was, and nobody knew, which started a round of annoyed grumbling. Well, at least I'd gotten someone's attention. But this was going to get interesting.

"Who started the alarm?" a guy in a security uniform called from the front door. He scanned the room, saw me, frowned even harder than he was already.

I raised my hand and pulled myself up, leaning on the desk to keep from sliding on the foam now covering the floor. "Me," I said redundantly.

The sprayers turned off, so at least foam stopped raining down. I wiped a layer of it from my face and looked up at the guy. He put his hands on his hips.

"Our infrared alert system didn't spot any fire," he said. "Where's the fire?"

"There isn't a fire," I said, and before he could start yelling added, "But there wasn't an option to report a kidnapping."

His brows lifted. "A kidnapping?"

"Yeah. I came into the lobby and saw these two big guys, body-guard types, drag George Lou Montes outside, but I don't think they were supposed to be here, and George was supposed to be with the field trip—"

"Who *are* you?" the security guy asked.

Deep breath, stay calm. "My name is Polly Newton, I'm with the group of students visiting from Galileo Academy. One of the other students was taken away against his will. Kidnapped. I saw it. I'm trying to report it. I swear, you guys are all up about security until something bad actually happens!"

"Wait, kid, say that again but slowly this time."

I enunciated as clearly as I possibly could. "I'm Polly Newton, I'm with a group of students from Galileo Academy, and one of the other students has been kidnapped—"

The guy shook his head, still obviously confused. "Polly Newton. Where are you from?"

"I told you, the Galileo Academy—"

"I mean, you're not from Earth, are you?"

I stared. It was my accent. He couldn't understand my accent. "What's that got to do with anything?"

Distraction arrived, and we all turned to look when Stanton walked into the lobby, followed by the rest of the Galileo group. The students clogged up behind her, because she stopped cold right inside the doorway, staring at the chaos. Her gaze went to me, and she didn't seem surprised to find me in the middle of it all. The security guy sighed as if relieved that someone else in a uniform who appeared to have some authority had arrived to explain things.

"Newton?" she inquired, glancing distastefully at the sticky floor as she picked her way over to us.

"Is this one yours?" security guy said.

"What's happened?"

"She activated the fire-alert system under false pretenses," he said.

"It was the only way I could get anyone's attention! Didn't you see my message?"

"You were supposed to stay in your room," Stanton said.

"But if I'd done that, no one would have seen George getting kidnapped!"

"And why do you think George has been kidnapped?"

"He's not here, is he?" I pointed to the milling herd of students that George should have been a part of. "So where is he?"

"Nonsense, he was at the theater with the rest of us . . ." She studied her charges, pointing at each one as she counted, then counted again. No George, just like I'd been saying.

"Can't you check the video footage?" I asked, getting desperate. The hotel lobby was probably ruined, soaking wet and stinking of soapy chemicals.

"Officer," Stanton said to the security guy, "is the building clear? There's no danger here?"

"We're checking it out now, but I'm pretty sure there's no fire."

"Fine. Everyone, go to your rooms and stay there. Newton—you wait right here." She waved everyone else to the lifts. Elzabeth and some of the others scrunched up their faces and made disgusted noises about the gunk getting all over their nice shoes.

Charles lingered. While Stanton was talking to security, he sidled up to me. I avoided meeting his gaze.

"What's going on?"

"Somebody kidnapped George," I muttered.

"For real?" he said. He didn't seem shocked our doubtful—just confirming.

"Totally for real! There's got to be security footage of it!"

"Do you know who did it?"

"The Terran Liberation Front? I don't know! It was just two guys in coats with comm pieces hooked into their ears! They might have had a gun." I looked at him, narrowing my gaze. "Were you expecting something to happen?"

Not even a flinch. "Calm down. We'll figure it out."

Stanton loomed over us. "Charles, you can go now."

"May I stay with my sister? I might be able to help her explain what happened." He blinked up at her, making his eyes look very round and sad.

I huffed. "I can explain what happened, I've been *trying* to explain—"

He shoved me with his elbow to get me to shut up.

This wasn't worth it. George wasn't worth it. Maybe I'd imagined the whole thing. At least I wished I had. I shouldn't have said anything. I should have stayed in my room. I should have stayed on Mars.

Stanton let Charles stay, and the security guy made us all go to an office in the back of the lobby. One of the hotel staff was there, along with a wall full of video screens where multiple images of the lobby, from several points of view, played out. Finally. I sat back, arms crossed, and waited to be vindicated.

The hotel person fast-forwarded through the various videos until the time stamps read a half hour before I called the alarm.

Charles leaned forward to study the one screen that looked across to the door. About twenty minutes before I pulled the alarm—maybe fifteen before I'd walked into the lobby—George came in from outside, accompanied by the man in the overcoat. The man held tight to his arm and leaned forward to mutter something into his ear. George scowled and crossed his arms. I searched the overcoated man's hands—and yes, he was holding something that looked like a weapon.

"There, do you see it?" I said, jumping up and pointing. Charles grabbed me and pulled me back to my chair.

The scene played out to the moment when I stepped out of the elevator and saw them. The second man walked in, and they dragged George out.

"That doesn't seem right," Stanton said.

"That's what I've been trying to tell you!"

The other two officials played with the video until the faces of the two men, and the shock guns in their hands, were visible.

"Do you recognize these men at all?" the security guy said to the three of us, and we shook our heads. "Do you have any idea who might want to take the boy?"

Stanton said, in a tone that expressed disgust that they didn't already know this, "George Lou Montes's father is on the cabinet of the South American Alliance. Other cabinet members have been receiving blackmail demands from crime syndicates in the region. Perhaps one of them thought George would make an easy target. I'd start there."

So, Earth: not quite the perfect place everyone made it out to be.

"If that's the case," the officer said, "we should be getting a ransom notice. We'll monitor incoming messages here at the hotel. We'll have to notify the boy's family—"

Stanton said, "Surely it would be better to find the boy first, before unduly worrying his family." She folded her hands together and gripped tightly. Her smile was strained. This sure wasn't going to reflect well on the school, was it? Made me suddenly wish, again, that I hadn't reported it, because how bad would that have looked, George being gone for hours and no one noticing? And did I really want George *back*? Well, too late now.

The security officer frowned. "I'll get these images to security. They'll be able to initiate a search. We'll find him quickly, don't worry. But we're contacting his family. Why don't you all go back to your rooms and get some rest."

Both the security office and the hotel staffers were looking pretty ashen. Yeah, a lot of people's reputations were on the line with this one.

Stanton repeated the order. "You two get back to your rooms.

You've done all you can here. More, really." The statement was an accusation.

"I had to do *something*, I wasn't going to just *stand* there," I argued.

"I suppose you expect some sort of medal?" she said.

"I don't expect anything," I muttered.

"Good. Because you're still restricted to your room. Stay there this time."

We retreated, and as soon as the lift doors closed, Charles started talking. "Something's not right. Those two guys in the security vid, the kidnappers—they're not acting right."

"How should they be acting?" I prompted.

"Don't you think it's odd that they're not doing anything to disguise their identities? They came into the lobby and posed, almost as if they wanted the vid to see them clearly. They had to know the security footage would see them."

"But that would mean they want to get caught," I said. He didn't say anything to that, which meant I'd gotten it right. "But that's messed up. Why would they do that?"

"That's the question, isn't it? They may be trying to send a message to George's family, or to the hotel, or to security, or to the rest of us. At any rate, it means George probably isn't in real danger."

"Can we take that chance?"

Charles went to his room, which he was sharing with Ethan, and I followed him.

"What's going on?" Ethan asked. "I heard something happened to George—"

"Something weird's going on," I said. "We just have to figure out what."

"Shouldn't city security be able to do that?" he said.

"Yeah, but did we mention the weird part?"

"Most of the city has vid coverage. We ought to be able to find something," Charles explained, pulling his handheld out of his luggage. He sat on the bed and hunched over it, punching in commands. With his hacking skills he'd figure this out in no time.

And we waited. If I tried to ask him what he was doing or how long it was going to take, he'd only get more inscrutable, so instead I asked, "How was the play?"

"What?" He looked up, blinking.

"The play that I didn't get to see. How was it?"

"It was okay," Ethan said.

Charles surprised me by looking thoughtful—pleased, even. "Not bad. It was vintage, first performed in the early days of the original theater district. About gangsters and a floating craps game. Everybody sang songs when they got emotional."

Had Charles actually *enjoyed* it? I thought theater would have been beneath him. "And what is a floating craps game?"

"I think it's a metaphor. Can we talk about that later?" He keyed in more commands and studied the handheld's screen intently.

I started thinking I should have just run after the bad guys rather than messed with the security nonsense. I bet I could have stopped them, or at least slowed them down. For whatever reason he'd been taken, George was probably long gone by now.

A knock pounded on the door, and when Charles didn't look up, Ethan went to answer. Ladhi, Angelyn, and Elzabeth pushed inside. Ladhi and Angelyn came to me, while Elzabeth stood apart; her eyes were red, like she'd been crying.

"What *happened*?" Ladhi begged. "What did you *do*?"

Elzabeth burst, "What happened to George? Is he okay?"

I slumped over and sprawled on the bed next to Charles, staring up at the ceiling. I didn't want to have to explain it. It seemed so stupid now, and I just got more angry that I couldn't do anything.

"Polly—" Ladhi said again. They sat on either side of me and obviously wouldn't leave me alone until I answered.

"George got kidnapped. I tried to help. It went badly," I said.

"So you're the one who triggered the fire alarm?" Angelyn asked. "Couldn't you just call security?"

"I *tried*," I grumbled. "But the computer at the front desk wouldn't let me talk to a real person and didn't have a selection for 'kidnapping'!" The room had suddenly gotten crowded. Elzabeth, pacing at a good fast clip, started crying again, and Angelyn tried to comfort her. I repeated, "And there's something weird going on."

"Yeah, obviously," Elzabeth said. "I honestly didn't know one person could cause so much trouble."

I shrugged, but the gesture didn't mean much with me lying down. "One person with a drill can do enough damage to the hull of a space station." That was me, it was like I had a diamond-tipped drill bit and didn't even know it.

"So what's going to happen to George?" Ladhi said.

"I'm almost certain the kidnapping was staged," Charles said.

"What?" everybody said. Everybody except me. Nothing Charles said surprised me, ever.

Charles explained, never looking up from his handheld. "Let's say, for the sake of argument, George really was going to get kidnapped. I'm sure plenty of people could come up with reasons for it, not the least of which is that generating ransom money is probably his only real talent."

"Hey!" Elzabeth exclaimed, but Angelyn hushed her.

"Manhattan Island is locked off, every single person who enters and leaves is recorded and tracked. Someone who wanted to kidnap anyone would have to recruit help from the staff already on the island, and they wouldn't be able to easily get George off it. They'd have to plan to keep him here until . . . well, whatever it was they were planning to do with him happened. It'd be easier to just kill him outright than hold him for ransom."

Again, Elzabeth gasped a sob, and we all hushed her.

"I've hacked into the port authority database," Charles said. "They don't show anyone entering the island in the last month matching the two kidnappers from the surveillance video. In fact, cross-referencing the security video with the island's staff database . . . and there they are."

Elzabeth rushed to look over his shoulder at his handheld. "You found who did it? Really?"

I crossed my arms. "If you could find that out just by hacking into the official database, the island's security will have already figured it out for themselves."

"Exactly," he said, smiling slyly. "They probably figured it out in a matter of minutes. But I'm guessing Stanton told them not to do anything about it."

"Then that would mean she was behind it," I said, and Charles smiled. "But why?"

"I'm still working on that."

"Charles," I said. "What is Stanton doing, right this minute?"

He punched a set of commands into his handheld, calling up the hotel-security feed, most likely. "Huh. She's in the lift, on her way up here."

"Want to bet she's going to do a bed check?" I grabbed Ladhi, Angelyn, and Elzabeth and hauled them toward the door. "We've got to get back to our rooms." I squeezed Ethan's arm on the way out. "Call us if you figure out anything else."

"Yeah, of course."

Elzabeth and Angelyn raced to their rooms, and Ladhi and I ran back to ours, closing the door just as the lift at the end of the hall slid open. We hurried to rip off our uniforms and grab our pajamas, pull back the sheets, and find our handhelds so we could pretend to be reading.

Stanton had the lock codes to all the rooms. Our door opened, and Ladhi and I were lying our beds, reading dutifully. Or pretending to read.

"Girls?" she asked, looking us over, frowning, like this wasn't what she'd expected to find.

"Yes, Ms. Stanton?" Ladhi asked, because she was the polite one.

"It's late. Lights out."

Dutifully, we turned off our handhelds and the lights. Stanton didn't close the door until we were under our covers and still. It kind of made me want to get up and scream and dance around, just to see what she'd do. Truly amazing how she brought out in the worst in me. She probably did it on purpose.

When the door finally closed, I sat up and turned the light back on. "Did you notice she checked our room first?"

"Does that surprise you?" Ladhi asked.

Not really. I had another hunch, so I jumped out of bed and went to the door, rattled the handle. Locked, from the outside this time. She'd locked us all in.

"She's on to us," I muttered.

"Can she do that? What if there really is a fire, what if—" Ladhi stopped there. She sat up in bed, gripping the blankets. "What are we going to do?"

I paced along the wall by the window. We had to be able to do something besides just *sit* here.

"George is going to be okay, right?" Ladhi said. "I'm sure it's just a big misunderstanding."

I ran my hands around the window frame, pressing on the glass, hoping for a way to open it, push it out, but no. Solid as a view port in a space station. Should have made me feel better, but it didn't. Even if I could open the window, what was I going to do, jump from the fifth story and shatter my fragile offworlder bones on the concrete sidewalk below? On Mars, I could jump out a fifth-story window and land like a soap bubble. Well, maybe not a soap bubble. Maybe more like a pillow. But soft enough.

"Polly, sit down, you're making me nervous."

I started to round on her, to yell and vent, which wouldn't have been fair to her but I was getting really anxious, when my handheld beeped—incoming call. We both jumped, and I ran to my bed to grab it. "Yes? What?"

"Polly." It was Charles. Of course it was. "I'm starting a group call . . . now." He lowered his gaze, pressed buttons, and three other boxes opened on the screen. Ethan in one, Tenzig in a second, and Angelyn in the other, with Elzabeth leaning over her shoulder, her eyes still red from crying. They all looked surprised—except Ethan, who was in the room with Charles—and talked over each other. "Who is this—" "How did you—" "What—"

Charles interrupted. "Everybody be quiet, we have work to do."

"Charles, what's happening?" I said.

"We have to track the men who kidnapped George, and since Stanton locked the rooms we have to do it here, over the network."

Tenzig sneered. "Why don't we let Dean Stanton and security find him? It's their jobs."

"They're not looking for him."

A chorus of arguments answered him. I didn't say anything, and Ladhi looked at me, pleading for me to explain.

Charles continued. "They're not looking for him because Stanton wants to see what we'll do. Like the accident at Yosemite."

I could believe that Stanton had rigged George's kidnapping, but the question I needed answered was, *Why?* Why would she do it? Especially so out in the open like this?

"It's a test," I said. Every minute of our days were planned and scheduled, we were watched so closely—and even the accidents were planned and monitored.

Out of curiosity, I called up the local news, an online site that gave a scroll of cultural events, residential information, and security alerts for the island. I went over the last hour of news—

nothing about a kidnapping, no alerts to be on the lookout for men matching the kidnappers' descriptions. This was totally out of any kind of public awareness.

"You're all crazy," Tenzig said. "And you're going to get in more trouble than you already are, if not kicked out of the school entirely. I don't want any part of it." He pushed a button, and his box went dark and vanished.

"That's okay, we didn't need him anyway," Angelyn muttered. "He's just worried about how all this is going to look on his record."

"I can't look at every security-vid feed myself," Charles said. "I'm tapping each of you in to a likely security feed and sending security pictures of the kidnappers from the hotel. We need to sync up the facial recognition program to go over the last hour or so of footage, to track them from when they left here. They're probably at one of a handful of addresses—I've found their residences and where they work—so we'll check those first. If you get a hit, tell me."

"Can you bring Ladhi in on this so she can help?" I asked, and a moment later Ladhi's handheld beeped.

We got to work. Charles sent me half a dozen links, and the boxes opened up on my screen. They all looked the same, security-vid views of streets and entranceways, gray sidewalks and redbrick walls, all well lighted. Even this late, the streets were crowded, partygoers and night owls bustling. Everyone seemed to be wearing coats and hats that hid their faces and made them hard to identify. But I didn't have to see the faces—we were looking for George, with two men who matched a certain description. The facial recognition program started isolating traits and rejecting mismatches. It still seemed to go slowly, even with all of us covering different video feeds.

I started with the most recent footage and worked backward, going through each camera, helping the software by rejecting near misses. Then the handheld pinged a match, and the vid showed three bulky male figures, two holding firmly to the one in the middle. They turned the corner and left my view.

I hit pause and called out, "There, I think I got him, on feed, um . . ." I recited the ID on the security feed.

"Got it," Charles said. "That's at Fifty-second and Broadway. Angelyn, that's moving into your territory, can you find them?"

"Looking, looking . . . Yes. I have them. They entered a building on Fifty-second, twenty minutes ago, I think."

"And there we go. We've got them."

"We can call security to go find him, now," Elizabeth said. "Right?"

"Because that worked so well the last time," I muttered.

"We'll do better than that," Charles said. "We'll find a way to get him out of there ourselves."

Angelyn said, "Can we, I don't know, hire our own security?"

"You going to pay for it?" Charles said.

"*I'll* pay for it," Elizabeth said.

"I don't think that'll be necessary. We're on an island that's a tourist resort, aren't we? There ought to be all kinds of services we can send to disrupt the kidnappers and give George a chance to escape."

"Assuming he's smart enough to take the opportunity," I said.

Charles's expression had turned pensive. "Good point. We

need to find a way to call him. We don't have to mount a rescue, just cause a disruption."

He was in thinking mode, lips pursed, scratching his chin.

"I've got an idea," Angelyn said. "Pizza delivery. We send over a pizza."

"A what?" I asked.

"Pizza, it's a kind of food—don't tell me we haven't made you eat pizza yet. Maybe I'll order one for here, too. Anyway, we order it, send it to that address, they'll bring it right to the door. Should be all kinds of distraction."

"Do it," Charles said. "Make it a big order. Charge it to Stanton's account."

"Wait, you have Stanton's credit-account number?" I said, impressed in spite of myself.

Angelyn was already punching in codes.

"Can we find a way to get a message to George? Give him some kind of warning?" Elzabeth said.

"Without tipping off the kidnappers," I added.

"Details," Charles muttered. "I wish we had a camera in that building."

"You have a handheld ID for one of those guys?" I suggested.

"Getting to that . . . and . . . thank you . . ."

Just like that, he hacked into one of the kidnappers' handhelds. He threw up a box with the image from the thing's camera eye, but since the guy kept it in his pocket, all we saw was a big shadow. We got sound, though.

George, being tough. "You won't get away with this, my family is very important, they'll hunt you down!"

The next voice was closer—the owner of the handheld. He sounded tired, frustrated. "Kid, you've said that ten times, please be quiet. Nothing's going to happen to you, we just have to wait."

"Wait for what?" George argued.

"Just wait. Okay? Seriously."

Angelyn interrupted. "Pizza's going to take twenty minutes."

"Why so long?" Charles shot back.

"Because they have to make it?" Angelyn offered nicely.

"Too bad you can't change the laws of physics, right Charles?" I said.

"Working on it," he murmured.

"You're joking, right?" I said.

"This is all theater," Charles said.

George provided some entertainment while we waited, by turns pleading with and threatening his kidnappers, who appeared to be waiting for some signal, just like we were. The amount of money he kept offering to ransom himself with increased, until the other kidnapper—also in the room, standing some distance away by the sound of his voice—said, "I'm inclined to take him up on his offer rather than wait for the cue."

"No kidding." Guy number one chuckled.

"What cue? What's going to happen?" George said.

"Oh, he sounds so scared," Elzabeth crooned from over Angelyn's shoulder on their end of the call. She might have been right. To me, he sounded as blustery and arrogant as he ever did, but there was an edge to his voice that might have been fear or desperation.

"It'll be good for him, being scared for once," Ethan said. And *he* sounded amused.

"Hey!" Ladhi called. "I'm watching the vid feed, a car just pulled up outside the kidnappers' building, I think it's the pizzas!"

"All right, here we go," Charles said, a gleeful tone in his voice. "Polly, order a taxi, they can pick him up right at the front door."

I found the contact number on the tourist info page and got Ladhi to double-check the address for me. ETA: five minutes.

"Taxi on the way," I said.

"Good. All right, turn your volumes up, it's showtime."

On the kidnapper's handheld feed, a door alert sounded.

"Is that it?" said the second guy. "Is that the signal?"

"No, we were supposed to get a call," said the first guy.

"Then who's at the door?"

"Stay here, I'll go check."

A bit of rustling while the guy moved through the rooms, padded down the stairs, and opened a door. "What?"

A younger male voice said, "Yeah, we have an order for a dozen pizzas to be delivered to this address for some kind of party?"

"What? I think there's been a mistake, we haven't ordered any pizzas . . ."

"But the order is right here, they've already been paid for and everything."

"Well, we don't want them, can you take them somewhere else? The employee mess hall maybe?"

I decided right then that this pizza-delivery thing must have been invented for its comic value.

"Let's wrap this up," Charles said.

A loud alarm rang, making Ladhi and me slap our hands over

our ears. Another fire alarm? I couldn't tell where it was coming from until I looked back at my handheld. The box showing the kidnapper's handheld suddenly got an image, blurring as it zipped past, as the guy took it out of his pocket to look at it. "What *is* that?!"

"What am I supposed to do about these pizzas?"

"Hey, you, get back here!" That was the other kidnapper, and I heard heavy footsteps slamming down a staircase.

Then things got very messy. I might have thought this would be like watching a vid, clandestinely eavesdropping while we got the audio and visual feed from the kidnappers' handhelds. Like sitting in the corner, watching events unfold. This wasn't like that at all. There was a lot of shouting and running, and the guy must have shoved his handheld back in his pocket because everything went dark again, and the alarm was still blaring, echoing off the walls in the house they were in, adding to the chaos.

"There, he's outside! Check the video feed!" Angelyn said, and then Charles sent the image from that camera feed to the rest of us, and finally this was like watching a vid. There was George, standing on the street, looking back and forth in a panic. A guy standing there in some kind of food-services uniform, holding a stack of flat boxes, blinked back at him in confusion, and the two kidnappers barreled out the door after him. George ran.

"And there's the taxi," Charles observed. The taxi was an electric-powered groundcar painted a mustard yellow with a lighted sign on top. Another one of the traditional modes of transport on the island. If George had listened to the orientation when we got here, he'd know that all he had to do was get in and it would take him wherever he wanted.

"Please, George, pay attention to the taxi . . ." Angelyn muttered, because it looked like George was going to run right past it in his panic. Poor guy.

But he didn't. Right at the edge of the security camera's range of view, George did a double take, stopped, and piled into the taxi's backseat. The car pulled away as the two kidnappers raced down the sidewalk. They glared at it and slouched, clearly discouraged.

Well, that was exciting.

"That's it," Charles said. "He's on the way back."

Elizabeth clapped, and Angelyn turned around to hug her tight. The rest of us sighed. For not having moved for the last half hour, I was exhausted. I blamed the gravity.

I heard a soft click from the door.

"Ladhi, try the door," I said.

She padded over, turned the handle—and the door opened. She looked back at me, holding the door open, uncertain.

"Hey, guys?" I said carefully, because I didn't quite believe it. "The doors are unlocked. We can leave."

"Do we dare?" Ladhi whispered, like someone was listening in on us, and maybe they were.

"I don't care," Elizabeth said. "I'm going to meet George."

I heard their door open and slam closed in the hallway.

"Let's go," I said, getting up to race after them.

Charles and Ethan joined us, and the six of us ran to the elevator. Elizabeth fidgeted the whole way down.

Me, I was waiting for bombs to drop. "What next?" I said. "Do we call out Stanton?"

"We don't do anything," Charles said. "We pretend we don't know anything."

"She has to know what we did, she monitors everything—"

"But she'll pretend she doesn't, and we'll pretend that we didn't."

"But then why is she doing this? Why set up these disasters just to see what we'll do? It's wrong, she's crazy—"

"Polly, be quiet, she's probably listening in on us right now."

"I don't care! I hate her and I don't care if she knows it!"

"She probably doesn't care how you feel about her."

"We can call Mom. All of us, we call our parents and tell them what's been happening—"

"And who are they going to believe?" Charles said, arcing his brow in that maddening smug way of his. "Stanton or us?"

"I don't care!" I shouted again, as if yelling it to the universe would actually change something.

"Then be quiet and let me handle it." He was so infuriatingly superior about it all.

"So what, I'm just supposed to pretend this wasn't all a setup?"

"Yes. You are going to keep your mouth shut."

"Make me!"

And he just stared down at me. Once again, I felt a shock that he was taller than me, staring down at me.

The others were watching us, pressed over to one side of the elevator, leaving the two of us alone to shout at each other in our hard Martian accents. Well, leaving me to shout. Charles never shouted. Charles had no emotion at all. He was a machine with flesh glued over him.

"What?" I muttered at them.

"Do you guys always argue like that?" Ladhi said.

"Yeah," I answered, deadpan. "It's because we love each other."

"Look up 'sibling rivalry,'" Charles said. "A well-documented psychological phenomenon. Polly falls victim to it often."

"Charles!"

"See?"

I growled. The elevator doors opened.

The lobby was filled with automated scrubbers and cleaners repairing the damage from the fire-retardant foam, making a soft, annoying hum. In their midst, a pair of uniformed security officers stood talking to Stanton, who appeared utterly calm and serene with her gray uniform and superior gaze. She should have been surprised to see us all marching out of the elevator, but she wasn't. Narrowing her gaze at us, she considered. Charles must have guessed that I was about to open my mouth and start yelling, because he grabbed my wrist and squeezed.

Before anyone could say anything, George came in the front door. He looked flushed, sweaty, exhausted, his shirt untucked, a spatter of mud on the hem of his trousers and shoes. He looked around, blinking like he'd left an air lock to emerge in bright sunlight.

"George!" Elzabeth called and ran forward. George's expression softened with relief and he opened his arms, catching her and hugging tight. They stood there for a long time, clinging to each other. Might have been the sweetest thing I'd ever seen. Even if it was George and Elzabeth.

They pulled apart only when Stanton said, "Mr. Montes. What a relief. You're not hurt, I assume?"

George and Elzabeth stared at her. The security guys moved in and asked a few questions—to make it all seem real. George went with the security guys to a corner of the lobby. Elzabeth

232 • CARRIE VAUGHN

refused to leave his side and no one argued. Stanton came to face down the rest of us.

Like Charles said—it was all theater.

I waited to see whom Stanton was going to yell at first, and what exactly she was going to yell about. But she didn't. She just stood there, her expression still, and said, "Well. Thank goodness it all turned out well. Everyone, go back to your rooms. We'll return to Galileo in the morning. Everyone needs to be packed and in the lobby by eight A.M."

"That's *it*?" I said, because I couldn't help it. Charles elbowed my arm.

"That's it, Ms. Newton," Stanton said. She acted like she'd won something. But what? This was some kind of foot race, but where was the finish line?

"Come on, Polly," Charles said, taking hold of my arm. "You must be very tired and should get some sleep."

How was I supposed to fight back if no one would let me, and if there wasn't even anything to fight against? Didn't change that I felt like I ought to be fighting *something*.

Maybe it was me. I was just going crazy. Again, I blamed the gravity. I could live with that.

20

And that was the trip to the Manhattan Cultural Preserve. I wanted to say I had a good time. The place could convince anyone that maybe Earth wasn't so bad after all, if it had horses. But I couldn't think about anything without thinking about Stanton and what was going to happen next. *Something* was going to happen next. My stomach hurt thinking about it.

Galileo Academy and its grounds were supposed to be beautiful and awe inspiring, but it felt more and more like a prison. The cameras felt like eyes, and every instructor seemed to be paying extra-close attention to me, making notes on every little thing I did wrong. Because everything I did was wrong, I was sure. Except in Ms. Lee's astrophysics class. *She* still smiled when I raised my hand.

George was fine. Acted like nothing had happened, even. He didn't treat me any different than he had before, which was fine. If it had happened to me, I'd have pretended nothing was different, too. You didn't want to draw too much attention to yourself, after all.

After a week, the routine had stayed routine, which was why

I didn't expect George to corner me at PE. We'd been running, and I'd been in the back with the rest of the offworld kids. We didn't wheeze and straggle like we used to, but we still lagged behind the others. We got back to the locker rooms about twenty minutes after everyone else, and George was waiting by the outside door, slouching with his arms crossed, until he caught my gaze.

He waited until everyone else was inside before calling out, "Polly."

I shouldn't have stopped, but I did, letting him pull me aside.

"What do you want?" I said flatly, too tired to be offended.

"I just wanted to say . . ." He looked at his feet, then up again. Scuffed a toe on the ground. Was he actually *nervous*? "I know we haven't really gotten along, and I probably could have been a little nicer and all . . ."

All I could do was stare. What was he *doing*? I braced to run, just in case.

He must have talked for a full minute, explaining: ". . . and whatever was really up with those guys and the kidnapping, I don't even know. But Elzabeth told me everything that happened, and you and Charles stuck your necks out for me. And, well. Thanks. I really appreciate it. If there's ever anything I can do for you, let me know. All right?" He was blushing a little, and his smile was tight and nervous, waiting for me to respond.

I didn't know what to say. This didn't seem like a trick. He was being genuinely . . . nice. I could tell because he'd never sounded like that before, at least not to me.

"I didn't do it to get any favors from you," I said finally. "I did it because it was the right thing to do."

"I can still be grateful. Just keep it in mind." He turned and walked into the building.

I would have gone through all that for anyone, if I thought he was being hurt. Did he even understand that? Maybe he did. Maybe this was the only way he knew how to say thank you. Because it was all about who could do what for you—Tenzig knew this, and proved it when he took me aside as we were walking back to the residence hall from class.

"You've figured out the system, I see," Tenzig said.

"What are you talking about?" I shot back.

"Sucking up to the Earth kids. First saving Angelyn, then George. Lots of grateful, influential people lining up behind you. Pretty soon even Stanton won't be able to give you a hard time."

I stared. "I don't even know what you're talking about."

"Yeah, you keep playing dumb. Makes you endearing. I get it."

The game Charles kept talking about. Didn't seem to matter how much I kept telling people I wasn't playing a game—I didn't know the rules, I didn't know how to play, and didn't even *care*—they saw what they wanted to see. I couldn't win.

Then I got a video message from Mom. An actual video message, not just a note, and she was gushing. She was actually smiling all the way to her eyes. She went on and on about how clever I was for helping that boy—that boy with the very important family. She'd even gotten a personal message from George Montes's father about what happened in Manhattan. After earning his praise, the reprimands from Stanton didn't matter.

"You're doing very well, Polly. I'm so proud of you. Just keep working hard and making friends, and everything will be *perfect*. Keep working hard, Polly."

I supposed that was pretty close to "I love you."

This was during the evening study period, and I tracked down Charles at his desk. I pulled a chair close and whispered, "I got a video from Mom."

He raised an eyebrow and waited, so I kept talking. "She's making me *very* nervous."

"Because she's being overly solicitous?"

"What?"

He glared. "She knows every detail of everything that happens here, and moreover she seems *pleased* about it."

"It's Stanton, isn't it?" I said. "Stanton is reporting to her."

He blinked in surprise. Like he didn't expect me to figure it out. "Yes. I assume she's reporting to all the parents—but she has staff for that. Automated review forms. Our mother seems to be getting much more detailed information."

"It's making me nervous," I repeated.

"It should." Then he glanced around, over his shoulder like he was in an actual old-style spy video. "Meet me outside the front doors of the weight room before your PE class tomorrow."

"Why, what—"

"Quietly," he whispered. "I have to show you something."

I was sure he wasn't going to be there and would leave me standing there like an idiot while everyone else did their weight rotations. Then Franteska, the upperclass student supervisor, wandered over to stand with me.

"He here yet?" she asked.

"What?" I replied stupidly.

She gave me a look. "Your brother said he wanted to talk."

"To *you*?"

"How is it you two are even related? I thought twins were supposed to be the *same*."

"Welcome to the infuriating world of genetics," I said. She huffed in agreement.

Just then Charles came down the corridor to the weight room. With him was Harald, Franteska's classmate, who was supposed to be supervising the running PE section.

Harald said, rather loudly and obviously in a way that made Charles wince, "Newton here might be interested in weight training, so I thought you both could talk to him about it." He glanced at the camera in the corner for only a second, but it was still really obvious.

So this was all staged for the benefit of anyone who might be spying on us. Crazy weird.

"Tell Polly what you told you me," Charles said as we clustered together, pretending we were discussing weights.

Harald said, "Everyone's talking about your class's field trips. Every year goes on trips—Yosemite and Manhattan are standard for first-years. But in the thirty years of the school's history, nobody's ever had an accident. Not the way your class has. Even in the middle of Yosemite, everything's controlled. It's part of Galileo's reputation."

Franteska added, "None of this is supposed to be dangerous. It's about building community. That's what Galileo is about—developing connections that will benefit us for the rest of our lives. Networking. We'll always work together."

"Well, *that's* kind of elitist," I muttered.

"Of course it is, that's the point," Harald answered.

"Tell her the rest," Charles said.

Harald took a deep breath. "I was doing an intern shift at administration and I overheard Stanton. I think she was recording a message rather than talking to someone. But she explained that you two were undermining her efforts to integrate you into the system. She kept insisting that Galileo wasn't structured to properly assimilate Martians and that she might need to take more extreme measures if you didn't start fitting in soon."

Charles nodded for my benefit. "If Galileo is meant to build community, we would never be a part of that community without serious intervention."

Franteska shrugged. "I don't know. You're not too bad, once people get used to you."

Both Charles and I glared at her for that.

"If Stanton's manipulating the system, it affects everyone here. Not just us," Charles said. "So what's the next field trip? I'm asking in the name of community, of course."

Franteska and Harald glanced at each other. "It's a secret," she said. "We're not supposed to talk about it. It's supposed to be a surprise."

Harald tried to sound comforting. "All the first-years do it. It'll be great. Especially for you guys."

"Even if you consider it in terms of accident potential?" Charles asked.

Franteska's eyes went wide. "Oh, no—"

"Shh," Harald hushed her when she started to say something. "I'm sorry, we can't talk about it. It's tradition. But I'm sure . . . I'm sure everything will be fine. I'm sure of it."

"Right. Thanks," Charles said flatly. "Have fun lifting weights, Polly." He stalked away. Harald shrugged and went after him.

"It'll be fine," Franteska repeated to me, but her smile was more of a wince.

"Sure it will," I said. I wondered if weight *throwing* was a thing.

After PE, I started thinking—would getting kicked out of Galileo really be so awful? I could go back to Mars. I could do *something* worthwhile there. I didn't believe I'd be cut off from piloting entirely. I could get another internship at the astrodrome. Somehow, I'd make it happen without all these so-called connections.

"What are you thinking?" Charles asked cautiously, suspiciously.

"It's like you said when we first got here. Earth has systems set up so that nobody starves, and anyone who wants an education can get one—but not everyone can go to a place like Galileo, and that's how they get an aristocracy. Family dynasties like the Chous and the Monteses. But Colony One isn't old enough to have dynasties, an aristocracy, anything like that. Maybe Mom is trying to start one, with us? Is that why we're here?"

"And what do you think about that?" he asked, like he was an instructor and I was the hapless student.

"I think if the Mars colonies are going to keep working, we have to look out for everyone. Mom's not doing that, is she?"

"I don't know," he murmured, and I didn't believe it. I didn't believe that he didn't know, that he didn't have an opinion.

"Never mind," I said, because I didn't want to think about it anymore. "It's like you said. If this is a game, maybe it's better not to play."

I totally blew off my homework that night. It felt great.

I worked on a plan to get myself kicked out of school. Steal a motorbike and take it off campus. Sabotage the plumbing in the dorm. Refuse to do any more PE. Punch Tenzig in the face during astrophysics. That would probably break my hand. It would be worth it.

Or maybe I could stick it out until the end of the year and convince Mom that I wasn't cut out for Galileo and could I please come home. Maybe that would work. I could already see the look on her face, how disappointed she'd be, and I could hear her explain how I was giving up. Failing. Pilot-training programs didn't accept failures. If I had known that going to Galileo would set me up for a failure that would not only not help me get into a good piloting program but actively prevent me from getting into *any* program . . . I felt like I'd been robbed. This was all a big con, and I was the biggest sucker in the universe.

But maybe I could take myself out of the game, as Charles kept calling it. Don't compete. Let go of the need to be the best.

Not be bothered at all when Tenzig tried to show me up. Maybe I could just get myself kicked off the next field trip, so at least I wouldn't have to deal with any more wild expectations and crazy accidents. Stanton would probably be happy to leave me behind, seeing how much trouble I kept causing.

Maybe I could get sick. I researched diseases that we hadn't been vaccinated against for something mild but annoying that I could catch so I wouldn't have to go anywhere. But all I found were diseases so horrible they'd been eradicated and existed only in petri dishes in labs. And they wouldn't just make me sick; they'd cripple me for life or kill me outright. Polio, smallpox . . . Maybe I could *invent* a disease. I could develop a severe allergy—to Earth.

Then I found out where our next field trip was going, the big secret Harald and Franteska wouldn't tell us: we were going offworld. To the Moon. A lunar expedition. That meant an orbital shuttle, time on a station in low gravity, and a trip on a real M-drive ship to lunar orbit. The closest thing to home I could get without going interplanetary. And then a week on not-Earth. I *really* wanted to go. I didn't want Stanton to know how much I wanted to go because then she'd put me on restrictions for sure. Grounded, really grounded. I hated that word.

I tried to stay very, very quiet for the next two weeks. I showed up with my uniform pressed and neat, my attitude adjusted, and my lips firmly closed. I wouldn't speak unless spoken to. I wouldn't even complain about PE.

"Are you okay?" Ladhi asked on day three of Operation Don't Piss Off Anyone. We were getting ready for bed, ten minutes before lights-out. Even Marie watched me, glancing out of the corner of her eye while she hung up her uniform.

"Fine. Why?" I said.

"You just seem kind of . . . tense."

"I'm *fine.*" I slammed a closet door and yanked back the covers of my bed.

Ladhi said, "If you're trying to stay out of trouble, you might want to rethink. You look like you're about to explode."

Wouldn't that be fun? "I'm just . . . I can't . . . I don't want to . . ." I sat down on the bed and sighed. "It's that obvious?"

Both Ladhi and Marie nodded. Ladhi came and sat next to me.

"If Stanton wants to boot you from the field trip, she'll figure out a reason and there's nothing you can do about it. If she wants you to go, because Charles is right and she's putting us through some kind of stress and disaster test, you could burn down the school and she'll still let you on the trip. So you might as well just . . . well, get back to normal."

"I don't know what normal is anymore. I haven't felt normal in weeks. Months."

"Just hold out another week," Ladhi said. "At least on the Moon we'll be able to breathe without thinking about it. Boris can show us the sights. He'll be so excited, you know?"

"And we can finally show up the Earth kids," Marie added.

I didn't even care about that anymore. Charles was right. Better to not play the game. But I was looking forward to the low gravity.

The schedule for the lunar expedition involved a lot of home-work. Well, it looked like homework on paper, but I already knew a lot of it. All of us from offworld did. Finally, the Earth kids were going to be at a disadvantage. Hard not to feel smug about it.

We'd take a shuttle to Cochrane Station, where we'd have a tour, emergency-procedure training, and then go for low-g and zero-g training, which I was really looking forward to. From there we'd take a short-hop M-drive ship to lunar orbit, then another shuttle to Collins City, where we'd stay for three days of classwork, including planetary geology and colony-systems engineering. Then we'd take a shuttle to a research station at the Sea of Tranquillity to collect our own geology samples, which we'd then take back to the lab and analyze. It wasn't like we'd be discovering anything new, but it was still exciting. At least I thought so. It was *real* work. On top of that we had to calculate orbital trajectories for the entire trip, which wasn't hard because we could use our handhelds, and if you didn't enter in the right variables, you'd come up with a mess. And if I asked nicely, maybe I could get onto the bridge of the M-drive ship. The possibilities were wide-open. Not to mention it felt a little like going home.

After a sudden paranoid notion that Stanton would see how excited I was about the trip and ground me out of spite, I settled down and took Ladhi's advice. Just act normal. Just play it cool.

At study hall a couple of days before we were due to leave, I asked Charles if he was looking forward to the trip.

"Can't say I am, particularly," he said.

I looked at him like he was crazy. "We'll finally be back in low g. We'll finally be in our element and we'll get to watch the others flail around like newbies. Tell me you're not looking forward to that at least a little."

He set aside his handheld and looked at me. "It's my hypothesis that on each field trip, Stanton has rigged some kind of event to test our responses to emergencies, and that in both cases we've exceeded her expectations with our proactive responses. So what do you think she has planned for us on this trip? Think about worst-case scenarios possible on a lunar field trip for a minute, then ask me again if I'm looking forward to it."

Charles really had an interesting way of looking at the world.

"We'll just have to keep a lookout, that's all," I said, trying to be blasé.

"Yes, we will."

And we would. We'd be in our element, in sealed space stations and colonies. We'd be able to spot it the minute something went wrong.

Stanton wouldn't dare rig anything truly dangerous, would she?

21

Boarding the shuttle to get to Cochrane Station, I couldn't stop grinning. I might have been vibrating, I was so excited. I might have annoyed some of the others.

"I think I'm gonna be sick," Angelyn muttered.

Turned out about half the Earth kids in our group had been off-planet before, at least to one of the orbiting stations on a vacation or whatnot, and didn't have any trouble. Some of the other half, though, weren't thrilled. Angelyn had gone pale, like the blood had drained out of her face.

"Zero g's nothing to be scared of," Ladhi said, trying to sound reassuring.

"I'm not scared of zero g, I'm scared of making an idiot of myself!" Angelyn said.

She wasn't wrong—making an idiot of yourself in zero g was way too easy if you didn't pay attention.

"Don't flail," I said. "Relax. No sudden moves. It'll be fine."

She closed her eyes. "Oh, my God."

We filed down the aisle of the shuttle and into our seats.

We had a cluster of familiar faces in our section of the shuttle.

The usual offworld clique—me, Charles, Ladhi, Ethan, Boris, Marie—plus some of the Earthers: Angelyn, Elzabeth, George, a couple of George's friends. And this time, they weren't teasing us, smirking at us, or acting superior.

A member of the shuttle crew gave us the safety briefing. Stanton ordered us to pay attention, but I had a hard time. I *knew* all this, about emergency oxygen and crash positions and inflatable escape bubbles and harnesses stored at the exits. The odds of anything going wrong were so vanishingly small—

Except for Stanton, standing in the front of the shuttle gazing over us during the briefing with her usual superior, calculating expression. With her in charge, I could throw the odds out the window. Anything could happen.

I started paying closer attention and checking to make sure the safety and escape devices actually were in place and labeled. I looked across the aisle to see Charles doing the same. He caught my gaze and pressed his lips in a grim line.

The engines whined, and the shuttle rattled as the launch module prepared to ignite and take us out of the gravity well. A hand closed over mine. Angelyn, sitting next me, had grabbed my hand and squeezed.

"I'm sticking with you this whole trip," she said, her voice tight with anxiety. She glanced back to include George and Elzabeth sitting in the row behind us. "We all are. If something awful happens, we're counting on you guys to get us out of it."

"We'll all get ourselves out of it."

So what should have been a really nice trip and the highlight of my time so far at Galileo ended up being anxious and stress ridden. We knew something was going to happen, we just didn't know what, or when. I hoped it didn't involve air locks.

As far as we could tell, everything went smoothly. We docked at Cochran Station, and the seal between the ship and station didn't blow and send us all tumbling into an explosive vacuum.

Being on the station, stepping on the rubber matting in the steel corridor, felt like coming home after a long and difficult journey. I took a deep breath of filtered air and relaxed as the walls safely closed around me.

"Why do I feel like my heart's in my throat?" Elzabeth muttered.

Funny, my internal organs finally felt normal, sitting lightly in my body cavity like they were supposed to, instead of sinking like rocks.

We could tell who'd never been off-planet before by how they acted once we got on the station. The station had simulated gravity, but it was less than Earth's, and you had to move carefully. Even the students who were excited about this took slow steps and reached out to grab on to things.

A couple of people got sick right off. We'd been given bags for that, fortunately. It was apparently pretty common. Secretly, I thought it was hilarious, because at least one of the sick kids was Franklin, who'd given us offworlders a hard time from the get-go.

"It's called payback," Charles said. "Part of the natural order of the universe. I think it's a corollary of Newton's Third Law of Motion."

"What are you *talking* about?" one of the other kids said.

"He's making a physics joke," I said. "He does that."

The entire list of activities on Cochrane Station:

Microgravity gym class. Charles's payback in spades, because here the offworld kids were the ones able to jump and zoom and spin and bounce without effort, reaching out to grab handholds or bounce off walls like it was second nature. We might have spent the last six months on Earth in too much gravity, but the instincts came back in moments. We had been like carp out of water, gasping for breath, now tossed back into our watery homes, and we celebrated. On the other hand, the Earth kids flailed like mindless blobs set loose in space. I couldn't really laugh, since the idea of the low-g practice wasn't to make anybody an expert—it was to make sure people didn't hurt themselves and everybody around them. Microgravity gym was like remedial PE for *them*. A tiny revenge.

Station-operations tour: Everything you needed to know to operate a space station, which was pretty much exactly what you needed to operate a Martian colony, so once again we were ahead. Life support, maneuvering thrusters to maintain spin and orbit, communications systems, daily operations. The kind of thing Mom did every day. It was like being home again.

Planetary-charting workshop. We used the telescopes in one of the station's observation lounges to photograph and then map various features of Earth's surface. I found Manhattan, a built-up gray splotch jutting into a twisting corner of water. It looked so innocuous from 160 kilometers up.

Introductory hydroponics and low-gravity health and nutrition. Which was, again, mainly for the Earth kids because it was second nature to those of us who grew up with it all. I still had to pay attention and take the tests. Another hoop to jump through.

Through just about all of it, us station and colony kids finally, finally took the lead. I was too happy to be functional again to gloat. If they'd just move Galileo Academy to a space station instead of insisting that it had be on Earth, I might actually enjoy it.

Except, weirdly, the pang of homesickness hit even harder than it had on Earth, because the station felt so much like home. But however much a station might have been *like* a colony, it wasn't, and I realized that what I really wanted to see was a rocky brown landscape stretching away outside a view port. Wasn't going to happen anytime soon. Moving on.

After three days of activities came the second leg of the trip, to Collins City. I was anxious to bursting. Not about the trip, but about making that all-important request.

We were eating breakfast in the student bunk area we'd been staying in. Stanton and several other instructors were supervising—probably because it would be especially embarrassing if I decided to go exploring on my own here. I hurried to finish eating, cleaned up my things, and approached her. Carefully, deferentially, hands clasped behind my back, gaze downcast. It was just me, harmless little student type. She watched me like she might an approaching missile. I only got as close as I needed for her to hear me talk, slightly softer than normal.

"Ms. Stanton," I said as carefully and politely as I could. "May I make a request? A small request." I winced. I had to strike a balance between making sure I was serious, but that it wasn't a big deal. Who was I kidding? She'd know exactly how important this was to me. She knew everything.

"Yes, Newton?"

"I'm deeply, very interested in the piloting and operations of M-drive interplanetary craft, and so I would like to observe the M-drive jump in the flight operations cabin, if I might be able to do so without being in the way, if at all possible. Please." Calm and quiet, that was me.

She raised a brow, studied me. This was possibly the most polite I'd ever been in my entire life, please let her not slam me for it. I had a sudden, terrible thought: she could leave me on the station. She could keep me off the lunar half of the trip just out of spite. Had I made a horrible mistake? I wanted to scream, but I just stood there wringing my hands behind my back and clenching my teeth so I wouldn't say anything stupid.

Finally, Stanton said, "I'll ask the captain. It will be her decision."

"Thank you, Ms. Stanton. Thank you for asking." At least I'd tried. I couldn't get down on myself for not trying.

She didn't say anything. Just frowned.

"You shouldn't even engage with her," Charles said, sidling up to me as we walked to the docks.

"Why, because it's not playing the game right? I don't care about the game, I want what I want and if I have to ask for it myself, that's fine, because no one else will. I'm not going to go around second-guessing myself all the time."

He didn't have a zinger for that.

The M-drive jump was short, seeing as how we only had some half a million kilometers to go, instead of hundreds of millions.

Just a hop, really. Less exciting than a truly interplanetary leap, but I'd take what I could get. Especially since Stanton said yes. I got to sit in the flight cabin for the entire jump maneuver.

We were boarding when she pulled me aside, calling me to the front of the passenger aisle. "Ms. Newton, will you come up here please?"

Nearby students gave me that *look*, wondering what I'd done wrong and hanging back to see how much trouble I was in. I knew I hadn't done anything wrong, I just *knew* it. At least, I hadn't in the last fifty hours or so. "Yes, ma'am?"

She looked down her nose, and I couldn't tell from her expression whether she was praising me or dressing me down. "You'll be allowed to observe flight operations on the bridge, but you must remain still and quiet, and I want a thorough written report of the experience as part of your classwork. Understood?"

The breath went out of me, but I managed to squeak, "Yes, ma'am."

Captain Arroz was obviously from Earth, short and stout, with olive skin and dark hair. And she was kind, showing me a little jump seat in the back where I could sit out of the way. She introduced me to her navigator, Lieutenant Nguyen, and asked if I had any questions. I had too many. I just wanted to see it all work. This was a smaller ship, so the bridge really was just a cabin, with two seats for the pilot and navigator, who doubled as engineer for the trip. The controls and displays were all scaled down, but I still recognized a lot of it. I stayed very quiet and didn't bother them with questions.

Powering under the M-drive felt much smoother and quieter than the conventional engine. There weren't vibrations through the hull, there wasn't the distant roar of thrust. It all seemed perfectly calm. Perfectly *perfect*. The ship was hurtling through folded space—speed was irrelevant, but I imagined zipping across tens of thousands of kilometers in seconds. The crew managed the ship without any fuss. Lights beeped, status reports scrolled across screens. Captain Arroz would ask for an update using some verbal shorthand of just a couple of words, and Nguyen replied, again with just a couple of words. They had been doing this a long time and were comfortable here. I wondered if I'd ever get that comfortable in a flight cabin and not too excited for words. About halfway through the M-drive jump, Captain Arroz leaned over the navigator's station and they had a quiet conversation that involved pointing at the screen, like something was wrong, but they didn't speak loudly enough for me to find out what. They were very calm about it. As if something going wrong was just part of the routine. I wondered if that came from training, or if that was just their nature—if you had to be super calm to be on a ship's crew. That was something I could probably work on.

Nothing was wrong, it turned out. This had all been routine.

I sat quietly, hardly moved at all, and tried to take it all in. I was desperate to remember everything so I could replicate it when I finally got into training. Be calm, be prepared, be focused. How wonderful to feel like I was part of it, even if just for an hour or two.

And then, too quickly, we were in lunar orbit and docking with a shuttle that would take us to Collins City. I let out a happy sigh.

"Thank you very much, Captain. I really appreciate it," I said when Stanton arrived to steer me back to the others.

"Still want to command a ship of your own? It's pretty boring."

"No," I said. "It's wonderful."

She got this glint in her eye, like she understood.

22

Collins City was even more like home than Cochran Station. It was partially underground, with all the expected support systems and rubber-matted corridors and hissing vents. But the gravity was scant. We had no trouble standing upright, anchored to the floor, but take a step too quickly or too hard, and you'd fling your body forward into a wall or the floor or someone else.

I could look out a view port here to an expanse of ground reaching to a horizon. But the landscape was gray, harshly lit by unfiltered sunlight, and the sky was black. Fiercely black. My homesickness got even worse. I wanted to see Mars so badly I almost cried. But I couldn't. Like Charles said, just put your head down and get through it.

I couldn't tell if he was feeling the same deep longing, the frustration that things were familiar but just off enough to be flat-out wrong. He kept his serious expression to the world, and I was sure that if I asked, he'd say he wasn't feeling anything at all. You didn't win the game by *feeling*.

We had to sit through another orientation and safety video, a lot like the one we had to sit through on Cochran. I imagined

Mars had a video new arrivals were made to watch, about what doors you were allowed to go through and what buttons you really shouldn't push, and about how the dust was so bad that if you went on EVA you had to be very sure you got thoroughly vacuumed in the air lock. I'd never seen that video, because why would I? We had a different set of videos we'd watched since we were babies, for people who lived there. I'd never thought about it before. This was all second nature. It would be easy to blow it off, not pay attention. But it was the little tiny differences between Collins and Colony One that would get me in trouble, so I paid attention.

Weirdly, *everybody* was paying close attention. Well, almost everybody. Me, Charles, Ethan, Ladhi, Angelyn, Elzabeth, George—the group of us who thought Stanton was up to something. Would she sabotage the life-support system? Cause an air lock to fail? Hard to believe she'd do something that life-or-death, something that had a good chance of getting someone killed. But that was the trouble with not being on Earth—if something went wrong here, there was a good chance someone would get killed.

Out here, so much could go wrong. Stanton had many opportunities to rig something, to test how we'd react in an emergency. The more attention we paid, the more we knew about the colony and its systems, the more likely we were to figure out what disaster she was going to throw at us. Ethan leaned forward, chin in his hand, staring at the screen like he was memorizing every image. Charles sat back in his chair, scowling.

After that, we were sent to the dorm area we'd been assigned. We shared rooms, which were clustered around a common area where we'd eat meals and hang out between coursework and tours.

We had this first day to rest and acclimate, but I was so mixed up about what time it was supposed to be, I didn't really care about resting. We were all wired, wandering around the dorm area, complaining, staring out observation windows at the fascinating bleakness. The only one who was really happy with the gravity and the constant sensation that our bellies were crawling up our rib cages was Boris, who'd grown up here. A couple of the Earth kids had to be medicated so they could keep food down.

I had to write that essay about observing flight operations for Stanton, so I barricaded myself in the dorm room while the others burned off energy and excitement. Pretty soon, though, I heard shouting. Two voices, male, muffled through the door. One of them was Ethan's. Ethan never yelled at anybody. I slid open the door a crack and peered out to the sofas and chairs where people had gathered. Angelyn, George, and Ladhi were sitting, cringing and watching with wide eyes. Ethan stood off to the side, arms crossed, staring down at Tenzig, who was pointing at him.

"That's messed up. *You're* messed up. I'm not spying on Stanton for you."

"We're just asking for everyone to keep an eye out, to watch out for each other—"

"I'm looking out for myself! You all should be looking out for yourselves. You're just too stupid to realize it, too stupid to not go begging everyone else for help."

Ethan sighed. "Looking out for yourself—that's you all over."

"You know what? I'm telling Stanton that you all think she's out to kill you." He took in the whole room, and his eyes were lit up, like he was on the hunt.

Ethan just smiled. "You're so into being her little stooge, you go right ahead."

"I'm not a stooge, I'm just better than you, you nutcase!"

"You don't get to decide that, stooge."

Tenzig lost it, then, and slammed into Ethan.

He probably just meant to smack Ethan on the chest, the finger-jabbing bullying kind of thing that would make Tenzig all smug and that Ethan never would respond to, normally. But Tenzig was angry. He was moving with force, and he wasn't completely acclimated to the low gravity, so instead of just stepping forward and jabbing Ethan, he launched himself, his whole body plowing into him, sending Ethan stumbling back. Ethan tried to shove him to his feet, but he, too, overcompensated against the gravity. It would have been funny, but they still managed to pummel each other in the face, even if it was mostly by accident.

More chaos ensued when everyone else jumped up and tried to move chairs out of the way to keep the guys from tripping over them. But again, the low gravity was almost worse than being weightless, because it didn't make everything float, it just made everything *slow*. Which meant when Tenzig and Ethan fell, stumbling over each other, they didn't fall all that hard, and they didn't seem hurt.

Enough. "Stop it!" I yelled, and took a couple of jumping steps toward them. I was thinking hard about the gravity so I didn't end up smashing my face on the floor like a couple of the others had done. I grabbed Ethan because he was closer, wrapping my fists into the shoulder of his jumpsuit, ducking while he swung back at Tenzig, who was driving him backward. Thanks to the low gravity, I could actually haul the very tall and solid Ethan out of the way. I just made sure I was braced extra well.

With Ethan out of the way, Tenzig stumbled, but he didn't fall, because across the space Boris had grabbed him to steady him. Here, he was the most the stable of all of us. I nodded a thanks to him.

The two guys were fought out, so they didn't struggle against us very hard.

"What's wrong with you?" I demanded, and I didn't even know whom I was asking.

They didn't answer except by glaring. I kept hold of Ethan, because he leaned into me as if looking for some stability. Tenzig, however, jerked away from Boris. This sent him bouncing a couple of steps, because he was still too angry to focus on keeping stable.

He jabbed his finger at Ethan, at all of us. "You screwed up big. Just watch. I'll prove it to you." He marched out of the common space to his room, taking big bounding steps. He had to grab the doorway to stop himself from careening. I bit my lip to keep from laughing, because it wasn't all that funny in the end.

No one said anything, no one explained, so I looked at Charles, who was standing out of the way and looking thoughtful. "What?" I asked him, in shorthand.

"Tenzig asked what we were talking about," he said. "We told him."

"And now he's going to tell Stanton that we're on to her?"

"Likely she has surveillance in the room and has been listening to everything already," Charles said. As if *that* didn't make my stomach twist into knots. The others glanced around, suspicious and uncertain.

"It doesn't change anything," Ethan said, wiping his mouth. Half of his lip was swelling from where Tenzig has smacked it.

"He's right," George added. "If Stanton's listening to us now, she's been listening to us all along. There's nothing we can do about it, and it doesn't change anything. We just stick together and keep a watch out."

The half dozen of us standing here were the ones who were in on it, who'd been with us from the start because of the accidents. We had a team. We had people watching our backs. I felt better.

I was still holding on to Ethan, who rested his hand on mine. "You can let go now, Polly." His swollen lips smiled. I hesitated, then brushed off his sleeve. Realized everyone was watching and took a step back.

"You should probably get a cold pack on that," I said, reaching for his lip before pulling away.

"Yeah. I'll do that."

Somehow, the idea of Stanton listening in on us made us not want to talk anymore.

"We should get some sleep," Angelyn said finally, and the party broke up. Ladhi took my arm and pulled me toward our room. I took another glance at Charles. He nodded at me, and I wasn't sure what he was trying to say. *Good work*, maybe? Or *keep watch, stay close*. Or maybe both. I was suddenly exhausted.

Before going to sleep I finished my report on the shuttle flight. In it, I talked about how practical interplanetary space travel was what separated us from other forms of life.

But not by very much.

23

We had two more days of orientation and classwork on planetary geology. Dirt and rocks. Meteors hurtling from space and crater formation. The whole time, we waited for something to go wrong, and nothing did, except everyone getting more and more anxious. Tenzig shoved a shoulder or elbow into Ethan whenever he could. By accident, of course. It got so that Ladhi, Angelyn, and I made sure to stand nearby to run interference by stepping into his path when Tenzig got close. Ethan must have enjoyed being surrounded by girls. But nobody was smiling much.

Tenzig tried going after Charles instead. The first time he did it, moving to the other side of the room and "accidentally" bumping into Charles, shoulder to shoulder, Tenzig started to say something surly about Charles watching where he was going. But Charles just stared at him—a cold, rocky stare, expressionless. It sent a chill down my back, and I was standing three meters away. Tenzig blinked a moment and stumbled back, not saying anything else. He left Charles alone. A rumor got back to me later that day, through George and Angelyn: Tenzig saying that

Charles was psychotic, that he was going to murder us all in our sleep if we weren't careful.

"Well, that's stupid," I said when I heard it. "Charles wouldn't do that. I mean, he *could*. If he really wanted to kill everyone in their sleep, he'd find a way to poison the air supply. Or maybe cut the air off entirely. Or blow up the whole colony. But Charles is more of a poison-the-air-supply kind of guy rather than a blow-things-up guy, you know?"

They stared at me, horrified, and I squeezed my lips shut.

"Polly, don't ever say that to anyone else," George said, letting out a nervous breath.

Angelyn said, "He wouldn't really do that, would he? Want to kill everyone?"

I glared. "No! He's totally normal!"

They looked back at me with what I thought was more skepticism than was entirely necessary.

On the third day of our Moon visit, we were scheduled to take a field trip to the Sea of Tranquillity. Part geology workshop, part history lesson. Gather rocks for later analysis, admire Neil Armstrong's first footprint under its protective shield. We'd make the trip in one of the small shuttles used to travel between the Moon's various bases. Not an M-drive vessel, but I was still going to find a way to sit in the cabin and watch. Mostly these were repurposed orbital shuttles, and in a pinch most of them could rocket their way to the stations in Earth orbit. There was some big evacuation plan, like if the power and life support went out on all the lunar colonies at once, officials wanted to make sure everybody could get off, so they kept a certain number of working shuttles around at all times. Seemed like overkill to me—what was the likelihood of *all* the life support going out at once? It probably seemed strange because we didn't have anything like that kind of plan on Mars. If we had to evacuate everyone on the planet—well, we just couldn't, and that was that. Made it feel more permanent, though. Did the lunar colonies ever really feel permanent if you could see the whole Earth, close enough to get to in a reasonable amount of time without an M-drive?

There I was, getting homesick again.

Along the corridor to the shuttle-boarding platform, Charles hung back. I hung back with him. We hadn't had much of a chance to talk after the fight in the common area. He didn't seem any more inclined to talk now.

"I think you won," I said to Charles.

He looked at me, raised a brow, and seemed genuinely confused. Which was rare, so I let the pause drag on a moment to savor the feeling.

"You won. Everyone's scared of you. No one's going to bother you, and you can pretty much do whatever you want. They've even stopped messing with me because they think you'll come after them if they do."

"You don't think I would?"

I smirked at him. "I suppose if it was a matter of life and death. But no, I think you'd stand back and watch me flail."

He made a sound that might have been denial, or meant that he was agreeing with me.

"If people don't mess with us," he said finally, "it means we can focus on more important matters."

"Like Stanton."

And just then, Stanton arrived to sort us into our various shuttles for the trip to Tranquillity.

I didn't get to sit in the cabin, mostly because the cabin was too small, but I did get the shuttle captain to leave the door open so I could watch from the front seat of the passenger compartment. The thing wasn't that big. A nice cozy trip.

The shuttle copilot was also the field-trip guide, a Collins City staffer who did this for a living, flying shuttles and escorting herds of students. Stanton didn't come with us—she was on a different shuttle.

I pointed this out to Ladhi, who passed it along to everyone else. We'd managed to keep our core group together, along with Angelyn, George, and a couple of others.

"Thank goodness," Elzabeth said with a sigh. "She's creepy."

"Just keep your eyes open, like always," Charles said.

The shuttle trip was expected to take an hour. The cabin was sparse, with thinly padded seats along both sides and small round view ports next to them, tubing and juncture boxes visible along the ceiling, and lots of warning signs about where emergency survival gear and first-aid kits were stored. And really big warning signs pointing to a lifeboat, a cramped automated lander accessible through a door in the back. In glaring red letters, the warnings didn't inspire confidence. If something went wrong out here, there wasn't a whole lot anybody could do about it. Even on Mars, if you were outside the colony structures, you could still theoretically survive for a while as long as you had a breathing mask because there was atmosphere, even if it was super thin. Here on the Moon, not so much. The stars glared as starkly as they did everywhere else, and the cratered surface below glowed silver, unreal almost. In another couple of hours, the Moon's rotation would take us into night, where everything would turn dark. That was the Moon, everything black and white. Fortunately, the soft rumble of the engines sounded fine. We wouldn't crash. Probably.

Most everyone was quiet, looking out their view ports and murmuring back and forth with each other. I leaned forward to look into the pilot's cabin with its wider view port, showing the lunar landscape scrolling under us.

So I saw it first, when the copilot leaned over to the pilot and murmured, "Baz, I'm not feeling well."

But Baz had already slumped back in his seat, eyes closed. The guide shook him once before slumping over herself with a deflating sigh. I spent the next few heartbeats in complete disbelief. Utter disbelief. There could be no greater disbelief. Both our pilots had just passed out.

Stanton poisoned our pilots. Just to see how good we were at getting out of *this* one.

"Charles!" I gasped, my voice squeaking. Then I unhooked my safety harness and clambered out of the seat and into the cabin.

Charles, Ethan, and a couple of the others crowded in behind me. I felt for the pulse at their necks, first the copilot and then the pilot. They both had pulses, both were still alive. I shook the pilot, yelling in his ear to wake up. He didn't budge.

"They're probably drugged," Charles said calmly.

"Then who's flying the shuttle?" Ethan asked. He hid his anxiety well, but not as well as Charles.

"Polly, help me get them out," Charles said, reaching around me to unbuckle their harnesses.

It was tough, because only one of us could squeeze into the cabin at a time, in the narrow spaces between the seats and instrument panels. I was thinnest, so I leveraged each of them out of the seats while Charles and Ethan waited to pull them into the main cabin. At least they were super light in microgravity. The others found survival blankets in the emergency gear to try to make them comfortable.

Somehow, Charles and I ended up in the seats, staring out the wide view port and at an immense panel of blinking lights, scanners, readouts, and buttons. I was in the pilot's chair. Where I'd always wanted to be. I was suddenly terrified.

The shuttle had an automatic-guidance system. It seemed to be working just fine. Everything looked normal. Nothing was flashing red, no alarms were blaring.

"Charles, what do we do?" I asked breathlessly.

His gaze flickered back and forth, taking in every control, and for once he looked on the edge of panic. "She must have drugged them somehow, with some kind of time release so we'd be halfway through the flight before they passed out. She's probably watching right now to see what we'll do."

Everyone in the passenger cabin heard that.

"Stanton wouldn't let us really get hurt, right?" Elizabeth said. "We all agree on that, *right*?"

"Random controlled accidents are one thing, but this is crazy," George added.

Ethan was actually smiling. "Except she knows that Polly knows as much about piloting as you can without actually being a pilot. Right?"

"Can you pilot this, Polly?" Angelyn asked, serious and hopeful.

"I don't know." I couldn't breathe. I closed my eyes and forced my lungs to inhale. Tried to focus. The most complicated thing I'd ever driven were the scooters back home. This was totally different. "The autocontrols will keep us going for a while, but we're due at Tranquillity soon. How far are we?"

Charles found a screen showing our route and destination. "Hundred and twenty kilometers, looks like."

"Can you make an emergency landing and let them find us?" Angelyn said.

I shook my head. "No, the surface is too rough, too full of debris and craters. We have to find a flat space or else get all the way to Tranquillity for landing. I don't know if I can do this . . ."

Charles found the comm headset and hooked it over his ear. "We'll find out what traffic control wants us to do. They'll send a rescue, or they can talk you through it."

That was a good plan. I let out a shaking breath and felt calmer.

Charles sounded very professional as he found the emergency channel and started talking to someone.

"What's the problem, shuttle, over?" a scratching female voice said over the speaker. Charles had switched the audio from the headphones.

"We're a student group on a shuttle from Collins to Tranquillity, and both our pilots passed out. No one here is qualified to pilot, but we have some trainees you might be able to talk through it."

A rushed conversation followed, the traffic-control official asking a bunch of questions—how many of us were there, how we were doing, the condition of the pilots. Charles said they might have been drugged, which would open up a whole other can of sewage. Worry about that later.

They decided to talk us through landing at Tranquillity. Because if something terrible happened, at least we'd be close to emergency crews and an air lock. My heart was racing.

Charles gave me the headset. "You can do it," he said softly.

"Who am I talking to?" the woman on the line asked as I fit the headset in place.

"Polly Newton, ma'am. I'm Polly."

"I'm Ms. Andrews. You're both from Mars? You have the accent." She sounded calm. Not worried at all. My heart rate slowed.

"Yes, ma'am."

"And you're the pilot-in-training?"

"Um. Not yet. But soon. I hope."

"How about starting now, kid?"

I thought I was going to throw up. "Yes. Yes, ma'am."

She explained where the automatic-system controls were and had me confirm that everything was running smoothly. I found the navigation screen and checked—the course to Tranquillity was already plotted and we were still en route. We activated a countdown—how long until we needed to start landing procedures. She had me tell everyone to get in their seats and strap in.

We strapped the unconscious pilots into Charles's and my empty seats.

"Okay, Polly. You don't have anything to do now, but let me know if something changes. When you get to Tranquillity, I'll talk you through the landing sequence, you'll have plenty of help. It's going to be super easy, okay?" I got the feeling she was talking down to me, but I didn't even care. "You all right?"

"Yes. Thank you."

"I'm here at Tranquillity control, so I'll see you soon. Good work, Polly."

Nothing to do now but wait.

I glanced over my shoulder and was relieved to find everyone sitting straight, breathing, and not freaking out. There were wide eyes, white-knuckled hands gripping each other. But no one having a meltdown.

I glanced sidelong at Charles. He'd settled back in the seat and was staring out the view port in front. His arms were crossed, his muscles tense.

"We're going to be okay," I said to him. He nodded. I had this urge to hug him. But I didn't.

The lunar landscape scrolled past, looking like molded talc. I ought to enjoy this front-seat view. Fifteen, twenty more minutes, this would all be over.

When you live on a space station or planetary colony with an artificial atmosphere, you live in fear of one specific noise: hissing air. It means something has happened to the hull, the bulkhead, the outer layer protecting you from vacuum or in-hospitable atmosphere—a micrometeoroid impact hole, a crack, some kind of damage, a malfunctioning air lock. There should be dozens of alarms, fail-safes, and emergency doors to seal off breaches, to warn you when something like this happens. You practice dozens of drills to go for air masks and survival suits, to use emergency-patch kits that can repair cracks and holes. It doesn't matter how many alerts and protections there are, a part of your brain is always listening for that soft hissing of air.

The shuttle had gone quiet, as if everyone shut up because they thought I needed absolute silence to concentrate on the controls. So I heard it.

"Does anyone else hear that?" I said, and somehow it got even quieter, because now everyone was holding their breath. And there it was, like someone blowing air through their teeth.

"Oh, no," Ladhi said, going pale.

"We have to find that," Ethan said.

"What?" George said. "What's happening?"

"We have a leak," Charles said.

I looked around, even though I probably wouldn't be able to see it. "Where's that coming from?"

Charles ordered, "Polly you stay there and monitor systems, we'll handle it."

Ethan already had one of the emergency packs down from the wall, which if it was like every other emergency pack included a kit for finding and patching hull leaks. He tore off a couple of plastic strips from the packaging and handed one to Ladhi. The two of them started crawling all over the cabin, along the corners, across the ceiling, holding out the thin flimsy strips, looking for the draft of air that would cause the strips to shudder.

Meanwhile, I called the Tranquillity control official. "Hi, Ms.

Andrews?" I said into the headset. "We . . . I think we have a hull leak."

She swore under her breath, like she was trying to hide it. But I heard it.

"Okay. Slow leak or explosive?"

"Slow."

"Have everyone put on masks. You don't have far to go; you should keep enough atmosphere to make it here. You have your mask?"

Charles retrieved it from its box on the back of the cabin wall and handed it to me. "Yes, ma'am."

He handed out masks to everyone else.

"Polly? How is everyone doing?" Ms. Andrews's voice crackled at me over the transmission.

"Fine. We're looking for the leak."

That was when the engine compartment exploded.

24

At least, I guessed it was the engine compartment, because it came from the bottom and rear of the shuttle, booming forward from there and throwing us all against our safety harnesses. Or against the bulkhead, because Ethan and Ladhi were still up and around looking for that leak. There were screams of shock that fell off quickly, mostly because no one knew what was happening.

All the alarm lights and warnings on the instrument panel turned red and blinking.

"Polly, what is it? What just happened?" the Tranquillity traffic control officer demanded.

"I don't know, something just blew up." The air seemed to be hissing louder now, as if the leak had gotten bigger.

"Is everyone all right?" Ethan called. Anxious murmurs answered him, except for Angelyn, who said, "Ladhi fell, I think she's hurt."

"It's just a little blood," she said, her voice woozy.

Elzabeth exclaimed, "No, you're *gushing!*"

My rushed breaths fogged the inside of my air mask. Had to

calm down. Had to look after the shuttle. I couldn't tell what the automatic systems were doing.

"Polly, please tell me you're still there, what's happening?" Ms. Andrews demanded.

"There's been an explosion. We've lost rear thrusting engine, we've started rolling." Momentum kept us moving forward, but it didn't keep us stable. The horizon outside the view port was slowly tilting.

Charles put a hand on my shoulder, and I jumped. He caught my gaze and frowned. The twin telepathy worked just fine then because I knew exactly what he was thinking: Stanton hadn't just drugged the pilots—she'd sabotaged the whole shuttle.

"How are we going to get out of this one?" I asked.

"One step at a time. What's traffic control say?" He nodded at the headset.

Ms. Andrews was talking. "You know where the lateral-thruster control is?"

"Yeah."

"Lean on that baby, stabilize the roll."

The lateral-thruster control was a lever on a square patch of control panel, lined up with several other levers—all controlling various thrusters that could get the shuttle pointed in any direction. I shifted it opposite the roll, hoping it worked.

The horizon line outside matched up with what the sensor display was telling me: we were still rolling.

"Ma'am, I think the thrusters are out completely," I said.

"Polly . . . everyone in the lifeboat . . . listen close . . ." Static had started creeping into the communication, drowning out her voice.

I held the headset close to my mouth as if that would help. "Control, can you repeat that? I think something's gone wrong with our antenna, or the power, or something."

"Roger that, Polly. You need . . . gain enough altitude . . . safely launch the lifeboat . . . under the instrument . . . open panel . . . bypass main fuel line . . ."

I had to figure out what she meant from half the instructions. I heard stuff going on in the passenger cabin, spared a glance at Charles, who was directing people—getting them into the lifeboat, helping them with the two unconscious pilots. I could feel air rushing out of the cabin now. My ears were popping, and my eyes felt dried-out and watery. Meanwhile, I listened as hard as I could, asked Ms. Andrews to repeat instructions, and I figured it out.

We weren't going to make it to the base with the shuttle falling to pieces, so we had to abandon ship. We needed at least a kilometer in altitude for the lifeboat to launch safely. We'd been slowly descending on the approach to Tranquillity and were now too low, about seven hundred meters, and dropping. Not far to go. Unless your thrusters were giving out.

Under the instrument board was a panel, easy enough to unhook and remove. This provided access to the actual guts of the ship, a mass of cables and wires that let the flight crew communicate with the rest of the shuttle. So many cables and wires. I was supposed to learn all this in flight school, not now. But Andrews talked me through it. There was a switch under here, a mechanical rather than electronic switch in case power went out, that would physically bypass the damaged fuel system and bring a backup system online.

White smoke was curling up from under the panel, and sparks jumped. The static on the line was getting worse—our antenna was also losing power, I guessed, and couldn't transmit the signal to my headset anymore.

"Ms. Andrews? Ma'am?"

"Pol . . . come in . . . are you . . . Po . . ."

Then nothing. But I had her instructions, I had the switch.

The slow roll had turned us on our side; I was braced against the copilot seat with my arms in the guts of the instrument panel. I didn't know how everyone else was doing; I couldn't take the time to look. But no one was screaming, so I assumed everything was okay. Okay as it could be, which meant people strapping into the lifeboat.

I turned the switch for the power bypass. The whole shuttle rattled as thrusters roared on. A short scream from the back as someone got knocked off balance. I jumped up to the maneuvering controls to get us pointed up, away from the surface. Outside the view port, the black of space spread out before us. Good.

Then we started spinning. Not a slow roll—a corkscrew. I fell, smashed up against the back of the cabin, then into the tops of the chairs. I grabbed hold of the pilot chair and worked against the centrifugal force to pull myself back to the instrument panel, got thrusters going in the opposite direction to counter the spin. Didn't stop it completely, but slowed it, so it was time to cut the thrusters and let inertia carry us on. I had to find the switch by feel. It was sticky, as if something held it in place, but I managed to get it switched back. With the bypass off, the power cut out again, and the thrusters died. That was okay, because we were pointed up now. In a couple of seconds we'd be high enough to launch the lifeboat. Then I wouldn't have to worry about it.

"What was that?" Ethan demanded.

I looked up to see both him and Charles hanging on the door of the cabin. Gravity was vanishing, no such thing as up and down anymore. I was sprawled on the floor in front of the pilot's chair, Ethan was standing on a wall, Charles was just hanging there, keeping his place while the passenger cabin spun slowly around him. Made me dizzy, and I swallowed back nausea. Their breathing masks hid their expressions.

"We had to gain altitude to be able to release the lifeboat," Charles explained, because of course he did.

"I lost contact with traffic control," I said. Sweat was dripping down my face inside the mask, even though the cabin was getting cold. The air was thin, heat bleeding out.

"Surely they've sent help by now," Ethan said.

"Polly, let's get going," Charles said.

I let go of the switch. Or I tried to let go of the switch, but it slammed back into place, turning the thrusters on again, throwing the shuttle into another corkscrewing spin. Fortunately, this time I was braced in place and was able to go through the process again, reaching the controls to turn on the counterthrust with one hand, stretching to reach the emergency switch with the other. Something in the mechanism had fried, and it wouldn't stay where I put it. The spring-loaded pressure was pulling against me.

For every action there is an equal and opposite reaction. Netwon's Third Law of Motion was going to kill us.

If the ship fell into a corkscrew spin, the lifeboat wouldn't be able to launch. To keep the ship from spinning, I was going to have to hold the switch in place to keep the thrusters from firing.

"Um. Charles? Do you have any tape or adhesive or loose wire or something?" I looked around but couldn't see much from where I sat. I didn't dare get up again, because every time the shuttle went into a spin, the damage got worse, and the chances of successfully launching the lifeboat went down.

"Why?"

"The switch is stuck," I said. He started digging through one of the emergency packs.

Ethan looked at me, and his eyes held despair. "We don't have much time. The atmosphere's almost gone, everyone else is in the boat, we have to go."

"Here." Charles shoved around him and threw me some white first-aid tape.

It wasn't sticky enough. The switch's pressure tore right through it.

"Can you make a run for it?" Ethan said.

Even my messing with the tape made the switch spring back, and the thrusters fired for a second, and the shuttle's spin got faster. During the time it would take me to run from here to the lifeboat, the spin would become so fast, the g's so forceful, we'd all get slammed into the hull and smeared into paste.

I shook my head.

Charles was still looking for tape, wire, glue. But we didn't have any more time. They had to get out, or we'd all be stuck in a vacuum.

"Go," I said.

Ethan hesitated, and I almost yelled again because we didn't have time to argue. But he was smart. I didn't have to explain. He nodded and squeezed my ankle, which was sticking out over the seat and the closest part of me he could reach. That touch steadied me. Convinced me I was doing the right thing.

"Get him out," I said.

"Charles, come on," Ethan said.

"No. We can fix this, we can figure this out—"

Ethan grabbed him around the middle and hauled back.

"No!" Charles screamed the word over and over again. I'd never heard him make a sound like that. I squeezed my eyes shut, because I hadn't even thought about crying until Charles started shouting.

The bulkhead door to the lifeboat slammed shut—I felt the vibration through the metal hull rather than heard it. Not much air left for sound to travel through. Charles's shouts cut off.

I concentrated on holding the switch in place, keeping the thrusters off-line long enough for the lifeboat to get away. Just another minute. A charge fired, sending another shudder through the hull. I craned my neck to look at the instruments—and yes, the lifeboat was gone, on its way to a thrust-assisted landing and rescue. The shuttle was quiet now, mostly, except for the faded beeping of a malfunction alert. I couldn't even hear the sound of air venting through a crack that couldn't be sealed. Most of the air was already gone.

I could let go of the switch now. But I didn't. People could survive in a vacuum longer than you'd think. Especially if you had oxygen. Sure, your blood started boiling and the internal pressure of your body caused your capillaries to burst and pretty soon your whole body failed. But that took time. I had oxygen. I'd survive for a little while.

On the other hand, all I had to do was let go of the switch, let the thrusters go out of control, and the high gravity would kill me.

I wondered what Mom would think when she got the news about what happened. Not exactly what she planned for me. Maybe she'd be proud.

My arm was cramping, so I shifted my body, trying to get to a different angle. The air coming through the mask felt stuffy. I didn't have a way out, and for some reason, I was kind of okay with it. Everyone else had escaped. Charles was alive. It was okay.

It was okay.

I didn't notice at first when my air canister started to run out. My lungs were hurting, but that could just have been nerves. I sucked deep breaths at the mask but couldn't seem to catch my breath. My vision started going splotchy, black with flares around the edges, like I was about to faint. It was sort of comforting—I'd pass out before I died and wouldn't feel a thing. When I passed out, I'd let go of the switch, and the shuttle would tumble out of control. At least I wouldn't feel anything at that point.

I hadn't wanted to pick a death, so I waited for the air to go. Now, it looked like I was going to get all three—vacuum, asphyxiation, g-forces—at once.

I listened to the alarm, beeping in time with my heart, until all I could hear was my heart, then nothing.

25

I don't even know where to start. Well. Let me start at the end: Why do you have to be so stupid? Scratch that. You're not stupid. So why do you have to be so brave? You wouldn't even realize it. You wouldn't call it bravery. You'd say something noble about how you just did what needed doing, you were just the one stuck holding the switch, and you're not really brave or a hero or anything, all the standard clichés, but that would be okay because you'd mean it. You'd get nervous that everyone was making a fuss.

People keep coming up to me and patting me on the back and telling me how proud I must be of you. And I am, I suppose, if I had to admit it. But I'm also very angry. One of these days I'll figure out how we could have saved everyone without leaving you behind. Then I'll be right and you'll be wrong, and you'll never have to do anything that brave ever again.

So next time just step back and let me fix things, all right?

Charles

I folded the note and held onto it. I had to think about it for a while. My brain seemed to be running at half speed, and the doctor said that was because they were keeping me sedated until some of the bruising healed. I'd apparently been tossed around the cabin of the shuttle pretty hard before the rescue ship got it stabilized. I didn't have brain damage from anoxia. At least, they didn't think I did. I couldn't really tell. I felt tired.

I'd woken up and hadn't known where I was. The room was pale, filled with light, and something beeped, just like the alarm on the shuttle. Then people came in, and I realized I was in a bed, and I wasn't moving—at least relative to the room, I wasn't moving. I didn't feel heavy or light. I didn't feel much of anything. One of the people—a guy in a white coat, a doctor—asked if I could hear him. I nodded and tried to talk, but my voice scratched, and there was a tube in my nose. The doctor seemed relieved.

Then I'd felt the square of paper under my hand. Polly's Eyes Only. I kept it hidden so people wouldn't try to take it away. Charles had been here, sitting by my bed, watching over me. I tried to look for him, to see if he was still here, but moving hurt and the guy put a hand on my shoulder, keeping me in place. Some medical folks did some tests and poked and prodded, asked some questions, and I asked them what had happened in a scratchy, dry voice that didn't sound like me at all. Rescued, they'd said, and taken to the hospital at Collins City. I'd been rescued at the very last moment, just as my air was going out and the g's were about to pound me to jelly. I'm a very lucky girl, they assured me.

I tried to ask them where Charles was, but my voice faded. They gave me a cup of water, explained about the sedation, and left me alone. I read the note. Charles had been here. I assumed that meant he and everyone else were okay, that they got rescued, too.

It seemed very much like a dream, so I went back to sleep and expected everything to be different again when I woke up. Maybe I'd be able to feel the gravity enough to figure out where I was.

When I did wake up, I felt clearer. The room wasn't as bright, and I could see the walls, the medical equipment, the blanket over my skinny body a lot better. And Charles was sitting by the bed. Neither of us said anything for what seemed a long time. He studied me like he was trying to figure out a problem.

"Hi," I said, because that was all I could think of.

"They said you'd woken up. That I should be here for you. A familiar face."

He didn't look comfortable. He didn't look in control. He must have hated this.

"Is everybody okay?" I asked.

"Mostly. Everyone got a little banged up. Ladhi had a concussion, but she's all right. Very proud of the scar she's acquired."

"Ethan?"

"He wants to see you, but the doctors are keeping everyone else out for now. How do you feel?"

"Not too good," I said. My head might have been less fuzzy, but even so I'd rather lie still than try to move.

"You almost died."

I hadn't really thought of it like that. I just did what I thought I had to, and now I was dealing with the consequences.

"Are you mad at me?" I asked.

He paused, pursed his lips. Charles, at a loss for words. "You saved my life," he said finally. "You saved everyone's lives."

I thought for a minute. "I don't really know what that means."

"It means you're getting into pilot training, when the time comes," he said. "I made a request, and they're holding a spot for you, when you're ready."

That was too big to think about right now.

"Charles, what happened? To the shuttle, what really happened? It was sabotage, wasn't it? Stanton?"

He glanced away, his lips curving into an inexplicable smile. "That's a complicated question, it turns out. Stanton did drug the pilots. A time-release dermal sedative in a patch stuck inside their headsets. They didn't even feel it. She knew the shuttle had enough automated systems we weren't likely to get in serious trouble. She expected exactly what happened to happen—we'd make an emergency call, we'd have a big adventure, and we'd all grow and learn as human beings." The cutting edge in his voice indicated exactly what he thought of this plan. It matched the pattern of the previous "adventures."

"But the air leak?" I prompted. "The explosion?"

"Not planned. The shuttle just broke. Freak accident, at the worst possible time."

"Seriously?"

"Yep. A seam in the hull by the engine compartment cracked—normal failure, not serious in itself. But the pressure differential caused one of the power cables between the fuel cells and the engine to rupture. Cascading failure after that. That's what they think happened, anyway. A trained crew probably could have handled it without it becoming a huge drama. But there wasn't any trained crew. Just us."

I chuckled, but my lungs hurt, so I stopped.

"There's more," he said, and he had the look of an astronomer discovering water on the Moon.

"More what?" I croaked.

"Stanton wasn't just being sadistic. She'd been hired."

"Hired to rig those accidents? Hired to mess with us like that?" If I could have sat up, I would have, but I was too snuggled into the pillows, too comfortable. My brain was getting very awake, though. "Who would do that?" But I had an idea.

As I talked, he reached to a bedside table for a tablet, scrolled up a file for me, and held it up so I could see the screen. I reach out to adjust it so I could see more clearly.

"Mom," I murmured at the image. Supervisor Newton of Colony One. Her face filled the screen, her brown hair slicked back, her uniform creased, perfect and professional. Of course this was a recorded message. Somehow I still thought she might look through the screen at me, see me with my burst veins and bloodshot eyes and banged-up body propped up in a hospital bed, and her eyes might go wide with shock and her lips purse with concern. She might even express some kind of sympathy and . . . love?

But knowing my mother, this could have been a live feed and

the image's expression still wouldn't have changed. Seeing me bruised and broken wouldn't have affected her at all.

She spoke like she would to an underling. "Charles, I received your message. Thank you for that. I'm not going to deny your accusations, you've collected too much evidence for me to embarrass myself like that, or to condescend to you. Though I am very, *very* disappointed that you would investigate my personal financial records. I thought you would trust me, trust that everything I've done has been for the good of you and Polly. Under normal circumstances, even a place like Galileo wouldn't give you a chance to prove yourselves. I simply made sure that you would have that chance. I had no doubt that given the opportunity, you would excel. And you have. Of course I never intended for Dean Stanton to take her mandate as far as she did. But my faith in your and your sister's abilities was not at all misplaced. You'll have to agree with me there. However, I'm sure you'll be glad to know that I've submitted a complaint about Dean Stanton's behavior. This won't happen again.

"And of course I'm glad that Polly isn't seriously injured. Let me know if anything changes with her condition."

Because it was a recording, I couldn't yell at her. Couldn't argue. And by the time I was able to record a reply, I'd have forgotten everything I meant to say right now. Maybe I could just take a picture of me glaring at her and send that.

"'This won't happen again.' Why don't I believe her?" I said disgustedly as he set the tablet back down. "What are we supposed to do, Charles? We can't just go back to Galileo, can we?"

His smile turned even more sly. How long had I been unconscious? How much conspiring had he gotten done in that time?

"Angelyn and Ethan and some of the other students told their parents what happened with Stanton. President Edgars's press releases are sounding increasingly panicked. Not only has Stanton been asked to resign, criminal charges may be pending. An independent advisory council is being convened to examine the school's entire operating structure. So much for Galileo's *great tradition*."

"Wow."

"No doubt."

"So what's next?" I asked. "What are we going to do?"

"This is a perfect opportunity for you to go back to Mars. If you want to."

I was very surprised to find myself shaking my head. I tried to explain it to myself, as much as to him. "I know you're not going to believe this, but I don't think I want to go back to Mars. At least not right now. Not while I'm this angry at Mom. And . . . I still have to finish school before I can start pilot training. Right?"

"Maybe you'll enjoy it more if you aren't so worried about getting into pilot training."

Charles had done that. For me. And because it was him, I could trust that there really would be spot waiting for me. Now I really did want to hug him. "What about you?"

His gaze turned thoughtful. "Like you said, we have to finish school. I may go back to Mars to do it, though. Start really learning the system there. After that, maybe I'll run for a spot on the governing council."

"But you're only seventeen, they'll never go for it!"

"Twenty Earth standard is the minimum age. That'll give me a few years to prepare. And someone has to stand up to Mother."

I really wanted to watch that fight. But I wasn't happy, because the future had suddenly become a huge, unmanageable void. Flight school, what I always wanted. Why was I suddenly scared?

"But Charles, what am I going to do without you watching my back?"

He smiled. An actual, real, nonsmirky, honest-to-goodness smile. And then it was gone. Like someone flashing a strobe light. "I'm sure we'll come up with something."

"I'm glad you're my brother. Thanks."

"Polly." He came to the head of the bed, leaned over, and kissed my forehead. He turned and walked out of the room without looking back.

Our twin telepathy still didn't work right, but I was pretty sure that meant he was glad he was my brother, too.